MAIGRET AND THE MADWOMAN
AND
MAIGRET AND THE KILLER

The little old lady with the clear trusting eyes, who hovers around the Quai des Orfèvres asking whether she can see the great Superintendent Maigret, has a strange tale to relate to Lapointe who interviews her instead. Someone is apparently going round her flat moving the position of various articles, and she feels that she is being watched. Lapointe is convinced that she is suffering from persecution mania, but a few days later she is found strangled, and Maigret is confronted with one of his most difficult cases.

*   *   *

In *Maigret and the Killer*, a young man is found lying in the pouring rain with seven knife wounds in his back; he dies in hospital without regaining consciousness. Maigret, almost the first person at the scene of the crime, slowly pieces together the events leading up to the brutal killing. Tape recordings taken by the victim lead him to three possible suspects, but that is only the beginning. Not until the murderer appears—actually in Maigret's flat—is this complex case finally solved.

Also by
GEORGES SIMENON

★

MAIGRET AND
THE MADWOMAN

and

MAIGRET
AND THE KILLER

*

GEORGES SIMENON

THE
COMPANION BOOK CLUB
LONDON

This edition, published in 1973 by
The Hamlyn Publishing Group Ltd,
is issued by arrangement with
Hamish Hamilton Ltd.

---

*Made and printed in Great Britain
for the Companion Book Club
by Odhams (Watford) Ltd.*

600871614
5.73/261

CONTENTS

*

CONTENTS

MAIGRET AND THE MADWOMAN

*

*Translated from
the French by*
EILEEN ELLENBOGEN

CHAPTER ONE

FLANKING THE MAIN GATE of Police Headquarters, Constable Picot stood guard on the left, and his old friend Latuile on the right. It was about ten o'clock on a fine morning in May. The sunlight was dazzling and Paris was aglow with colour, like a pastel drawing.

Picot could not have said exactly when he first noticed her. It did not seem important at the time. She was a tiny little old woman in a white hat, white cotton gloves and a dress of gunmetal grey. Her legs were very thin, and slightly bowed with age.

Had she been carrying a shopping basket or a handbag? He could not remember. He had not been aware of her approach. She was only a few feet away from him, standing on the pavement, peering at the rows of little cars parked in the forecourt of Police Headquarters.

Not that sightseers were uncommon at the Quai des Orfèvres, but mostly they were tourists. She drew nearer, went right up to the gate, inspected the policeman from top to toe, then turned and made off in the direction of the Pont-Neuf.

Picot was on duty again the following morning, and at about the same time as on the previous day he saw her once more. This time, after some considerable hesitation, she came up and spoke to him.

'This is the place where Chief Superintendent Maigret has his office, isn't it?'

'Yes, madame. On the first floor.'

She raised her head and gazed up at the windows. She had very delicate, finely modelled features, and her clear grey eyes were full of wonderment. 'Thank you, officer.'

She went on her way with little mincing steps. This time he noticed that she was carrying a string shopping bag, which would seem to indicate that she lived somewhere nearby.

9

On the third day Picot was off duty. His replacement paid no attention to the little old woman, who sidled through into the forecourt. She wandered around for a minute or two, and then went in through the door on the left and began climbing the stairs. On the first floor she stopped and peered down the long corridor, apparently feeling a little lost.

Old Joseph, the messenger, went up to her and asked, in his friendly way, if he could be of any assistance.

'I'm looking for Chief Superintendent Maigret's office.'

'Do you wish to see the Chief Superintendent?'

'Yes. That's what I'm here for.'

'Have you an appointment?'

Looking very downcast, she shook her head.

'Can't I see him without an appointment?'

'Would you care to leave a message?'

'I must speak to him personally. It's terribly important.'

'If you'll fill in one of these forms, I'll see if the Chief Superintendent can see you.'

She sat down at a table covered with a green baize cloth. They had just had the decorators in, and the whole building smelt strongly of paint. Unaware of this, she was struck by the cheerful look of things, not at all what one would have expected of a Government Department.

Having filled in one form, she then proceeded to tear it up. She wrote slowly, composing her sentences with great care, and underlining a word here and there. A second form followed the first into the wastepaper basket, and then a third. It was not until after her fourth attempt that she appeared satisfied.

She went over to Joseph with the form.

'You'll see that it's handed to him personally, won't you?'

'Yes, madame.'

'He's very busy, I daresay.'

'Very.'

'Do you think he'll see me?'

'I couldn't say, madame.'

She was at least eighty-five, eighty-six or seven perhaps, and as light and slender as a little girl. Age had fined her down, and her delicate skin was translucent. She looked up at Joseph, good-hearted fellow that he was, and gave him a shy smile, anxious to win him over.

'You will do your best, won't you? It's so terribly important to me!'

'Take a seat, madame.'

He went up to one of the doors, and knocked. Maigret was in conference with Janvier and Lapointe, who were both standing by the window, which was wide open, letting in all the hubbub of the street outside.

Maigret took the form from Joseph, glanced at it, and frowned. 'What's she like?'

'A very respectable old lady. A little shy. She was most insistent that I should beg you to see her.'

On the dotted line at the head of the form, she had written her name in a surprisingly firm, neat hand:

Madame Antoine de Caramé.

And below, the address:

8b Quai de la Mégisserie.

She stated as the object of her visit:

The caller has something of the utmost importance to communicate to Chief Superintendent Maigret. It is a matter of life and death.

Here the handwriting was more shaky, and the words irregularly spaced. 'Chief Superintendent' and 'utmost importance' were underlined. 'A matter of life and death' was underscored twice.

'Is she mad?' muttered Maigret, sucking at his pipe.

'That isn't how she strikes me. She's very quiet and composed.'

Everyone at the Quai des Orfèvres had at some time or other had to deal with letters from lunatics or cranks, and the underlining of words was a characteristic of most of them.

'You'd better see her, Lapointe. Unless someone does, we'll have her calling here every day.'

A few minutes later, the old woman was ushered into the little office at the back. Lapointe was waiting there alone, standing near the window.

'Please come in, madame. Take a seat.'

She looked him up and down in some bewilderment.

'Are you his son?'

'Whose son?'

'The Chief Superintendent's.'

'No, madame. My name is Inspector Lapointe.'

'But you're only a boy!'

'I'm twenty-seven.'

And so he was. All the same, he didn't look a day over twenty-two, and was more like most people's idea of a student than a police officer.

'It was Chief Superintendent Maigret I asked to see.'

'Unfortunately, he can't spare the time at the moment.'

She hesitated, standing in the doorway, fidgeting with her white handbag, uncertain whether to stay or go.

'What if I were to come back tomorrow?'

'He still couldn't see you.'

'Does Chief Superintendent Maigret never grant interviews?'

'Only in very special cases.'

'Mine is a very special case. Just that. It's a matter of life and death.'

'So you said on the form.'

'Well, then?'

'If you will tell me what it's all about, I'll report to the Chief, and let him be the judge.'

'You think he might agree to see me?'

'I can't promise, but he very well might.'

She remained standing for quite some time, pondering the pros and cons, and then, apparently having made up her mind, sat down on the very edge of a chair facing Lapointe, who was now seated at the desk.

'What's the trouble?'

'I should explain first of all that I've lived in the same flat on the Quai de la Mégisserie for the past forty-two years. On the ground floor, there's a man who sells birds. In the summer, when he puts all the cages out on the pavement, I can hear them all day long. It's company for me.'

'You said you were in some sort of danger, I think.'

'I'm in danger all right, but I daresay you think I'm

drivelling. The young always seem to imagine that old people aren't quite right in the head.'

'No such thought ever occurred to me.'

'I don't quite know how to put this. My second husband died twelve years ago, and since then I've been on my own in the flat, and no one other than myself ever has occasion to go into it. It's too big for me now really, but I've set my heart on living my time out there. I'm eighty-six, and I can still manage the cooking and housework without any help.'

'Do you keep a pet? A dog or a cat?'

'No. As I said, I can always hear the birds singing. My flat is on the first floor, just above the shop.'

'What is it that's worrying you?'

'It's hard to say. At least five times in the past fortnight, I've noticed that my things have been moved.'

'What do you mean? Are you saying that, when you've been out, you've come back to find your things disturbed?'

'That's right. A frame hanging slightly crooked, or a vase turned round. That sort of thing.'

'Are you quite sure?'

'There you are, you see! Because I'm an old woman, you think I'm wandering in my wits. I did tell you, don't forget, that I've lived forty-two years in that same flat. Naturally, if anything is out of place, I spot it at once.'

'Has anything been stolen? Have you missed anything?'

'No, Inspector.'

'Do you keep money in the flat?'

'Very little. Just enough to meet my monthly expenses. My first husband was in local government. I still draw a pension from the Hôtel de Ville. Besides that, I have a Post Office Savings account.'

'Do you have valuables, jewellery, ornaments, anything of that sort?'

'I have things that are of value to me, but I doubt if they're worth much in terms of cash.'

'Were there any other signs of an intruder, such as a damp footprint, for instance?'

'There hasn't been a drop of rain for the past ten days.'

'Cigarette ash?'

'No.'

'Have you ever given anyone a key to your flat?'

'No. I have the only key, and I always keep it in my bag.'

He was hard put to it to conceal his embarrassment.

'In other words, all it amounts to is that, from time to time, you find some of your things not precisely as you left them?'

'That's right.'

'You've never caught any unauthorized person in the flat?'

'Never.'

'And you've no idea who the intruder might be?'

'None.'

'Have you any children?'

'Much to my sorrow, I never had a child.'

'Any other relations?'

'One niece. She's a masseuse. I don't see her very often, though she lives not far from me, just across the river.'

'What about friends? Men friends, women friends?'

'Most of the people I used to know are dead. And there's something else as well.'

She said it quite casually. There was no underlying note of hysteria, and her bright glance never wavered.

'I'm being followed.'

'In the street, do you mean?'

'Yes.'

'Have you actually seen the person who's following you?'

'Whenever I stop suddenly and look back there's someone there, but not always the same person. I don't know who it can be, really.'

'Do you go out much?'

'Every morning, for a start. I go out at about eight to do my shopping. I miss Les Halles very much, now that it's been moved. It was so convenient, just round the corner, and old habits die hard. Since then I've shopped around a bit locally, but it will never be quite the same again.'

'Is it a man who's following you?'

'I don't know.'

'I presume you get back at about ten?'

14

'Thereabouts. And then I sit by the window and shell peas, or whatever.'

'Do you stay in in the afternoon?'

'Only when the weather's bad. I like to get a bit of fresh air whenever I can. Usually, I sit on a park bench, preferably in the Tuileries Gardens. I have my own favourite bench. I'm not the only one. People of my age are like that, you know. I see the same old faces there, year in, year out.'

'Are you followed as far as the Tuileries?'

'Only part of the way. So as to make sure I won't be coming back immediately, I think.'

'Have you ever done that?'

'Three times. I pretended I'd forgotten something, and turned back.'

'And, needless to say, you found no one there?'

'That doesn't alter the fact that, on other occasions, my things have been moved. Someone has it in for me, though I can't think why. I've never done any harm to anyone. There may be more than one person involved.'

'You said your husband was in local government. What did he do?'

'He was Clerk to the Council. He had very heavy responsibilities. Unfortunately, he died young, of a heart attack. He was just forty-five.'

'And you married again?'

'Not till almost ten years later. My second husband was chief buyer at the Bazar de l'Hôtel de Ville. He was in charge of agricultural implements, and tools in general.'

'Is he dead too?'

'He'd been retired for some years when he died. If he'd lived, he'd have been ninety-two.'

'When did he die?'

'I thought I told you. Twelve years ago.'

'Had he any family? Was he a widower when you married him?'

'He only had one son. He lives in Venezuela.'

'I'll tell you what, madame, I'd best go and report all you've just told me to the Chief Superintendent.'

'Do you think he'll agree to see me?'

'If he does, he'll get in touch with you.'

'Have you got my address?'

'It's on the form you filled in, isn't it?'

'That's true, I'd forgotten. The thing is, you see, I think the world of him. It seems to me he's the only one who could possibly understand. I don't mean any disrespect to you, but you do seem a bit on the young side to me.'

He accompanied her to the door, and down the long corridor to the head of the main staircase.

When he got back to Maigret's office, Janvier was no longer there.

'Well?'

'I think you're right, sir. She must be a bit cracked. All the same, you wouldn't think it. She's very soft-spoken, very cool and self-possessed. She's eighty-six, and all I can say is I hope I'll be as bright as she is when I get to her age.'

'What about this threat or whatever it is that's hanging over her head?'

'She's lived in the same flat on the Quai de la Mégisserie for more than forty years. She's been married twice. She claims that, while she's out, some of her things get moved.'

Maigret re-lit his pipe.

'What sort of things?'

'Picture frames hanging crooked, vases turned back to front . . .'

'Has she a dog or a cat?'

'No. She makes do with bird song. Apparently, there's a man who sells birds on the ground floor.'

'Anything else?'

'Yes. She has persuaded herself that she is always being followed.'

'Has she actually seen anyone following her?'

'No, that's just it. But she seems to have an obsession about it.'

'Will she be coming back?'

'She's set her heart on seeing you personally. She talks about you as if you were the Good Lord Himself. You're the only one, it seems, who could possibly understand. What am I to do?'

'Nothing.'

'She's sure to be back!'

'We'll cross that bridge when we come to it. Meanwhile, you might go along and have a word with the concierge.'

Maigret turned his attention once more to the file which he had been reading, and young Lapointe went back to the Inspectors' Duty Room.

'A nut-case, was she?' Janvier asked.

'Probably, but a very unusual one.'

'Do you know many nut-cases?'

'One of my aunts is a patient in a mental hospital.'

'The old girl seems to have made quite an impression on you.'

'She did, in a way. To her, I'm just a kid who couldn't possibly understand her problem. She's pinned all her hopes on Maigret.'

That same afternoon, Lapointe strolled along the Quai de la Mégisserie, where almost every shop window was filled with birds and other small pets. In response to the glorious weather, there were tables and chairs on the pavement outside every café. When he got to number 8, Lapointe looked up at the first floor windows, and saw that they were wide open. He had some difficulty in finding the lodge, which was across a court-yard at the back of the building. The concierge was sitting in a patch of sunlight, darning a pair of men's socks.

'Looking for anyone in particular?'

He showed her his official card.

'I'd be grateful for anything you could tell me about Madame Antoine de Caramé. That is her name, isn't it, the old lady who lives on the first floor?'

'I know, I know. Actually, Antoine was her second husband's surname, so, legally, her name is Madame Antoine. But she's very proud of her first husband, who was something quite high up in the Hôtel de Ville, so she likes to be known as Madame Antoine de Caramé.

17

'What do you make of her?'

'How do you mean?'

'Is she at all peculiar?'

'What I want to know is why the police should be taking such an interest in her, all of a sudden?'

'She came asking for our help.'

'What seems to be the trouble?'

'Apparently things get moved about in her flat while she's out. Hasn't she said anything to you?'

'She just asked me if I'd ever seen any strangers going up to her flat. I said I hadn't. I wouldn't anyway, not from here. I can't see the front entrance or the staircase.'

'Does she get many visitors?'

'Only her niece, who comes once or twice a month. And even she sometimes doesn't show up for three months at a stretch.'

'Have you ever noticed anything odd about her behaviour?'

'She's very much like any other old woman living on her own. She's a real lady, you can see that, and she's always very polite to everyone.'

'Is she at home now?'

'No, she never misses a chance of sunning herself on her favourite bench in the Tuileries.'

'Does she talk to you at all?'

'Just a few words when we happen to meet. Most days she asks after my husband, who's ill in hospital.'

'I'm much obliged to you.'

'I take it you'd rather I didn't mention your visit?'

'It doesn't matter one way or the other.'

'At any rate, I don't think she's mad, if that's what you're getting at. She has her fads, all old people do, but no more than anyone else.'

'You may be seeing me again.'

Maigret was in high good humour. For ten days, there had not been a drop of rain, the pale blue sky was cloudless, and a gentle breeze was blowing. In this perfect spring weather, Paris was as gay and colourful as the backcloth of an operetta.

He stayed on rather late in his office to check through a report, which he had been working on for some time and was anxious to get rid of. He could hear the passing traffic, cars and buses, and occasionally a tug on the river sounding its siren.

It was nearly seven when he opened the communicating door to the inspectors' room, to tell Lucas and the two or three other inspectors on night duty that he was leaving.

He went downstairs, toying with the idea of dropping into the Brasserie Dauphine for an aperitif. As he went out through the main gate, he exchanged greetings with the two constables on guard.

After a moment or two of hesitation, he decided that he would rather go straight home. He had gone a few yards in the direction of the Boulevard du Palais, when the tiny figure of a woman stepped into his path. He had no difficulty in recognizing her from Lapointe's description.

'It really is you, isn't it?' she said with great fervour

She saw no need to address him by name. Whom could she mean but the great, the famous Chief Superintendent, every detail of whose cases she had read avidly in the newspapers? She even went so far as to paste into scrapbooks every word that was written about him.

'Please forgive me for accosting you in the street like this, but in there they wouldn't let me near you.'

Maigret felt a little foolish. He could just imagine the two constables exchanging amused glances behind his back.

'Mind you, I can see their point. I don't hold it against them. After all, it's their job to see that you're not disturbed when you're busy, isn't it?'

It was her eyes that made the deepest impression on the Chief Superintendent, clear, light grey eyes, very gentle and yet full of sparkle. She smiled at him. Clearly, she was in the seventh heaven. But there was something else about her too, an intense vitality, quite extraordinary in such a tiny little woman.

'Which way are you going?'

He pointed towards the Pont Saint-Michel.

'Would you mind very much if I walked with you?'

Trotting along at his side, she seemed tinier still.

'The main thing is, do you see, that you should realize that I'm not mad. I know how we old people look to the young, and I am a very old woman indeed.'

'You're eighty-six, are you not?'

'I see that the young man I spoke to has told you all about me. He seems very young for the job, but you can see he's been well brought up. He has beautiful manners.'

'Have you been waiting here long?'

'Since five to six. I thought you left your office at six. I saw a great many gentlemen come out, but you weren't among them.'

So she had stood there waiting a whole hour, ignored by the two incurious policemen on guard duty.

'I have this feeling that I'm in danger. Someone is sneaking into my flat and rummaging among my things. There must be some reason for it.'

'You say someone has been searching your flat. How do you know?'

'Because I find things not quite as I left them. I'm extremely tidy. It's almost an obsession. In my flat there is a place for everything, and, for more than forty years, everything has been in its place.'

'And this has happened more than once?'

'At least four times.'

'Do you have anything valuable?'

'No, Chief Superintendent. Nothing but the sort of odds and ends that one accumulates over the years and keeps for reasons of sentiment.'

She stopped suddenly, and looked back over her shoulder.

'Is anyone following you now?' he asked.

'Not at this moment, no. I beg you to come and see me. You'll understand it all much better when I've shown you over the place.'

'I'll do my very best to try and fit it in.'

'For an old woman like me, can't you do better than that? The Quai de la Mégisserie is just around the corner from here.

20

Drop in and see me sometime in the next day or so. I promise I won't keep you long. And I promise I won't bother you at your office again.

She was nothing if not artful.

'I'll come as soon as I can.'

'This week?'

'This week, if possible. Otherwise, at the beginning of next week.'

They had arrived at his bus stop.

'Please forgive me, I must be on my way home now.'

'I'm relying on you. I trust you.'

At that moment, he would have been hard put to it to say what he really felt about her. There was no denying that she might have made the whole thing up. That, at any rate, was what it sounded like. But when one was actually with her, looking into her face, it was almost impossible not to take her seriously.

He arrived home to find the table already laid for dinner. Kissing his wife on both cheeks, he said:

'It's been such a lovely day. I hope you managed to get out.'

'I went and did some shopping.'

And then he said something that surprised her.

'Tell me, have you ever sat on a bench in a public park?'

She was taken aback by the question. After a moment's reflection, she said:

'I suppose I must have done, when I was too early for a dental appointment, for instance.'

'I had a visitor this evening, who spends pretty well every afternoon sitting on a bench in the Tuileries.'

'There are lots of people like that.'

'Have you ever got into conversation with any of them?'

'On one occasion, at least. The mother of a little girl asked me to keep an eye on her while she got something from a shop just across the square.'

Here, too, the window was open. They had several kinds of cold meat, and a salad with mayonnaise. It might have been the height of summer.

'What would you say to a short walk?'

21

There was still a rosy glow in the sky from the setting sun, and it was quiet in the Boulevard Richard-Lenoir. Here and there they could see people looking down into the street, their elbows resting on the window sills.

They enjoyed walking for its own sake. It was pleasant to be together, though they had nothing much to say to one another. Together, they watched the people crossing the roads, together they looked at the window displays in the shops, and occasionally one or other would make a remark. They went as far as the Bastille and came back along the Boulevard Beaumarchais.

'A very strange old lady came to see me this evening, though actually it was Lapointe who interviewed her. I didn't see her until later, when she accosted me in the street as I was leaving.

'From the story she tells, you'd think she was mad, or at least a bit touched.'

'What seems to be the trouble?'

'Nothing, really. It's just that she says that sometimes, when she's been out, she comes back to find some of her things slightly out of place.'

'Has she a cat?'

'That was the first thing Lapointe asked her. She doesn't keep pets. She lives above a shop which sells birds, and she can hear them singing all day long, which she says is company enough for her.'

'Do you think there's any truth in it?'

'When she was actually there, looking up at me, yes, I did. She's got wonderfully clear grey eyes, full of kindliness and honesty, utterly without guile, at any rate. She's been widowed twelve years. She lives alone. Except for a niece whom she hardly ever sees, she has no one in the world.

'Every morning she goes out to the local shops, in a white hat and gloves. She spends most of her afternoons sitting on a bench in the Tuileries. She doesn't complain, she's never bored, and loneliness doesn't seem to worry her.'

'That's true of a lot of old people, you know.'

'I daresay you're right, but there's something a little

22

different about her, though I can't quite manage to put my finger on it.'

It was dark by the time they got home, and much cooler. They went to bed early, and, next morning, seeing that it was another lovely day, Maigret decided to walk to work.

As usual, there was a formidable pile of letters for him. He just had time to glance through them, and have a word with his inspectors, before the Chief Commissioner's daily briefing. There was nothing very important on hand.

He spent the morning clearing up a few routine matters, and then decided, on the spur of the moment, to have lunch at the Brasserie Dauphine. He rang his wife to tell her he would not be lunching at home. He had intended, after he had eaten, to call on the old lady at the Quai de la Mégisserie, and was prevented from doing so only by the merest chance. He ran into an old colleague, whom he had not seen since his retirement, and they lingered for a quarter of an hour or more, chatting in the sunshine.

Twice that afternoon, he thought again of going to see the old lady, whom the inspectors had already nicknamed 'Maigret's old madwoman,' but each time he found some excuse for putting it off, telling himself that tomorrow would do just as well.

If the newspapers were ever to get hold of the tale of the wandering ornaments, he would be the laughing stock of Paris.

That evening, they stayed in and watched television. Next morning he overslept, and had to go to work by bus. A few minutes before noon, the Divisional Superintendent of the 1st *Arrondissement* was on the phone to him.

'Something has happened here that I think may be of interest to your people. The concierge of the flats tells me that one of your inspectors, a young fellow, very handsome, called to see her the other day.'

He had a sudden foreboding.

'At the Quai de la Mégisserie?'

'Yes.'

'Is she dead?'

'Yes.'

'Are you ringing from the flat?'

'I'm downstairs in the bird shop. There's no telephone up there.'

'I'm on my way.'

He put his head round the door of the Inspectors' Duty Room, and said to Lapointe:

'Come with me.'

'Anything wrong, sir?'

'As far as you and I are concerned, yes, very wrong. It's the old lady.'

'The one with the grey eyes and the white hat?'

'Yes. She's dead.'

'Murdered?'

'I presume so. Why else should the Superintendent have thought fit to get in touch with me?'

They didn't bother with a car. It was quicker to walk. Superintendent Jenton, well known to Maigret, was standing on the edge of the pavement, next to a parrot chained to its perch.

'Did you know her?'

'I only saw her once. I'd promised to come and see her as soon as I could. Yesterday, I very nearly did.'

Would it have made any difference if he had?

'Is there anyone up there?'

'One of my men, and Doctor Forniaux has just arrived.'

'How did she die?'

'I don't know yet. At about half past ten this morning, one of the second-floor tenants noticed that her door was ajar. She didn't attach any importance to it, and went out to do her shopping. When she got back at eleven, and saw that it was still open, she called out:

' "Madame Antoine! . . . Madame Antoine! . . . Are you there?'

'When there was no answer, she went into the flat and nearly tripped over the body.'

'Was it lying on the floor?'

'Yes. In the sitting room. The neighbour had the good sense to ring through to us at once.'

Maigret went slowly up the stairs. His expression was grim.

'How was she dressed?'

'She must have been out earlier. She was still wearing her white hat and gloves.'

'Any visible injuries?'

'None that I could see. The concierge told me that one of your men was round here three days ago, asking questions about the old lady, so of course I rang you at once.'

Doctor Forniaux, who was kneeling on the floor, stood up as the three men came into the room.

They shook hands.

'Can you tell us the cause of death?'

'Suffocation.'

'Do you mean she was strangled?'

'No. Some sort of cloth, a towel, perhaps, or even a handkerchief, was held over her nose and mouth until she stopped breathing.'

'Are you sure?'

'I'll be able to tell you for certain after the autopsy.'

The window was wide open, and they could hear the birds twittering in the shop below.

'When did she die?'

'Sometime yesterday. Late afternoon or early evening.'

In death, the old woman seemed even tinier than she had when she was alive. Lying there, so small, with one leg bent at an awkward angle, she looked like a disjointed puppet.

The doctor had closed her eyes. Her face and hands seemed carved in ivory.

'How long before the killer could be sure she was dead, would you say?'

'It's hard to tell, especially with a woman of her age. Five minutes perhaps, a little more, a little less. . . .'

'Lapointe, ring Public Prosecutions and the Laboratory. Tell Moers to send his men along right away.'

'Unless there's anything further I can do for you,' said the police surgeon, 'I'll be on my way. I'll arrange for the mortuary van to collect her and take her to the Forensic Laboratory, as soon as you've done with her.'

A small crowd was beginning to collect outside the building. The Divisional Superintendent sent his man down to speak to them.

'Move them on. This isn't a public entertainment.'

Murder was scarcely a new experience to either of them, but they were none the less deeply affected on that account. She was so very old and—what made it seem worse—there was not even a mark on her.

Then there was the atmosphere of the place, recalling the Edwardian, if not the Victorian era. The furniture was of solid mahogany, massive pieces, all beautifully polished to a high gloss. The chairs, of the kind still to be found in provincial drawing rooms, were covered in crimson plush. There were a great many ornaments, and masses of photographs were hanging on every wall, against a background of flowered paper.

'All we can do now is to wait for the D.P.P.'

'He won't be long. They'll send the first available Deputy. He'll arrive with his clerk in attendance, take a quick look round, and that will be that.'

This, indeed, was a fair description of what usually happened, as a prelude to the arrival of the forensic technicians, with all their cumbersome apparatus.

The door swung open without a sound. Maigret gave a start. A little girl sidled in, probably a neighbour's child, from one of the upper floors, curious to see what all the comings and goings were about.

'Do you often come here?'

'No. I've never been before.'

'Where do you live?'

'Just across the landing.'

'Did you know Madame Antoine?'

'I used to see her sometimes on the stairs.'

'Used she to talk to you?'

'She always smiled at me.'

'Did she ever give you anything, sweets or chocolates?'

'No.'

'Where's your mother?'

'In the kitchen.'

'Take me to her, will you?'

He turned to the Superintendent.

'Excuse me a moment. I'd be grateful if you'd let me know when the Deputy gets here.'

It was an old building. The walls were bulging in places, and there were gaps between the floorboards.

'There's a gentleman to see you, mummy.'

The woman came out of the kitchen, wiping her hands on her apron. Her arms, just below the elbow, were still spattered with soapsuds.

'I'm Chief Superintendent Maigret. I just happened to be in the flat across the landing when your daughter walked in. Was it you who found the body?'

'What body? Go to your room, Lucette.'

'Your neighbour, opposite.'

'So she's dead? I always said it was bound to happen sooner or later. A woman of her age ought not to live alone. I daresay she was taken bad, and hadn't enough strength to call for help.'

'She was murdered.'

'I never heard a thing! But then, of course, with all the noise of the traffic . . .'

'There was no shooting, and it happened not this morning, but yesterday afternoon or evening.'

'Poor woman! She was a bit too high and mighty for my taste, but I had nothing against her.'

'Were you on friendly terms with her?'

'I doubt if we exchanged a dozen words in all the seven years I've lived here.'

'Do you know anything about her personal life?'

'I often used to see her go out in the morning. She wore a black hat in winter and a white one in summer, and she never went out without her gloves, even round the corner to the shops. Well, live and let live, I say.'

'Did she ever have visitors?'

'Not that I know of. No, wait, come to think of it, she did have one, a woman, rather on the heavy side, and a bit

27

mannish. I have seen her two or three times ringing the door-bell.'

'Was this during the day?'

'In the evening, as a rule. Soon after dinner.'

'Have you noticed any unusual comings and goings in the building recently?'

'There are always people milling about. The concierge hardly ever leaves the lodge there, across the yard. She takes no interest at all in the tenants.'

The little girl had sidled back noiselessly into the room. The woman turned to her.

'Didn't you hear what I said? Go straight back to your room.'

'You'll be seeing me again, I daresay. I shall have to have a word with all the tenants.'

'I suppose you've no idea who did it?'

'None.'

'Who found her?'

'Someone from the second floor. She noticed on her way out that the door was ajar, and when she came back and found it still open, she called out, and then went in.'

'I can guess who that was.'

'Why do you say that?'

'It must be old mother Rochin. She's the nosiest woman in the building.'

They could hear footsteps and voices outside on the landing. The men from the Department of Public Prosecutions had arrived. Maigret went across to join them.

'This way,' he said. 'Doctor Forniaux has been, but he has a great many calls this morning, so he couldn't wait.'

The Deputy was a tall young man, distinguished-looking and strikingly well-dressed. He looked about him in some surprise, as though he had never seen anything quite like it. Then he stood for a moment staring down at the crumpled little grey figure on the carpet.

'How did she die?'

'She was suffocated.'

'She can't have put up much of a fight, that's for sure.'

Judge Libart arrived a few minutes later. He too looked round the flat with interest.

'It's just like an old film set,' he remarked.

Lapointe, by this time, had returned. He and Maigret exchanged glances. While neither of them actually shuddered, their feelings were plain enough.

CHAPTER TWO

'MAYBE I'D BETTER send along two or three men to keep the sightseers on the move,' suggested the District Superintendent.

Already the residents were pouring out of their flats and gathering on the landing and staircase. The Public Prosecutor's men would be arriving at any minute, not to mention the stretcher-bearers from the Forensic Laboratory.

Lapointe, glancing at Maigret, noted that he was looking unwontedly pale and grave. It was only three days since he had first set eyes on the dead woman. Up to that time, he had never even heard of her. Yet, in her distress—real or imagined —it was to him that she had turned for help. She had put her trust in him. She had sought a personal interview, and, failing that, had accosted him in the street. He could still see her looking up at him, her eyes glowing with hero-worship.

He had thought her mad, or at least not perfectly sane. And yet, all the while, there had been that little nagging doubt at the back of his mind. And so he had promised to go and see her. And probably would have done so, this very afternoon.

It was too late now. She had been well and truly done to death, just as she had feared.

'See that they go over every inch of every room for finger-prints. Make sure they don't miss anything out, not even the least likely surfaces.'

There was a sudden commotion on the landing. He opened the front door. At least a dozen reporters and cameramen were crowding round the door, with a solitary constable struggling to hold them back.

A camera clicked in his face.

'Can you give us a statement, Chief Superintendent?'

'Not at the moment, gentlemen, I'm afraid. You might say that the inquiry hasn't really started yet.'

'Who was she?'

'An old lady.'

'Madame Antoine de Caramé. That much we got from the concierge. What's more, she says that one of your men was here earlier in the week asking questions about her. What was that in aid of? Had you any reason to think she was in danger?'

'All I can say at present is that I'm as much in the dark as you are.'

'Is it true that she lived alone, and never had any visitors?'

'As far as we know, that's correct, except for a niece—I don't know her name—who used to come and see her from time to time. She's a masseuse, and lives quite near here, just across the river not far from the Pont-Neuf.'

A brief statement to this effect had already been broadcast, and would also feature in the afternoon editions of the newspapers. As a result, no doubt the niece would in due course come forward.

'May we go in and take pictures?'

'Not yet. The men from Criminal Records haven't finished. For the time being, I'd be obliged if you would leave the landing and staircase clear.'

'We'll wait downstairs in the courtyard.'

Maigret closed the door. He had not yet had time to look round the flat. Overlooking the street was the sitting room, where Madame Antoine had been attacked, no doubt on returning from her daily outing to the Tuileries.

Had she been right in suspecting that someone was in the habit of entering the flat while she was out? It seemed more than likely. If so, there was something here that the intruder very badly wanted.

But what could it possibly be?

She must have got home earlier than usual, and caught the intruder red-handed. At any rate, he had not hesitated to put her out of the way. That seemed to suggest that he was someone she recognized. If not, he could easily have taken to his heels. It therefore looked as if he had had no choice but to murder her.

'Any fingerprints?'

31

'None but the old lady's so far. Oh, and the Police Surgeon's on the table in the sitting room. I'd know them anywhere.'

There were two windows in the sitting room, which was low-ceilinged like the rest of the flat. A communicating door led into the dining room. Both rooms were quaintly old-fashioned, as old-fashioned as Madame Antoine herself. On a pedestal table in the corner stood an enormous green plant in an earthenware pot, which was swathed in drapery.

It was all spotlessly clean, and there was not a thing out of place.

There was only one window in the dining room, and, facing it, a door which led into the kitchen. The loaf in the bread-bin was still fresh. Maigret opened the refrigerator. It contained, neatly wrapped in pieces of greaseproof paper, a slice of ham and half a veal cutlet. There was also a lettuce and a half bottle of milk.

There was only one other room, the bedroom. Like the kitchen, it looked out on to the courtyard. The bedroom suite, which included a massive mirror-fronted wardrobe and an imposing bed, was of walnut. The floorboards were covered by a faded, threadbare carpet, vaguely oriental in design.

There was an indefinable air of dignity about the whole place. He would have to come back later, after lunch, probably, and examine the old lady's possessions one by one, including the contents of the cupboards and drawers.

'We're through now, Chief.'

The police photographers were dismantling and removing their cameras. No fingerprints had been found, other than those of the old lady herself.

Maigret instructed the constable at the door to admit no one except the Inspector, whom he would be sending up in a moment. He went slowly down the dark staircase, with its worn treads, and banister polished to a high gloss by two or three hundred years of use.

In the courtyard, the pressmen were bombarding the concierge with questions, and getting short shrift for their pains. Lapointe, unusually silent, followed Maigret downstairs He, too, was much shaken. He had a mental picture of

Madame Antoine as he had seen her in the little office where he had interviewed her, and formed the impression that she was not quite right in the head.

The owner of the birds—Monsieur Caille presumably, since that was the name painted over the pet shop—wearing a long grey denim overall, was standing on the pavement beside a row of cages.

'I wonder if I might use your telephone?'

'With pleasure, Chief Superintendent.'

He gave a knowing smile, very pleased with himself for having recognized Maigret. The telephone was at the back of the shop where, in addition to more birds in cages, there were several tanks full of goldfish. An old man, also in a grey overall, was engaged in feeding the fish.

'Hello! . . . Lucas? . . . I shall be needing another man here . . . Quai de la Mégisserie . . . 8b . . . Janvier? . . . Fine. . . . Tell him to go straight up to the flat, and not let anyone else in . . . and I'd be obliged if you'd ring my wife and tell her I won't be home to lunch. . . .'

He put down the receiver and turned to the pet-shop owner.

'Have you lived here long?'

'Ever since I was ten years old. My father owned the shop before me.'

'So you've known Madame Antoine ever since she moved in?'

'Yes, it must be forty years. That was in the time of her first husband, Monsieur de Caramé. A fine-looking man, he was. Impressive. He was very high up in local government, and whenever there was a do at the Hôtel de Ville, he always gave us complimentary tickets.'

'Did they do much entertaining in those early days?'

'There were two or three married couples who were close friends of theirs. They used to get together for a game of cards about once a week.'

'What was Madame Antoine like?'

'She was a dear little thing. Very pretty. It's strange how things turn out, though. She was so frail and delicate, you'd never have thought she'd make old bones. He, on the other hand, was strongly built, and, as far as I know, never had a day's illness. He enjoyed the good things of life. Yet he was the one who died suddenly in his office, when he was in the prime of life, while his wife lived on—until yesterday.'

'And she remarried soon after?'

'Oh, no! She was alone for the best part of ten years. Then she met Monsieur Antoine somewhere or other, and eventually married him. I have nothing to say against him. He was a thoroughly decent chap, but, compared with her first husband, he lacked distinction.

'He worked in the Bazar de l'Hôtel de Ville. He was head of one of the departments, I believe. He was a widower. I daresay you've seen his little workshop up in the flat. He loved nothing better than to be pottering about in there. He never said much beyond passing the time of day. They hardly ever went out.

'He had a car, and used to take his wife for a drive in the country on Sundays. In the summer, they always went on holiday to a place somewhere near Etretat.'

'Were any of the other tenants friends of theirs?'

'I fancy I must be the only one left. The others have all died off in the course of the years, and new people have moved in to take their place. I never see any of the old faces nowadays.'

'There's Monsieur Crispin, don't forget, father,' interpolated the son, who was still standing in the doorway.

'True enough, but as one never sees him about now, it's hard to remember that he's still alive. He's paralysed—has been for the past five years. He has a couple of rooms on the fifth floor, and the concierge takes him up his meals and cleans the place for him.'

'Was he friendly with the Antoines?'

'Let me think. At my age, you tend to lose track of time. He moved in a little while before Madame Antoine. So Monsieur de Caramé must still have been alive. But I don't think they were on visiting terms at that time. It was only later, when Madame de Caramé married Monsieur Antoine, that they became friends. He was in business too, you see, haberdashery, I think. He worked in a shop in the Rue du Sentier.'

34

'I'm much obliged to you, Monsieur Caille.'

Janvier was waiting for him in the front hall.

'Have you eaten?'

'A snack, but what about you?'

'Lapointe and I are just off to lunch. I want you to go up and wait for us in the flat. It's on the first floor. Don't touch anything, anything at all, however insignificant. You'll find out why later. Oh! there's just one person you'll have to let in if she turns up, and that's the niece.'

Ten minutes later, Maigret and Lapointe were seated at a table in the Brasserie Dauphine.

'A small aperitif?' suggested the proprietor.

'No, bring us a carafe of Beaujolais right away. What have you got on the menu today?'

'*Andouillettes*. They arrived fresh from Auvergne this morning.'

Maigret ordered fillets of herring as a first course, to be followed by the *andouillettes*.

'What do you think, yourself?' asked Maigret, a little uncomfortably.

Lapointe scarcely knew what to say.

'It never entered my head that she was telling the truth. I could have sworn that she was just imagining things, the way old people so often do.'

'She's dead.

'And if the door hadn't been left ajar, it might have been days before anyone found her. The murderer must have been someone she knew, otherwise there'd have been no need to kill her.'

'I wonder what it was he was looking for.'

'When we know that—if we ever do—the case will be virtually solved. Very shortly, we shall be going over the flat inch by inch. There must be something there that the murderer very much wanted to find. He searched the place several times without success, so it's probably well hidden or not immediately recognizable as such.'

'What if he's already found what he was looking for?'

'In that case, there's not much hope of catching him. All

the other tenants will have to be questioned. How many floors are there in the building?'

'Six, excluding the attics.'

'And there are at least two flats on every floor. . . .'

The Beaujolais could not have been better, and the *andouillettes*, served with chips, were quite delicious.

'There's one thing that puzzles me. Madame Antoine was eighty-six. She'd been a widow for twelve years or more. Why wait until now to start searching her flat? Surely that must mean that whatever it is that the intruder was looking for had only recently come into the old lady's possession?'

'If that were so, she would have known what it was. Whereas, if I'm not mistaken, she told you that she hadn't the least idea what it was all about.'

'She seemed just as puzzled as we were.'

'There was no mystery about either of her husbands. Quite the reverse. Both were typical middle-class Frenchmen, except that one was rather better-looking than the other.'

Maigret beckoned the proprietor:

'Two coffees, Léon.'

The sun was still shining in a cloudless blue sky. The Quais were crowded with tourists with cameras slung round their necks.

The two men made their way back to the Quai de la Mégisserie.

All but one of the reporters had left, and he was pacing restlessly up and down the courtyard.

'I don't suppose there's anything you can tell me?' he muttered, somewhat sourly.

'Nothing for the present.'

'There's a woman up there. She arrived about ten minutes ago, but she wouldn't give her name.'

It was not long before Maigret and Lapointe were making her acquaintance. She was a heavily built woman of somewhat mannish appearance, aged about forty-five to fifty. She was seated in one of the armchairs in the sitting room.

Janvier, apparently, had not attempted to engage her in conversation.

'You are Chief Superintendent Maigret?'

'Yes, and these two gentlemen are Inspectors Janvier and Lapointe.'

'I am Angèle Louette.'

'Madame?'

'No, I'm not married, though I have a son of twenty-five. I'm not ashamed of it. Quite the reverse.'

'You are Madame Antoine's niece, I take it?'

'She and my mother were sisters. She was the elder, for all that my mother was the first to go. She's been dead more than ten years now.'

'Does your son live with you?'

'No, I'm on my own. I have a small flat in the Rue Saint-André-des-Arts.'

'And your son?'

'He moves around a good deal. At present, I believe he's on the Côte d'Azur. He's a musician.'

'When did you last see your aunt?'

'About three weeks ago.'

'Did you visit her often?'

'About once a month. Sometimes once in two months.'

'Did you get on well with her?'

'We didn't have rows.'

'Which means . . . ?'

'We were never at all close. My aunt was a mistrustful old woman. I'm certain she believed I only came to see her so as to keep on good terms with her, in the hope of inheriting her money.'

'Had she anything to leave?'

'She must have had savings, but I shouldn't think they amounted to much.'

'Do you know if she had a bank account?'

'If so, she never told me. What she was always on about was that I should see to it that she was buried beside her first husband in the Montparnasse cemetery. She has a plot there.

'If you want my opinion, I believe she only remarried for the sake of company. She was still young. I don't know where

37

she met my uncle Antoine. The first I heard of it was one day when she announced, out of the blue, that she was getting married again, and asked me to be a witness. . . .'

Maigret was taking in every word, having indicated to Lapointe, who had got out his shorthand pad, that he did not wish him to take notes. She was the kind of woman who would probably shut up like a clam if subjected to an official interrogation.

'Tell me, Mademoiselle Louette, do you know of any reason why your aunt should have gone in fear of her life?'

'None at all.'

'Did she tell you that she had found traces of a mysterious intruder in the flat?'

'No, never.'

'Did she ever ring you up or call to see you?'

'No. I always came to see her. Just from time to time, you know, to make sure she was all right, and to find out if there was anything she needed. It worried me that she lived on her own. Anything might have happened to her, and not a soul would have known.'

'Did she never consider having a daily woman in to do the housework?'

'She could well have afforded it, on her two widow's pensions. I begged her to get someone to live in, but she wouldn't even entertain the idea of a daily. You can see how she kept the flat. Not a speck of dust anywhere.'

'You are a masseuse, I believe.'

'Yes, my time is fully occupied. I have nothing to complain of.'

'Tell me about your son's father.'

'He left me when my son was born. I wasn't sorry to see him go. He wasn't the man I thought him. I lost my head over him, as they say. I've no idea what's become of him, and I daresay I shouldn't recognize him now if I met him in the street.'

'I take it, then, that your son bears your name, and has a "father unknown" birth certificate?'

'Yes. His name is Emile Louette. But since he took up the

38

guitar and became a night club entertainer, he's become known, for professional purposes, as Billy Louette.'

'Are you and he on good terms?'

'He comes to see me occasionally, usually when he's short of money. He's an out-and-out Bohemian, but he's a good lad, all the same.'

'Did he ever come and see his aunt?'

'I used to bring him with me when he was a child. The last time was when he was fifteen or sixteen, I think. As far as I know, he's never seen her since.'

'Might he not have come to her for money, as he did to you?'

'He wouldn't do a thing like that. I'm his mother, so that's different, but he would never ask anyone else. He's too proud.'

'Do you know your way around this flat?'

'Pretty well.'

'Where did your aunt spend most of her time?'

'Here, in this very armchair, drawn up close to the window.'

'How did she keep herself occupied?'

'First of all, she had the housework to do. Then she'd go out and do her shopping. When she got back, she cooked herself a meal. She wasn't the sort to make do with a slice of cold meat eaten off a corner of the kitchen table. In spite of the fact that she lived alone, she took her meals in the dining room, and the table was always properly laid, with a clean cloth.'

'Did she go out much?'

'On fine days, she liked to go and sit on a bench in the Tuileries.'

'Did she read a lot?'

'No. She had weak eyesight, and it tired her to read for any length of time. She enjoyed watching the people out for a stroll, and the children playing among the trees. She almost always wore a rather sad little smile. I daresay she lived in the past a good deal.'

'Did she never confide in you?'

'What could she possibly have had to tell me? Her life was an open book.'

'Hadn't she any friends?'

39

'All her old friends had died, and she didn't feel like making new ones; and that was why she moved away from the bench she had always sat on. I've just remembered.'

'How long ago was this?'

'Towards the end of last summer. For years she'd always sat on the same bench in the Tuileries Gardens. One day, she was approached by a woman of about her own age, who asked if she might share the bench with her. Presumably she said yes. Anyone is at liberty to sit down on a park bench. At any rate, this woman tried to strike up an acquaintance with her from the very first day. She told her that she was of Russian origin, and that she had been, in her day, a famous ballerina.

'Next day, she was there again, and spent an hour regaling my aunt with tales of her former glory. She had lived in Nice for years, and she went on and on about the awful Paris weather.

'My aunt wasn't given to idle chatter as a rule.

'"I had become so attached to that bench!" she said, with a sigh.

'"Not only was I forced to move away from it, but I had to go right to the other side of the Gardens, otherwise she'd have found me out, and I would never have got away from her." '

'Did this Russian woman ever visit her here?'

'Not that I know of. My aunt being what she was, I'm pretty sure she never got the chance.'

'You can't throw any light on the identity of the murderer, I suppose?'

'I'm afraid not, Chief Superintendent. What am I to do about the funeral arrangements?'

'You'd better let me have your telephone number. I'll be in touch. By the way, do you happen to have a recent photograph of your aunt?'

'Only one taken by my uncle Antoine about twelve years ago. I'd be grateful if you'd ring me in the evening, as I'm out at work most of the day.'

The police constable detailed to keep watch on the entrance was still there.

'What do you make of her, Chief?'

'She seems ready enough to talk. Rather a bossy woman, I'd say.'

Janvier looked about him in astonishment.

'Is it all like this?'

'Yes. The bedroom, if anything, is even more old-world. Lapointe, you know the layout of the building, more or less. I want you to call at all the flats. Find out which of the tenants knew the old lady by sight, and whether any of them were at all friendly with her. Also, of course, whether they ever saw anyone entering or leaving the flat.'

The only concession to the twentieth century was the television set in the sitting room. It stood in a corner, opposite an armchair upholstered in flowered chintz.

'Now,' said Maigret to Janvier, 'we're going to go over the flat inch by inch, recording the exact position of everything in it. It was the fact that she found some of her things very slightly displaced that first gave her cause for anxiety.'

The shrunken floorboards, with gaps between, were covered not with a carpet but with scattered rugs, on one of which stood a round tripod table covered in a lace cloth.

They moved the table and took up the rug, to satisfy themselves that nothing was hidden under it. Having done so, they returned the table to its original position and carefully put back the ornaments, a large seashell with *Dieppe* carved on it, an earthenware plant pot, and a fake bronze statuette of a schoolboy in a sailor suit with a satchel on his back.

The mantelpiece was covered in photographs, photographs of two men, the two husbands of the old lady, who, towards the end, it seemed, had almost forgotten which was which. One of them, round-faced, plumpish and clean-shaven, had struck a dignified attitude before the camera. He, no doubt, was the one who had been a senior official at the Hôtel de Ville.

The other, somewhat less impressive, had a greying moustache. Men like him were to be seen in their thousands every day on the buses and the underground. He looked more like a shop assistant or a cashier than the manager or buyer of a large store, which was what he had actually been. He wa smiling in the photograph, a cheerful smile. He had been content with his lot.

'By the way, Janvier, how did the niece get in? Had she a key?'

'No, she rang the bell, and I let her in.'

'This drawer is locked. The key must be somewhere about.'

First he searched through the contents of the old lady's handbag, the white leather handbag which she must only recently have got out of her wardrobe, for use in the spring and summer. There was no lipstick, just a powder compact—the powder had a bluish tinge—and a handkerchief embroidered with the initial 'L'. Madame Antoine's Christian name, as the two men were soon to find out, had been Léontine.

No cigarettes. Obviously she didn't smoke. A small bag of violet-scented sweets from a shop in the Rue de Rivoli. The sweets must have been there for some time, as they were all stuck together.

'Here are the keys.'

He had been almost sure that he would find her keys in the handbag that went everywhere with her. There were three drawer keys, a key to one of the rooms and the front door key.

'She opened the door and put the keys back in her bag before coming in. Otherwise, they would have been left in the lock, or we should have found them on the floor. She must barely have had time to put her bag down on the chair before she was attacked.'

Maigret was not so much addressing Janvier as thinking aloud. He could not get rid of a nagging sense of uneasiness. Yet, even supposing he had been to see the old lady, would it have made that much difference? He would not have been able to find enough evidence to justify keeping a twenty-four-hour watch on the flat. And the murderer, unaware of his visit, would still have acted as he did.

He tried the smaller keys, one after the other, and finally succeeded in opening the locked drawer of the chest.

It was full of papers and photographs. On the right-hand side lay a Post Office Savings book in the name of Léontine Antoine, Quai de la Mégisserie, recording deposits amounting to ten thousand francs; nothing but deposits, not a single withdrawal. She had been paying money into the account for twenty-five years, which was why the name Caramé could still be read, with a line through it, below the name Antoine.

Twenty-five years of thrift. Shopping in the morning. An hour or so on a park bench in the afternoon, perhaps an occasional visit to a cinema when the weather was bad. There was also a Savings Bank book, recording a total of twenty-three thousand two hundred francs. A few days before Christmas in the previous year, there had been a withdrawal of two thousand five hundred francs.

'What does that suggest to you?'

Janvier shook his head.

'The television set. I bet you anything you like that's where the two thousand five hundred francs went. In other words, she decided to give herself a treat for Christmas.'

The only other recorded withdrawal was twelve years old, and no doubt represented the cost of her second husband's funeral.

There were numerous postcards, most of them signed 'Jean'. They bore the postmarks of various towns and cities in France, Belgium and Switzerland. The sender, no doubt, had been attending conferences in these places. All the cards bore the same message: 'Much Love, Jean' in a distinguished, roundish hand. 'Jean' was Caramé. Antoine, apparently, had seldom been away on his own. There was not a single card from him. But there were innumerable photographs both of him alone and of him and his wife. The camera with which they had been taken, rather a sophisticated one, was also in the same drawer. Monsieur and Madame Antoine, it seemed, had gone to a different place each year for their holiday. Apparently, they had been great travellers. They had visited Quimper, La Baule, Arcachon and Biarritz. They had toured the Massif Central, and spent summers on the Riviera.

The photographs had been taken at different times, in some the couple appeared older than in others. It would have been a simple matter to arrange them in chronological order.

There were a few letters, mostly from Angèle Louette, the

43

niece who was a masseuse. These, too, came from towns outside Paris.

'Emile and I are thoroughly enjoying our holiday. Emile is growing up fast. He spends all day rolling over and over in the sand. . . .'

There was just one photograph of the boy, Emile, who was now calling himself Billy. It was taken when he was fifteen. He was looking straight in front of him, with an expression that spelt defiance of the whole world.

'No secrets. No surprises,' sighed Maigret.

In the drawer of a little occasional table they found nothing but some pencils, a pen, a rubber, and a few sheets of plain writing paper. Of late, Léontine had probably written few letters. Who was there left for her to write to?

She had outlived most of her contemporaries. Her niece and great-nephew were her only remaining relatives, and the boy scarcely counted. There was no trace of him among her effects, except for that one photograph, and the references in his mother's letter.

Sorting through the kitchen utensils, Maigret came upon several gadgets which were unfamiliar to him, and which did not look as though they were mass-produced. There was, for instance, a tin opener of highly sophisticated design, as well as a simple but ingenious potato-peeler.

It was not until he discovered the little cubby hole across the way that he understood the significance of these appliances. The key to the door was on Madame Antoine's key-ring. It opened on to a tiny annexe, quite separate from the flat itself, which was lit by a skylight overlooking the courtyard. This annexe was furnished with a workbench and a wide selection of tools, hanging neatly from hooks all round the walls.

This, then, was where Monsieur Antoine had pursued his hobby. On a shelf in one corner stood a pile of technical journals, and there was a drawer full of exercise books filled with working drawings of all kinds, including a drawing of the potato-peeler.

There must be thousands of people like him all over Paris, thought Maigret, thousands of couples like the Antoines, living modest, tidy, well-organized lives. There was only one discordant note, the murder of the tiny little old woman with the marvellously clear grey eyes.

'There's still the bedroom and the cupboards.'

The entire contents of the wardrobe consisted of a Persian lamb coat, another of black wool, two winter dresses, one of which was mauve, and three or four summer dresses.

No men's clothes. After the death of her second husband she must have given away his things, unless she had stored them somewhere, possibly in the attics? He must find out from the concierge.

Everything was very clean and tidy, and all the drawers were lined with white paper.

But the lining paper of the bedside table drawer, which incidentally was empty, was discoloured by a large oil or grease stain.

Maigret, intrigued, took the paper out of the drawer and held it up to his nose. He called Janvier over to see what he would make of it.

'What do you think this is?'

'Grease.'

'Yes, but not just any sort of grease. It's gun-grease. The old lady must have kept a revolver or an automatic in this drawer,'

'Where is it now?'

'Not in the flat, that's for sure. We've searched every inch, and we haven't found it. All the same, it looks quite fresh to me. Do you suppose the old woman's killer . . .'

It seemed highly unlikely that the murderer, whether man or woman, would have spent time looking for the revolver before making his or her getaway.

This grease-stain, which he had not discovered until the very end of his search, was a complication that he had not anticipated.

Had the old woman actually gone to the length of buying a gun to defend herself with? It seemed unlikely. From what Maigret had seen of her, she was hardly the sort to look upon firearms with anything but alarm. Moreover, he simply could

45

not imagine her going into a gunsmith's, asking for a pistol, and trudging down to the basement for a few practice shots.

And yet, when all was said and done, why not? Hadn't he been struck by her extraordinary vitality? Frail she certainly had been, with her delicate wrists no thicker than a child's, yet her flat was as well cared for as any in the land, even better perhaps.

'It must have belonged to one of her husbands.'

'But where has it got to then? See that this paper is handed in to the lab for analysis. Though I'm quite sure in my own mind what the answer will be.'

A bell rang, and Maigret instinctively looked around for the telephone.

'It's the front door,' said Janvier.

He went to open it. It was Lapointe, looking absolutely worn out.

'Have you spoken to all the tenants?'

'All except those who were out. The worst of it is, I could hardly get a word in with any of them. It was nothing but questions, questions, questions! How did she die? What was the murder weapon? How come that no one had heard a shot?'

'Go on.'

'The flat immediately above is occupied by an elderly bachelor of about sixty. Apparently, he's quite a well-known historian. I saw some of his books on his library shelves. He seldom goes out. He lives alone with his little dog. He has a housekeeper who comes in daily to clean the flat and cook his meals. I say a housekeeper because that's how he described her. I saw her for myself. She's known as Mademoiselle Elise, and she's full of her own importance.

'It's almost as old-fashioned as this flat, except that it's furnished in better taste. In passing he said:

'"If only she hadn't bought that wretched television set! She had it on almost every night until eleven. And I'm up every morning at six, so as to get in my regular walk before breakfast." '

Lapointe went on:

'They never exchanged a word in all the twenty years he's

46

been living here. When they met on the stairs, they merely nodded. He remembers the husband because he was noisy too. Apparently he had a workshop and a regular armoury of tools, and he would be sawing, hammering, filing, and heaven knows what else until all hours.'

'What about the flat opposite?'

'There was no one at home. I went down to the concierge to enquire about them. They're youngish people, apparently. He's a film technician, some sort of sound engineer, and his wife works in the cutting room. They usually dine out, and get home very late. They're late risers too, and they don't leave for work until midday.'

'And the third floor?'

Lapointe glanced at his notes.

'Some people called Lapin. There was no one in but the grandmother and the baby. The wife works in a men's wear shop in the Rue de Rivoli, and the husband is an insurance salesman. He's away a lot.'

'What about the flat opposite?'

'I'll come to them in a minute. I spoke to the grandmother, and she said:

'"No, young man, I did not know her. That woman was too clever by half, if you ask me. Look at the way she behaved with those two husbands of hers. I'm a widow myself, but did I go out looking for another husband? You wouldn't catch me setting up house with another man, in the same flat, with the same furniture."'

Once again, Lapointe consulted his notes.

'Father Raymond. I don't know which order he belongs to. He's very old, and scarcely ever sets foot outside his flat.

'He didn't even know of the existence of Léontine Antoine, formerly Léontine de Caramé. . . .

'On the floor above, there's an empty flat, let to people who will be moving in in two weeks' time. The workmen are there now, redecorating. The new tenants are a couple of about forty, with two children at the lycée.

'I interviewed the old man the concierge does for. He's confined to a wheelchair, and you should just see how he gets

47

around in it! I was expecting to see a querulous old dodderer, but not a bit of it, he's as chirpy as a cricket:

'"You don't say!" he exclaimed. "So she's actually gone and got herself murdered! I've been here fifty years or more, and nothing of any interest has ever happened before. And now we have a murder of our very own! Do you know who did it? I don't suppose it could possibly he a *crime passionel*, do you?"'

Lapointe went on:

'It was really comical. He was enjoying himself hugely. If it had been physically possible, he would have asked permission to visit the scene of the crime.

'The woman opposite is a Madame Blanche. She's about sixty, and works as a cashier in a brasserie. I didn't see her, as she doesn't get in before midnight.'

It was a tight little world that all these people lived in side by side.

Yet the murder of the old lady on the first floor had caused scarcely a ripple.

'How was she killed?'

'Who did it?'

'Why didn't she call out?'

Most of these people knew one another by sight, and would nod in passing, without exchanging a word. A lot of little private cells, with the doors shut tight.

'I want you to stay here until I send someone to relieve you,' Maigret said to Janvier.

'It may seem far fetched, but I have a notion that the man or woman who searched this flat before may well be minded to do so again.'

'Send Torrence, if you can spare him. He's potty about television.'

Maigret took the grease-stained lining paper with him. As soon as he got back to the Quai des Orfèvres he went straight up to Moers in his domain in the attics.

'I want this stain analysed.'

Moers sniffed at it, nodded to Maigret as if to assure him that this was no problem, and went over to one of the many

48

technicians at work in the huge laboratory under the sloping roof of the building.

'It's as I thought, gun-grease.'

'I shall need an official report. It's the only clue we've got so far. Is it an old stain, would you say?'

'My man says that that will take a little time to establish.'

'Thanks. Send down the result when you have it.'

He returned to his office, calling into the Inspectors' Duty Room on the way. Lapointe was writing up his report, with his notebook open beside him. Torrence was also there.

'See here, Torrence, are you hungry?'

Fat Torrence stared at him in amazement.

'At five o'clock in the afternoon?'

'You probably won't get a chance to eat later on. Go and get a snack now, or if you'd rather, buy yourself some sandwiches. I want you to go to the Quai de la Mégisserie and relieve Janvier. It's the first floor flat. I'll send someone to relieve you first thing in the morning. You'll find the keys on the round table in the sitting room.

'Watch yourself, though, because the murderer must have a key to the front door. Otherwise there would have been signs of a forced entry.'

'Do you think he'll come back?'

'In this extraordinary case, anything might happen.'

Maigret rang through to Doctor Forniaux.

'Have you finished the autopsy yet?'

'I was just about to dictate my report. Would you believe it, that diminutive little old woman could well have lived to be a hundred? You wouldn't find many young girls with organs in a healthier condition.

'As I suspected from the first, she was suffocated; almost certainly with a scarf with scarlet threads in it. I found one lodged in a tooth. She tried to bite through it. She almost certainly put up a struggle, before she blacked out for want of air.'

'Thanks, doc. Let me have your report as soon as you can.'

'You'll get it tomorrow, by the first post.'

Léontine Antoine did not drink, at least she kept no wines

or spirits in her flat. She ate a lot of cheese. The Chief Superintendent, standing by the window watching the traffic flow across the Pont Saint-Michel, pondered, trying to recreate the details of her life. A string of barges went under the bridge, drawn by a tug with an enormous white clover leaf painted on the funnel.

The sky was a delicate pink faintly tinged with blue; the trees, not yet in full leaf, were pale green, and full of twittering birds.

It was at this moment that the con.table who had first noticed the old lady arrived, asking to speak to the Chief Superintendent.

'I don't know if it's important—I've only just seen the photographs in the papers—but, you see, I recognized the old lady at once. What I mean to say is, that I saw her almost a week ago. I was on guard duty at the main gate. She wandered up and down outside for some time, gazing up at the windows, and peering into the forecourt. I thought she was about to speak to me, but then she seemed to change her mind, and she went away without saying a word.

'She was back next day, and, this time, she plucked up the courage to go through into the forecourt. I didn't attempt to stop her. I thought she was just an ordinary tourist. We get so many of them. . . .

'The following day, I was off duty. Lecoeur was on in my place, and he saw her go through the gate, and make straight for the Police Headquarters entrance. She looked so determined that he didn't even think to ask her if she had an appointment.'

'Thanks. Let me have a statement in writing, and one from Lecoeur too.'

So several days had gone by before she had been able to pluck up the courage to ask to see Chief Superintendent Maigret. And he had fobbed her off with Lapointe, whom she had at first taken to be his son.

But this had not prevented her from accosting the Chief Superintendent later, in the street.

Old Joseph was knocking at the door. There was no mistaking that distinctive knock. He opened it before Maigret had time to say 'Come in.'

He handed him a slip bearing the name *Billy Louette*.

Yet, only a few hours earlier, the masseuse had claimed that her son was away, somewhere on the Riviera.

'Bring him in, Joseph.'

CHAPTER THREE

'YOU'VE BEEN TRYING to get in touch with me, I daresay?'

'Not yet. I understood from your mother that you were on the Côte d'Azur.'

'Oh, pay no attention to her!. . . . May I smoke?'

'Certainly, if you wish.'

The young man appeared by no means overawed. The precincts of Police Headquarters held no terrors for him, and, as far as he was concerned, Maigret was a policeman like any other.

But the impression he created was not that of a rebel or exhibitionist.

His red hair was on the long side, but he was certainly no hippy. He wore a check shirt, suede waistcoat, beige corduroy trousers, and moccasins.

'As soon as I read about my aunt in the paper, I felt sure you would want to see me.'

'I'm very glad you've come.'

He bore no resemblance to the masseuse. Whereas she was tall and heavily built, with shoulders like a man, he was small-boned and rather thin, with eyes as blue as periwinkles. Maigret, seated at his desk, motioned to the armchair facing him.

'Thank you. What was it exactly that happened yesterday? There's very little in the papers.'

'We know no more than they have reported, which is that she was murdered.'

'Was anything stolen?'

'Apparently not.'

'Anyway, she never kept much money in the flat.'

'How do you know that?'

'I used to go and see her occasionally.'

'When funds were low?'

'That goes without saying. There was nothing else for us to talk about. We had no interests in common.'

'Did she give you money?'

'As a rule, a hundred-franc note, but it wouldn't have done to ask too often.'

'You're a musician, I believe?'

'Of a sort, yes. I play the guitar. I work with a small group. We call ourselves the Bad Lads.'

'Do you make a living out of it?'

'We have our ups and downs. Sometimes we get a booking at a high-class night club, at other times we play in cafés. What did my mother say about me?'

'Nothing in particular.'

'Don't imagine she's overflowing with mother love. For one thing, we're so very different. She thinks of nothing but money, saving up for her old age, she calls it. If she could do without food, she would, so as to have more in the kitty.'

'Was she fond of your aunt?'

'She couldn't stand her. Many a time I've heard her say, with a sigh:

'"I do believe the old fool will live for ever!"'

'Why should she have wished her dead?'

'For the money, of course. The old woman, with her two widow's pensions, must have had a tidy bit put by.

'Mind you, I was fond of the old girl. And I think she liked me. She always insisted on making coffee, and serving it up to me with biscuits:

'"I'm sure there are days when you can't afford to eat. Why don't you take a training course of some sort, and get a decent job?"'

'My mother felt the same way. She'd made up her mind before I was fifteen what she wanted me to be . . . she had dreams of turning me into an osteopath:

'"They're in such demand that patients often have to wait a month for an appointment. It's not uninteresting, and the pay is good."'

'When did you last go and see your great-aunt?'

'About three weeks ago. We'd been to London on spec. We

53

were hoping to get a booking, but they've got all the groups they want over there, and most of them are a lot better than we are. So we had to give up and come home, and I went to see the old girl.'

'Did she give you your hundred francs?'

'Yes. And my biscuits.'

'Where do you live?'

'I move around a good deal. Sometimes I'm with a girl, sometimes on my own, as I am at the moment. I've got a furnished room in a small hotel in the Rue Mouffetard.'

'Are you in work?'

'In a manner of speaking. Do you know the Bongo?'

Maigret shook his head. The young man seemed surprised that there should be anyone who had not heard of the Bongo.

'It's a little café-restaurant in the Place Maubert. The proprietor comes from Auvergne. It didn't take him long to see what was happening in the Saint-Germain district. He sets up to run a hippy joint, and he sometimes lets them have free drinks. He's always glad to give a free dinner, and a few francs over, to any performer willing to put on a show. That's us. We do two or three shows a night. And then there's Line. She's a singer. She's got a fabulous voice.

'That's how he fetches in the customers. They come in droves to get a closer look at the notorious hippies, and when we tell them we don't smoke pot or hash, they won't believe us.'

'Do you intend to go on playing?'

'I should hope so. It's the only thing I care about. I've even started composing, though I haven't found my form yet. I can say this, at any rate. I didn't kill the old girl. First of all, killing people isn't my thing, and, secondly, I'd have known I'd be a prime suspect.'

'Did you have a key to the flat?'

'What on earth for?'

'Where were you round about six yesterday evening?'

'In bed.'

'Alone?'

'Alone at last, yes. We'd been at the Bongo nearly all night.

I picked up a swell chick. She was Scandinavian, Danish or Swedish, I think. We'd had a lot to drink. In the small hours I took her back to my room. And it wasn't until three o'clock in the afternoon that I was able to get some sleep.

'Sometime later, I felt the bed creak, and heard noises. I was still half asleep. All I knew was that there was no longer anyone beside me in the bed.

'I felt battered, drained, and my mouth was like the bottom of a birdcage. I didn't get up until after nine.'

'In other words, no one saw you between, say, five and eight?'

'That's right.'

'Could you get in touch with the girl again?'

'If she's not at the Bongo tonight, she'll be in some other joint nearby.'

'Was she someone you already knew?'

'No.'

'She's a new one, then?'

'It's not like that at all. They drift in and they drift out. I told you we'd been to London. Well, we went to Copenhagen on spec as well. Wherever we go, we make friends right away.'

'Do you know her name?'

'Only her Christian name. It's Hilda. I also happen to know that her father is something quite high up in the Civil Service.'

'How old is she?'

'Twenty-two, or so she said. I don't know who it was she had arranged to meet up with. If she hadn't, she'd probably have stayed with me for weeks. That's how it goes. Then, after a time, one drifts apart, without quite knowing why. No hard feelings, though.'

'Tell me about you and your mother.'

'As I said, we don't get on.'

'She brought you up, didn't she?'

'Not from choice. That was one of the things she had against the old girl. She hoped she'd offer to look after me. As she had to go out to work, she dumped me in a day nursery every morning, and fetched me on her way home at night. It was the same when I was at school.

'She didn't want a child about the place, especially when there was a man around. I was an embarrassment.'

'Were there many men?'

'They came and went. One lived with us for six months. He spent most of the day loafing around the house. I was made to call him "Daddy". . . .'

'Didn't he have a job?'

'He was supposed to be a commercial traveller, but he did precious little travelling. At other times, I'd hear noises in the night, but there was no one there in the morning. They were nearly all young men, especially of late.

'About a fortnight ago, I ran into her in the Boulevard Saint-Germain. She was with a bloke I've often seen around the night clubs. Everyone calls him Le Grand Marcel.'

'Do you know him?'

'Not personally, but he's reputed to be a pimp. And then, of course, she's fond of the bottle.'

He was cynical, yet at the same time refreshingly candid.

'Mind you, I'm not saying I suspect my mother of having killed the old girl. She is what she is, and I am what I am, and there's no changing either of us. Maybe I shall become a star, and maybe I'll be a flop, like so many others in Saint-Germain. Was there anything else you wanted to ask me?'

'A number of things, I daresay, but for the moment they escape me. Are you happy as you are?'

'Most of the time, yes.'

'Wouldn't you have been better off if you had done as your mother wished, and become an osteopath? You would probably have been married with children by this time.'

'It wouldn't suit me. Later, perhaps.'

'How did you feel when you heard of your great-aunt's death?'

'My heart missed a beat. I didn't know her well. To me she was just a very old woman, who, by rights, should have been put underground long ago. All the same, I was fond of her. It was those eyes of hers, and her smile.

'"Eat up," she used to say.

'And she used to watch me eat those biscuits of hers with

a kind of loving concern. Apart from my mother, I was all she had in the way of a family

'"Are you really quite set on wearing your hair so long?"'

'That was the thing that upset her most.

'"It makes you look something different from what you really are. Because underneath it all, you're a good boy."'

'When is the funeral to be?'

'I can't say yet. Leave your address with me, and I'll let you know. It will probably be the day after tomorrow. It really depends on the Examining Magistrate.'

'Did she suffer, do you think?'

'She put up very little resistance. Do you, by any chance, own a red scarf, or at least one with red in it?'

'I never wear a scarf. Why do you ask?'

'No reason. I'm feeling my way, that's all.'

'Do you suspect anyone?'

'I wouldn't go as far as that.'

'Could it be some sort of perverted sex crime?'

'Why pick on Madame Antoine in particular, and why attack her at home, with the building swarming with people? No, the murderer was looking for something.'

'Money?'

'I'm not sure. If he was someone who knew her, he would have been aware that she never had more than a few francs in cash. Besides, he visited the flat several times while the old lady was out. Do you happen to know if she owned anything of value?'

'She had a few bits of jewellery, nothing of great value, just trinkets given her by her two husbands.'

Maigret had seen them, a garnet ring with earrings to match, a gold bracelet and a small gold watch.

There were, in the same box, a pearl tiepin and a pair of silver cufflinks, which must have belonged to Caramé. All old-fashioned stuff, worth virtually nothing on the open market.

'Had she any papers?'

'What do you mean by papers? She was just an ordinary old woman, who lived a quiet life with her first husband, and then later with her second. Caramé died before I was born,

57

so I never met him, but I knew the other one, Joseph Antoine. He was a good sort. . . .'

Maigret stood up with a sigh.

'Do you often visit your mother?'

'Hardly ever.'

'You don't happen to know, do you, whether she's living alone at the moment, or whether this Monsieur Marcel you mentioned is with her?'

'I don't, I'm afraid.'

'I'm very grateful to you for having come, Monsieur Louette. I'd like to see your show some night, if I can find the time.'

'About eleven is the best time to come.'

'I'm usually in bed by then.'

'Am I still a suspect?'

'Until I have evidence to the contrary, everyone is suspect, but you are no more suspect than anyone else.'

Maigret shut the door behind the young man, and went across to lean out of the window. It was already dusk. Everything looked a little blurred. He had learned a great many new facts, but none of them was of any use to him.

What could anybody possibly want from the old woman's home in the Quai de la Mégisserie?

She had lived in the same flat for over forty years. There was no mystery about her first husband, and after he died she had lived on there alone for nearly ten years.

As far as one could tell, there had been no mystery about her second husband either. He had been dead for years, and since his death she had led an uneventful existence, seeing no one except her niece and great-nephew.

Why had no one ever tried to break into her flat before? Was it because what the intruder was looking for had been there only a short time?

With a little grunt and a shrug, he opened the door to the Inspectors' Duty Room.

'See you all tomorrow.'

Travelling home on the bus, he reflected that there was no other calling quite like his own. He did not know the names of his fellow passengers, yet he never knew from one moment to the next whether he might be having to shoulder his way into the life of any one of them.

He rather liked the young man with the long red hair, but his only interest in the mother was to find out the answers to several very personal questions.

As usual, Madame Maigret had the door open almost before he was across the landing.

'You look worried.'

'And with good reason. I'm caught up in something I simply don't understand.'

'The murder of the old woman?'

Naturally, she had read the paper and heard the news broadcast.

'Did you ever see her alive?'

'Yes.'

'What was she like?'

'I thought she was mad, or at least not quite right in the head. She was a tiny little thing, she looked as if a puff of wind would blow her away. She begged me to help her. The way she talked, you'd have thought that I was the only person in the world who could.'

'Didn't you do anything?'

'I couldn't very well detail an inspector to keep watch on her night and day.

'There was so little to go on. All she could say was that, once or twice, she had come home to her flat to find some of her things very slightly out of place.

'I confess I thought she was imagining things, or that her memory was playing her tricks. All the same, I had made up my mind to go and see her, if only to reassure her. Yesterday, she must have got home earlier than usual, and found the intruder still in her flat.

'It was all too easy to silence her. It needed no more than a scarf or a dishcloth held over her face for a minute or two. . . .'

'Had she any family?'

'Just one niece, and a great-nephew. I've seen them both. The niece is a great hefty woman, more like a man. She's a

59

masseuse. The young man, on the other hand, is small and thin and red-headed. He plays the guitar in a night club in the Place Maubert.'

'Has anything been stolen?'

'Impossible to say. There's just one thing, and it's not much to go on. She used to keep a revolver in her bedside table drawer, but it's not there now.'

'Surely no one would kill an old woman in cold blood just for the sake of a revolver? And it wouldn't need several visits to find it.'

'Let's eat!'

They dined facing one another across the table near the open window. Neither of them felt like watching television. It was a very mild evening. The air was still. As the night drew on, a pleasant light breeze blew up, creating a faint whisper among the leaves of the trees.

'As you weren't home for lunch, I've warmed up the lamb stew.'

'I'm delighted to hear it.'

He ate with relish, but his thoughts were elsewhere. He could not forget his meeting with the old lady in grey, on the pavement of the Quai des Orfèvres. He could still see her looking up at him, her eyes bright with trust and admiration.

'Why don't you forget it, just for tonight?'

'I wish I could. I can't help myself. If there's one thing I hate, it's letting people down, and, as things turned out, it cost the poor old dear her life.'

'Let's go for a walk.'

He agreed. There was no point in moping around the flat all evening. Besides, it was his way—one might almost call it an obsession—when he was on a case, to establish a routine and adhere to it day after day.

They walked to the Bastille, and sat for a little while on a café terrace. A long-haired youth with a guitar strummed as he made his way among the tables, followed by a black-eyed girl holding out a saucer.

Needless to say, he was reminded of the red-head who, no

doubt, when times were hard, had also done his stint as a café entertainer.

Maigret's contribution was more than generous, a fact which did not escape his wife. She said nothing, however, but merely smiled to herself. They sat on for some time, in silence, gazing out at the lights of the city.

He puffed gently at his pipe. At one point, he almost suggested going to the Bongo. But what was the use? What could he hope to find out beyond what he already knew?

The tenants of the building in the Quai de la Mégisserie were also suspects. Any of them might have known the old lady better than they were prepared to admit. It would have been easy enough for anyone to take a wax impression of the lock, and get a key cut to fit it.

But why? This was the question that haunted Maigret. Why? Why? What was the object of those repeated visits to the flat? Certainly not for the sake of the few francs the old lady kept there. There had been several hundred francs in the chest of drawers, just lying there for anyone to take. But they had not been taken. Maigret had found them inside the cover of the old lady's Post Office Savings book.

'Tomorrow, I'll start inquiring into the lives and backgrounds of the two husbands.'

It was absurd, really, especially taking into account how long the second husband had been dead.

Nevertheless, there was a secret somewhere, a secret important enough to warrant the taking of a human life.

'Shall we go?'

He had drunk a small glass of Calvados, and had just stopped himself in time from ordering another. His friend Pardon would have been displeased with him for even contemplating it. Maigret remembered his solemn warning just in time:

'One can drink wines and spirits for years without any ill effects, but a time comes when the system will no longer tolerate them.'

He shrugged, got up, and threaded his way between the tables. In the street, Madame Maigret took his arm. The

Boulevard Beaumarchais. The Rue Servan. At last the Boulevard Richard-Lenoir and their much-loved, shabby old flat.

Contrary to his expectations, he fell asleep almost at once.

The night passed without incident in the flat in the Quai de la Mégisserie, and fat Torrence was able to enjoy a full night's sleep in the old lady's armchair.

At eight in the morning, Loutrie arrived to relieve him, and found the concierge deep in conversation with a newspaper reporter.

At nine, Maigret, brooding and grumpy, pushed open the door of the Inspectors' room, and beckoned to Janvier and Lapointe.

'On second thoughts, Lucas, you'd better come too.'

He sat down at his desk, and proceeded to make a ceremony of choosing a pipe from his pipe-rack.

'Well, lads, we're no further forward than we were this time yesterday. As we don't seem to be able to find any lead in the present, we're going to do a little probing into the past. I want you to go to the Bazar de l'Hôtel de Ville, Lucas, the ironmongery department. There must still be people working there who knew old Antoine.

'Ask as many questions as you like. Find out all you can about the old boy, his personality, his interests, everything.'

'Will do, Chief. Mightn't it be better if I got the consent of the management first? They couldn't very well refuse, and the members of staff would probably feel freer to talk than if I approached them in an underhand way.'

'Agreed. As for you, Janvier, I want you to go to the Hôtel de Ville and do the same for Caramé. It will be more difficult, because he's been dead so much longer. If any of his contemporaries are still living in retirement, get their addresses and go and see them.'

All this was just routine, of course, but sometimes routine paid off.

'Lapointe, I want you with me.'

Downstairs in the forecourt, the young inspector asked:

'Shall we need a car?'

'No, we're just going across the bridge to the Rue Saint-André-des-Arts. A car would only slow us up.'

It was an old building, similar to that in the Quai de la Mégisserie and, indeed, all the other buildings in the neighbourhood. There was a picture-framer's shop to the right of it, and a confectioner's to the left. The glass door of the lodge was accessible from the entrance hall, which ran right through to a courtyard at the back.

Maigret went into the lodge, and introduced himself to the concierge. She was a plump little woman, with a high colour. As a child, she must have had dimples. Indeed, she still had when she smiled.

'I thought someone would be coming from the police.'

'Why?'

'When I read what had happened to that poor old lady, I had an idea that the niece they spoke of was one of my tenants.'

'Angèle Louette, you mean?'

'Yes.'

'Has she ever mentioned her aunt?'

'She's not very communicative, but, all the same, she does drop in for a chat occasionally. I remember once we were discussing people who don't pay their bills. She remarked that sometimes it was the high-ups who were the worst. Some of her own clients were in that class, she said, and she dared not press them too hard, they had too much influence.

'"It's a mercy that I've got my aunt's money to look forward to!"

'She brought it out just like that. She told me that the old lady had been twice widowed, and that she was drawing two pensions, and must have quite a bit put by.'

'Does she have many visitors?'

The concierge looked uncomfortable.

'How do you mean?'

'Does she often entertain women friends?'

'Not women friends, no.'

'Clients?'

'They don't come to her, she goes to them.'

63

'What about men?'

'Well, I don't suppose there's any harm in telling you. There are men from time to time. There was even one who stayed for nearly six months. He was ten years younger than she was, and he did all the housework and the shopping.'

'Is she in now?'

'She went out about an hour ago. She always starts on her rounds pretty early. But there is someone up there.'

'One of her regular visitors?'

'I don't know. She got in rather late last night. After I'd let her in, I heard two lots of footsteps. And if the person who was with her had left the building, I'd have known.'

'Does it happen often?'

'Not often. Just once in a while.'

'What about her son?'

'He hardly ever comes here. I haven't seen him for months. He looks like a hippy, but he's a good boy really.'

'Thank you. We'd better have a look round up there, I think.'

There was no lift. The flat was at the back, overlooking the courtyard. The door was not locked, and Maigret and Lapointe went in, to find themselves in a living room fitted out with fairly new, mass-produced furniture.

There was not a sound to be heard. There was a door, obviously leading to the bedroom. Maigret opened it, and saw a man asleep in the double bed.

He opened his eyes, and stared in amazement at the Chief Superintendent.

'What is it? What do you want?'

'It's really Angèle Louette I came to see, but as you're here . . .'

'Aren't you . . . ?'

'That's right, Chief Superintendent Maigret. We've met before, years ago. In those days, you worked in a bar in the Rue Fontaine. You were known as Le Grand Marcel, if I'm not mistaken?'

'I still am. Would you be so good as to leave me for a moment to get dressed? I haven't a stitch on.'

64

'Don't trouble yourself on my account.'

He was tall, thin and bony. Hastily he slipped on a pair of trousers, and searched about for his slippers, which he found eventually under the bed.

'You know it isn't the way you think between me and Angèle. We're just good friends. Yesterday, we spent the evening together and, by the end of it, I wasn't feeling too good. So, instead of trekking right across Paris to my own place in the Boulevard des Batignolles . . .'

Maigret opened the wardrobe. There were two men's suits in the hanging section, and, in the drawers, several shirts and two or three pairs of socks and underpants.

'I see! Well, what have you got to say for yourself?'

'Can I make myself a cup of coffee?'

Maigret followed Le Grand Marcel into the kitchen, and watched him make the coffee. It was obvious that he knew his way about.

'There's nothing to tell. I've had my ups and downs, as you very well know. I'm not a pimp, and never have been, in spite of what people say. You know yourself that the charges were dropped for lack of evidence.'

'How old are you?'

'Thirty-five.'

'How old is she?'

'I don't know exactly. Fiftyish, I suppose. Yes, she could be fifty.'

'The great love of your life, I daresay!'

'We understand one another. She can't do without me. I've kept away from her for as long as a week before now, and when that happens, she comes looking for me in all my old haunts.'

'Where were you in the late afternoon of the day before yesterday?'

'The day before yesterday? Let me think. I must have been somewhere in the neighbourhood, because I was due to meet Angèle at seven.'

'She didn't mention it.'

'It probably slipped her mind. We had a dinner date. I had

an aperitif on the terrace of a café in the Boulevard Saint-Germain.'

'And did she meet you at seven, as arranged?'

'She may have been a bit late. Yes, come to think of it, she was very late. She was kept waiting by one of her clients. It must have been about half-past seven when she arrived.'

'Did you have dinner together, as arranged?'

'Yes, and afterwards we went to a cinema. You can check on it, if you don't believe me. The restaurant is Lucio's in the Quai de la Tournelle. They know me well there.'

'Where are you working at present?'

'To tell you the truth, I'm between jobs. It's not so easy to find work these days.'

'Does she keep you?'

'That's unkind. You've no call to go out of your way to wound me. For years, you people have been trying to pin something on me, and I'm not guilty, I tell you. It's true she lends me a little money now and then. It's the most she can do. She doesn't earn all that much herself.'

'Were you intending to sleep all morning?'

'I'm expecting her back any minute. She's got an hour free between two appointments. She went to see you yesterday, and told you all she knew. What I want to know is what you're doing here now.'

'Taking advantage of the opportunity to make your acquaintance!'

'Would you mind waiting in the other room while I take a shower?'

'You have my permission to shave as well,' retorted Maigret, a little unkindly.

Lapointe could not get over the presence of such a man in Angèle Louette's flat.

'He's been arrested four or five times for procuring. He was also suspected of being tied up with that Corsican gang that caused so much havoc in Paris a few years back. But he's as slippery as an eel, and nothing was ever proved.'

Someone was coming up the stairs. The door opened. Madame Antoine's niece stood transfixed in the doorway.

'Do come in! I was hoping for a word with you.'

She shot a furtive glance towards the bedroom door.

'Yes, he is in there. He's just having a shower and a shave.'

Defeated, she shut the door with a resigned shrug.

'After all, it's nobody's business but my own. Well, is it?'

'You may be right.'

'What do you mean?'

'He just happens to be an old acquaintance of mine, and in the past he's had one or two brushes with the law.'

'Are you telling me he's a thief?'

'No. At least, not to my knowledge. But in the days when he was a barman, there were always two or three women working for him, not to mention the lady in charge of the establishment.'

'I don't believe you. If what you say is true, he'd have been sent to prison.'

'The only reason he wasn't is that we didn't have enough evidence.'

'You still haven't told me why you're here.'

'First, let me ask you a question. Yesterday, when you mentioned your son to me, you told me he was on the Côte d'Azur . . .'

'I said I thought he was.'

'In fact he's still in Paris, and he's been good enough to tell me some very interesting things.'

'I'm well aware that he dislikes me.'

'But you didn't dislike your aunt, of course?'

'I can't imagine what he's been saying. He's full of crazy notions. Mark my words, he'll come to no good.'

'On the day your aunt died, you had an appointment with Le Grand Marcel for seven o'clock on the terrace of a café in the Boulevard Saint-Germain.'

'If that's what he says, it's the truth.'

'What time did you in fact get there?'

She was caught off her guard for a moment. She hesitated, then said:

'I was kept waiting by one of my clients. I must have arrived at about half-past seven.'

'Where did you have dinner?'

'At an Italian restaurant on the Quai de la Tournelle, Chez Lucio.'

'And then?'

'We went to the Saint Michel cinema.'

'Do you know what time your aunt was murdered?'

'No. I know nothing but what you told me.'

'It was between five and half-past seven.'

'What's that supposed to mean?'

'Do you possess a revolver?'

'Certainly not. I wouldn't know what to do with it.'

Le Grand Marcel emerged from the bedroom, nonchalantly tying a knot in his blue silk tie. He was freshly shaved, and wearing a white shirt.

'What do you know?' he said, making a jest of it. 'I woke up suddenly to find these gentlemen standing at the foot of the bed, towering over me. For a moment, I wondered if I was taking part in a gangster film.'

'Do you own a revolver?' barked Maigret.

'Not likely! Can you think of a more certain way of getting nicked?'

'You live in the Boulevard des Batignolles, I believe. What number?'

'Twenty-seven.'

'I'm much obliged to you both for your co-operation. As to your aunt, Mademoiselle, the Forensic Laboratory have completed their work, so you are at liberty to send for the body, and make arrangements for the funeral at any time convenient to yourself.'

'Have I got to pay for it out of my own pocket?'

'That's entirely up to you. As her next-of-kin you will inherit enough and to spare to give her a decent burial.'

'What am I to do? Ought I to see a solicitor?'

'If I were you, I should see her bank manager. He'll tell you all you need to know. If you don't know the name of her bank, you'll find it on her bank book in the chest of drawers in the sitting room.'

'Thank you.'

'Don't mention it.

'Don't forget to let me know the date and time of the funeral.'

She was looking at him unblinkingly. He had seldom seen eyes colder or more steely than hers. As to Marcel, he was doing his best to appear as though all this was no concern of his.

'I bid you good day, Monsieur Maigret,' he said with studied insolence.

Maigret and Lapointe left. The Chief Superintendent stopped at the bar on the corner.

'Those two have given me a thirst,' he said, and led the way in.

'A half of beer please. What will you have?'

'The same.'

'Two halves.'

Maigret got out his handkerchief and mopped his brow.

'What a way to conduct an investigation into the death by violence of an old lady with grey eyes! Calling on people, and asking them a lot of more or less pointless questions! Oh well, those two have got the laugh on us for the time being, but not for long, I hope!'

Lapointe wisely said nothing, but it troubled him to see the Chief so moody.

'Mind you, it's always like this at some stage. Things grind to a halt, and one doesn't know what to do next. Until something happens, often it's something quite trivial, and one doesn't realize its significance at the time. . . .'

'Cheers!'

'Cheers!'

It was still quite early. Maigret was cheered by the sight of so many busy housewives bustling from shop to shop. They were not far from the Buci market, of which he was particularly fond.

'Come on.'

'Where are we going?'

'Back to the office. We'll see whether Lucas and Janvier have fared any better.'

Janvier was back, but not Lucas.

'No trouble at all, Chief. His successor is still there. He knew Caramé extremely well, right from the time when he joined the service.'

'Go on.'

'It's all perfectly open and above board, except that they all called Caramé "His Majesty" behind his back. He had an air about him, and he was very fastidious in his dress. He was highly conscious of the dignity of his position. He had been promised the Légion d'Honneur, and was greatly looking forward to receiving it. He never missed an opportunity of appearing in a morning coat, in which he looked particularly well. His brother was a Colonel.

'He was killed in Indo-China. Caramé was always ready to talk about "my brother the Colonel".'

'Is that the lot?'

'More or less. Apparently he had no vices. His one great sorrow was that he had no children. One of the messengers, a very old man, told me something, though he couldn't guarantee that it was true. . . .

'After they'd been married three or four years, he sent his wife to a gynaecologist, who subsequently asked to see him, the inference being that it was he, not she, who was sterile. From that time onwards, he never referred to the subject of children again.'

Maigret paced up and down his office, still wearing the same surly expression. From time to time, he would pause by the window and gaze at the Seine, as though calling upon the river to witness that, of all men, he was surely the most hard done by.

There was a knock at the door.

It was Lucas. He was out of breath, having taken the stairs at a run.

'Take your time.'

'I found a chap in the ironmongery department, who had been Antoine's number two. He's sixty now and head of the department.'

'What did he say?'

70

'Apparently, Antoine was a bit of a nut-case. In the nicest way, of course. It seems he had a bee in his bonnet. When anyone asked him what he did for a living, he invariably replied that he was an inventor.

'And it is a fact that he patented a very ingenious design for a tin-opener, and sold it to a hardware manufacturer. He invented several other things as well. . . .'

'Such as a potato peeler?'

'How did you know?'

'I saw one in the flat at the Quai de la Mégisserie.'

'He was always at work on some new invention or other. Apparently he had fitted up a workshop in the flat, and spent every spare minute pottering about in it.'

'I've seen the workshop, too. Were all his inventions household gadgets? Did he never try his hand at anything more ambitious?'

'Not as far as the man I spoke to knew. But, apparently, he had a way of wagging his head and dropping dark hints, such as:

'"One day I'll come up with something really big, something that will make me a household name."'

'Did he go into any detail?'

'No. Except when he was on his hobby-horse, he was rather reserved, although he was very conscientious in his work. He didn't drink. He never went out at night. He seemed very fond of his wife, fond of her rather than in love with her, which isn't surprising, considering that they were both well on in years. They got on well, and had a great respect for one another. The man I spoke to had been to dinner twice at the flat, and he was impressed by the pleasant, homely atmosphere.

'"She was a charming woman," he said. "Such distinction! There was just one thing I found a little embarrassing. When she talked of her husband, one couldn't be quite sure whether she meant her first or her second. I had the feeling that the two had become confused in her mind."'

'Anything else?'

'No, Chief, that's the lot.'

'There's only one thing we can be sure of. Until quite

recently a pistol was kept in the old lady's bedside table drawer. And it isn't there now. It's vanished.

'I feel like paying a call at the Boulevard des Batignolles. Care to come with me, Lapointe? Whichever car you pick, make sure it isn't the one with the engine-rattle.'

Before leaving his office, he put his pipe in the rack, and selected another.

CHAPTER FOUR

THE FAKE MARBLE PLAQUE beside the entrance to the little hotel bore the legend:

Furnished rooms to let by the day, the week or the month. All mod. cons.

Most of the rooms were let to monthly tenants, and the 'mod. cons.' consisted of a wash-basin in every room, and a bathroom shared between two floors.

Inside, on the right, was a desk, and behind it a row of pigeon-holes and a board with a great many keys hanging from hooks.

'Is Le Grand Marcel in his room?'

'Monsieur Marcel? He's just gone up. That's his car at the door.'

It was a bright red convertible, several years old. Two teen-age boys were inspecting it, if not with envy, at least with interest.

No doubt they were wondering how fast it could go.

'Has he lived here long?'

'Over a year. He's a very pleasant gentleman.'

'I fancy he seldom sleeps in his room.'

'He usually gets home in the early hours of the morning, which isn't surprising, seeing that he's a barman in a night club.'

'Does he ever bring a girl?'

'Not often. And, anyway, it's no concern of mine.'

The landlord was fat, with two or three bristly chins. He was wearing a pair of very old, misshapen bedroom slippers.

'What floor?'

'Second. Room number twenty-three. I hope you're not going to cause trouble. I know who you are. I don't much like having policemen tramping about the place.'

'You've nothing to hide, have you?'

'With you lot, one can never tell.'

Maigret went upstairs, followed by Lapointe.

Dangling from the banister was a cardboard notice, which read:

Please wipe your feet.

And underneath, written in by hand:

No cooking is permitted in the bedrooms.

Maigret knew what that meant. No doubt every single tenant had smuggled in his own spirit stove, on which to heat up the ready-cooked food that he regularly bought from the nearest delicatessen.

He knocked at the door of number twenty-three. There was a sound of approaching footsteps, and the door was flung open with some violence.

'Good heavens!' exclaimed Le Grand Marcel. 'You here already!'

'Were you expecting us?'

'Once the police start poking their noses into one's business, they're liable to turn up at any time.'

'Are you leaving here?'

There was a suitcase on the floor, and another on the bed, into which the ex-barman had been stuffing his clothes when they arrived.

'Yes. I'm quitting. I've had just about enough.'

'Enough of what?'

'Of that female sergeant-major.'

'Have you quarrelled with her?'

'You could say that. She called me every name under the sun, and all because I was still in bed when you arrived. She may be a masseuse, having to be up at crack of dawn to go poking and prodding people in their beds, but I'm not.'

'That doesn't explain why you're giving up your lodgings.'

'I'm not just giving up my lodgings. I'm giving up altogether. I'm off to Toulon. I've got friends there, real friends. They'll fix me up with something right away.'

Maigret recognized, folded on top of one of the cases, one of the suits he had seen earlier in the day, hanging in the wardrobe in the flat in the Rue Saint-André-des-Arts. Le

Grand Marcel was wearing the other. His surname was Montrond, but no one ever called him by it. Even his landlord addressed him as Monsieur Marcel.

'Is that red car parked outside yours?'

'She's a bit past it. She's almost ten years old, but she can still rattle along.'

'I take it you intend to drive to Toulon?'

'As you say. Unless you lot take it into your heads to stop me.'

'Why should we want to do that?'

'You tell me. You're the cop.'

'Just one thing; have you ever been to the flat in the Rue de la Mégisserie?'

'Whatever for? To pay my respects to the old girl?

'"Greetings, dear lady. I'm your niece's boyfriend. As I'm in a bit of a spot at the moment, she's keeping me. She always has to have a man, you know. She's a right trollop, and it was a great mistake to get mixed up with her."'

He went on calmly packing his suitcases, looking through all the drawers to make sure he had not forgotten anything. He pressed down the contents of the cases to make room for a camera and a record-player.

'There! Now, unless I can be of any further use to you, I'm off.'

'Where can we get in touch with you in Toulon?'

'Write to me care of Bob, at the Bar de l'Amiral, Quai de Stalingrad. He's the barman, and a very old friend of mine. Do you think you'll be needing me again?'

'You never know.'

He had not yet closed the suitcases. Maigret felt about in them, but found nothing of interest.

'How much did you get out of her?'

'The sergeant-major? Five hundred francs. And that, mark you, was only on condition that I wouldn't stay away too long. You never can tell with her. One minute she's cursing you up hill and down dale, and telling you never to darken her doors again, and the next she's whimpering that she can't live without you.'

'*Bon voyage!*' murmured Maigret with a sigh, as he made for the door.

On his way out, he paused at the desk and said to the landlord:

'I fancy you're about to lose one of your tenants.'

'So he tells me. He's going to spend a few weeks in the South.'

'Is he keeping his room?'

'No, but I daresay I'll be able to fit him in somewhere.'

The two men drove back to the Quai des Orfèvres, and Maigret lost no time in putting a call through to Toulon.

'Would you get me Superintendent Marella? Maigret, Police Headquarters, Paris, speaking.'

It was pleasant to hear the familiar voice of his old colleague. They had joined the force at about the same time, and now Marella was the senior man in Toulon.

'How are things with you?'

'Mustn't grumble.'

'Do you know the Bar de l'Amiral?'

'Do I not! It's the favourite haunt of all the villains.'

'And a man of the name of Bob?'

'The barman. They all use him as an accommodation address.'

'Sometime tonight or tomorrow, a fellow called Marcel Montrond will show up in Toulon. I've an idea he'll make straight for l'Amiral. I'd be much obliged if you'd have him watched.'

'What's your interest in him?'

'It may be nothing. It may be something very serious indeed. I don't know. All I know is he's mixed up in some way in a case that's giving me a monumental headache.'

'The old lady at the Quai de la Mégisserie?'

'Yes.'

'Queer business, that. I only know what I've heard on the radio and read in the papers. All the same, it strikes me as damned odd. Have you caught up with the laddie who plays the guitar?'

'Yes, but I don't think he's our man. At the moment, I

76

haven't a shred of evidence on any of them, and I can't for the life of me see any reason at all why the poor old dear should have been killed. . . .'

'I'll be in touch. This Marcel fellow wouldn't by any chance be a character known as Le Grand Marcel?'

'That's the one.'

'He's a bit of a gigolo on the side, isn't he? He's quite well known around these parts, and he always seems to latch on to some woman or other.'

'Many thanks. I look forward to hearing from you.'

As soon as he had put down the receiver, the telephone rang.

'Chief Superintendent Maigret?'

'Yes.'

'Angèle Louette speaking. First of all, I thought you'd like to know that I've given that layabout his marching orders.'

'I know. He's on his way to Toulon.'

'Please believe me, he's not my type at all. I won't be taken in so easily another time.'

'What have you got against him?'

'He sponges on women, and loafs about in bed most of the day—and not even in his own bed! I had a job getting rid of him. He'd be here still if I hadn't paid him off.'

'I know.'

'He surely wouldn't boast about it?'

'He certainly did, and, incidentally, he called you "the Sergeant-Major".'

'The other thing was about the funeral. It's to be tomorrow morning. The body will be arriving at the Quai de la Mégisserie some time this afternoon. As my aunt had no friends, I won't be turning the place into a memorial chapel. The funeral will be tomorrow at ten.'

'Will there be a church service?'

'Just a memorial prayer at Notre-Dame-des-Blancs-Manteaux. Are you any further forward with your inquiries?'

'No.'

'Have you got my son's address?'

'He did leave it with me, yes.'

77

'I'd like to let him know. He may, in spite of everything, want to attend his great-aunt's funeral.'

'He's staying at the Hôtel des Iles et du Bon Pasteur, Rue Mouffetard.'

'I'm much obliged to you.'

Maigret, familiar with the ways of Examining Magistrates, knew that they did not like to be kept waiting, so, as soon as he could, he let himself through the communicating door between Police Headquarters and the Palais de Justice. The corridors of the Offices of the Examining Magistrates were lined with benches, on which sat witnesses waiting their turn and, here and there, handcuffed prisoners between two warders.

Judge Libart was sitting alone in his room except for his clerk.

'What news, Chief Superintendent? How is that little matter of ours progressing?'

He rubbed his hands together, obviously in high good humour.

'As you know, it's my policy to leave you in peace to get on with the job. All the same, I trust you have made some progress?'

'None at all.'

'No likely suspects?'

'Not really, and nothing much to go on, except that the intruder was searching for something, when the old lady came back unexpectedly and found him.'

'Money?'

'I believe not.'

'Jewellery?'

'She had none worth stealing.'

'A lunatic?'

'Not very likely. Whoever it was had searched the flat several times before the afternoon of the crime. That doesn't look to me like the behaviour of a lunatic.'

'A family affair, perhaps? Someone in too much of a hurry to get whatever the old lady had to leave?'

'That's a possibility, but a somewhat remote one. The old

lady's sole heir is her niece. She's a masseuse, and quite comfortably off.'

'Don't let it get you down.'

Maigret forced a smile.

'I'm sorry. It's just that I seem to have hit a bad patch. The funeral is tomorrow.'

'Will you be going?'

'Yes. I always make a point of it. I've been put on the right track before now by watching the mourners at a funeral.'

He went home for lunch, and Madame Maigret, noting his preoccupied expression, was careful to ask no questions.

She went about on tiptoe, and watched him anxiously as he ate the *fricandeau à l'oseille* which she had cooked for him, knowing it to be one of his favourite dishes.

Soon after he got back to the Quai des Orfèvres, there was a knock at his door.

'Come in.'

It was Lapointe.

'Sorry to bother you, sir, but you haven't given me any instructions.'

'I have none to give you. Do what you think best. If anything occurs to you . . .'

'I'd like another word with the man in the bird shop. Not many people would be able to enter or leave the building without his seeing them. Maybe, if I jog his memory a bit, he'll come up with something useful.'

'It's up to you.'

He hated himself for feeling as he did, bereft of inspiration and a prey to inertia. Thoughts buzzed in his head until he was sick of them, but none of them seemed to be leading anywhere.

Foremost in his mind was the thought that Madame Antoine had been as sane as he was himself.

Why had she hesitated so long, pacing up and down the Quai des Orfèvres, before plucking up the courage to speak to the constable at the gate? Had she known more than she was prepared to tell?

She must have realized that her complaint, namely, that

she had found some of her ornaments almost imperceptibly displaced, was bound to be received with scepticism.

All the same, she had been right. The flat had indeed been subjected to a thorough search on several occasions.

But why? What had the intruder been looking for?

As he had explained to the Examining Magistrate, certainly not money or jewellery.

But one thing was certain: whatever it was, it was important enough to warrant the murder of the old lady, when she came back unexpectedly while the intruder was still there.

Had he or had he not in the end found what he was looking for?

Was he perhaps on his way out with his booty, when he heard Madame Antoine's key in the lock?

What could a very old woman, twice widowed, living quietly and modestly on her own, possibly possess that was worth committing murder for?

While these thoughts were going through his head, Maigret was doodling absent-mindedly on a large sheet of paper. Suddenly, he realized that what he had been doing was to make a rough sketch of an old lady, not unlike Madame Antoine.

By five o'clock he was beginning to feel stifled in his office. Taking with him a photograph of Le Grand Marcel, which he had got from the Vice Squad, he set off for the Quai de la Mégisserie.

It was a poor likeness—the man appeared more hard-featured than he was in real life—but it was still recognizable. He went first to the concierge.

'Have you ever seen this man?'

She went to fetch her spectacles, which were on the kitchen dresser.

'I wouldn't really like to say, though he does seem vaguely familiar. On the other hand, there are lots of people about who look a bit like him.'

'Take a closer look. If you saw him, it was probably quite recently.'

'Actually, it's the suit that rings a bell. I saw a check suit like that somewhere a week or two back, but I can't for the life of me think where.'

'Here, in the lodge?'

'No, I don't think so.'

'In the courtyard? On the stairs?'

'Honestly, I can't say. Your inspector was here again, asking questions, just a short while ago. You wouldn't want me to start inventing things, now, would you? You know they've brought her back?'

'Madame Antoine, you mean?'

'Yes. Her niece is up there with her. She's left the door open, and lit candles on either side of the bed. One or two of the tenants plucked up the courage to go in and say a little prayer. If I'd had anyone to look after things here, I'd have gone to the funeral tomorrow, but I'm all on my own. My husband is in a mental hospital. He's been there for three years.'

Maigret went out on to the pavement, where the birdcages were standing outside the petshop. Monsieur Caille's son recognized him immediately.

'Hello! One of your inspectors, the young one, has been here. He's only just left.'

'I know. I'd be obliged if you'd look carefully at this photograph.'

He did so, shook his head, held it up close, and then at arm's length.

'I can't exactly say I recognize him, but there is something . . .'

'Is it the suit?'

'No, not specially. It's his expression. That sort of devil-may-care look.'

'One of your customers, perhaps?'

'Oh no, I'm sure not.'

'Hadn't you better show it to your father?'

'I will, of course, but he's so terribly short-sighted.'

He came back shaking his head.

'He doesn't recognize him. Though you must remember that he spends most of his time in the shop, and really cares

81

for nothing but his birds and his fish. In fact, he's so devoted to them that it wouldn't take much for him to refuse to sell them.'

Maigret went back into the building, and climbed the stairs to the first floor. The woman who lived opposite Madame Antoine came out, with a string shopping bag over her arm.

'She's there,' she whispered, pointing to the half-open door.

'I know.'

'The funeral is tomorrow. It seems her first husband bought a plot in the Montparnasse cemetery, and she wanted to be buried beside him.'

'Who knew of her wishes?'

'Her niece, I daresay. And I know she told the concierge. She used to say that Ivry was too far out, and that she felt lost among all those thousands of graves.'

'There's something I'd like to show you. Could we go into your flat for a moment?'

It was very neat and tidy, somewhat darker than the old lady's, because the windows were almost entirely obscured by the overhanging branches of a tree.

'Have you ever seen this man before?'

Once again, he produced the little photograph taken by someone in Criminal Records.

'Is it someone I know?'

'I've no idea. You tell me.'

'You asked me if I'd ever seen him before. Well, I certainly have, not very long ago. He was smoking a cigarette. I knew there was something missing. That's it. The cigarette.'

'Take your time. Try to think back.'

'It isn't one of the tradesmen, nor anyone I've seen going in and out of the yard.'

She was obviously doing her best.

'I suppose it's important?'

'Yes.'

'Something to do with Madame Antoine?'

'I think it likely.'

'So if I identify him positively, it will mean trouble for him?'

'I'm afraid so.'

82

'You see my difficulty. I wouldn't want to get an innocent person into trouble.'

'If he's innocent, we shall soon know it.'

'That's not always the case. Even the police can make mistakes. Oh well, never mind! I was on my way out . . .'

'What day was this?'

'I don't remember. One day last week. I was going to fetch my daughter from school.'

There was a little girl of about twelve doing her homework in the next room.

'That would have been a little before four?'

'Or it might have been lunch-time. That's what I'm trying to remember. More likely it was four, because I had my shopping bag with me, and that's when I always buy the things I need for dinner. My husband doesn't come home for lunch, and my daughter and I just have something very light.

'I was on my way downstairs, not looking where I was going, when I bumped into someone. He was coming up the stairs four at a time. He nearly sent me flying. That's why I remember him.

'He turned round, and asked me if I was hurt. I said no, it was nothing.'

'Do you happen to know where he was going, which floor?'

'No. I was in a hurry. My daughter doesn't like to be kept hanging about outside the school gates, and, with all the traffic, I daren't let her come home alone.'

Maigret heaved a sigh. At last, a faint ray of hope!

A moment or two later he was in the bedroom gazing intently at the delicately modelled features of the old woman whom he had thought to be mad.

The curtains were three-quarters drawn, and the room was almost in darkness, except for a narrow strip of shimmering sunlight. Two wax tapers were burning, one on either side of the bed, making everything look strange and different.

Angèle Louette was there, sitting in an armchair, silent and motionless. At first Maigret thought she was asleep, until he looked again, and saw her sombre eyes fixed upon him.

He stood facing the dead woman for a minute or two, to

give himself time to recover, then went into the sitting room. It was a relief to be back in daylight. As he had expected, she came out after him.

She looked even more hard-featured than usual.

'What have you come here for?'

'To pay my last respects to your aunt.'

'If you ask me, nothing was further from your mind. And the same goes for the neighbours. Only two of them bothered to put their heads round the door. Any more news of that scoundrel Marcel?'

'He got into his car and drove off to Toulon.'

This was a shock to her, he could see.

'Good riddance! I had trouble enough getting rid of him. Do you know, I had to give him five hundred francs to get him to leave?'

'That's demanding money with menaces. You could lay a charge.'

'Maybe I will. At any rate, if he makes any attempt to come back. . . .'

'Did you know that he was here, in this building, one day last week?'

She started violently, and frowned.

'Do you know what day?'

'No.'

'What time of day?'

'Round about four.'

'Did he tell you himself?'

'No.'

'Have you asked him about it?'

'I haven't had a chance. How did he come to have your aunt's address?'

'One day, about a month ago, when we were crossing the Pont-Neuf, I pointed to the windows of the flat in the distance, and said:

'"My old aunt lives up there."'

'And I suspect you went on to say that you were hoping for a nice little legacy from that quarter in the not too distant future.'

'I can just hear him feeding you lies like that. All I said was that she had had two husbands, and was very comfortably-off. Where is he?'

'At this moment, unless he's changed his mind, he's on his way to Toulon.'

'He never stopped talking about Toulon, and all the friends he had there.'

'Do you know anything about his family?'

'No.'

'Did he never talk about his childhood?'

'No. All I know is that his mother is still alive, and that she lives in some little town in Central France.'

'Are you quite certain you never came here at any time during the past week or fortnight?'

'Not again, please!'

'Think before you say anything.'

'I'm quite sure.'

'Do you know what your aunt kept in her bedside table drawer?'

'I've never looked.'

'Not even this morning, when you were rearranging the furniture for the laying out of the body?'

'Not even then.'

'Did you know that your aunt had a gun?'

'Of course not! She wouldn't have dared even to pick it up.'

'Wasn't she nervous, living on her own as she did?'

'She was afraid of nothing and no one.'

'Did she ever talk about her second husband's inventions?'

'She showed me a little potato peeler once. She promised me one like it, actually, but I never got it. That was while Antoine was still alive. She showed me over his workshop as well, if you can call it that. It's hardly bigger than a cupboard, and there isn't room to swing a cat.'

'I'm much obliged to you.'

'Will you be at the funeral?'

'If I can possibly get there.'

'The hearse will be leaving here at a quarter to ten, arriving at the church at ten.'

'Till tomorrow, then.'

She was tough, all right, more like a man than a woman, but at times he could almost forgive her her brusque manner. Perhaps it was only the bluntness of plain speaking. She was no oil painting. She had never been attractive, and had coarsened with advancing years.

She behaved like a man, indulging in amorous adventures when the whim took her. Was that really so very reprehensible?

She was quite open about it. When she felt like it, she had a man in to stay for a night, or a week. The concierge had seen them come and go. The neighbours, too, must have realized what was going on.

On the other hand, she was very much on her guard, watching Maigret intently, always suspecting a trap.

On his way back to the Quai des Orfèvres, Maigret stopped at the Brasserie Dauphine for a glass of white wine from the Loire. He didn't feel like beer. The white wine in the frosted glass, with just a hint of a sparkle, seemed more appropriate on this lovely spring day.

It was the slackest time of the day. Except for a delivery man in a blue apron, there was no one in the café.

He decided to order another.

Doctor Pardon would never know. Besides, Pardon had done no more than warn him against excess.

Lapointe was waiting for him at the Quai des Orfèvres. He had once again combed the flats from top to bottom, showing the photograph of Le Grand Marcel to all the tenants.

'Any luck?'

'None at all.'

'I shall need you tomorrow morning to drive me to the funeral.'

He walked home, going over the old ground in his head. It was all very discouraging.

'The only thing we know for certain is that a revolver has disappeared.'

But were they really sure even of that? They had found gun grease on the lining-paper of a drawer. Might it not have got there in some other way?

Moers's men had stated positively that it had not been there for more than a month at most.

He was beginning to distrust everyone, himself included. If only he could find a new lead, however slender, he was ready to go back and start all over again, right from the beginning.

'You're early!'

For once, she had not been waiting for him in the doorway, and he had had to use his key, which he very seldom did.

'I shall probably be going out later.'

'Where to?'

'To a place where I think I'd better not take you, a little hippy bistro in the Place Maubert.'

He read slowly through the newspaper, and took a shower before dinner. As on the previous evening, they dined at the table drawn up under the open window.

'Tomorrow, I shall be going to the funeral.'

'Will there be many people?'

'Apart from the niece, I may well be the only one. Only two of her neighbours bothered to go and pay their last respects.'

'What about the press?'

'This case hasn't made the headlines. It only rates a small paragraph on page three of this evening's paper.'

He switched on the television. It would be ten at the earliest before he could hope to find Billy Louette at the Bongo.

On the corner of the Boulevard Voltaire, he hailed a taxi. The driver looked at him curiously when he gave the address, amazed that a thoroughly respectable-looking man from a district like this should lower himself by going to such a disreputable dive.

The place had been decorated with the minimum of expense. The walls were painted white, with a few meaningless squiggles of colour splashed on here and there.

This was the only attempt at originality. The bar was an ordinary zinc counter, with the proprietor, in shirt sleeves and a blue apron, serving behind it himself. An open door at the back led into a smoke-filled kitchen, from which came a stench of rancid fat.

There were ten or a dozen couples having dinner, which consisted mainly of spaghetti, this apparently being the speciality of the house.

Some of the younger people were in jeans and flowered shirts, but it was not these whom the crowds came to see.

To see, and, above all, to hear, because the group, which consisted of three players, was making as much noise as a full orchestra. Besides Billy and his guitar there was a saxophone and drums.

All three players had long hair, and were wearing black velvet trousers and pink shirts.

'Do you wish to order dinner?'

The proprietor had to shout to be heard at all.

Maigret shook his head, and ordered white wine. Billy, who had seen him come in, seemed to take his presence there quite as a matter of course.

The Chief Superintendent knew nothing whatever about pop music, but, as far as he could tell, the Bad Lads were no worse than many of the groups regularly to be heard on radio and television. The three young men went at it with great verve, building up to a positively frenetic climax.

They were loudly clapped.

An interval followed, during which Billy joined Maigret at the bar.

'I take it it's me you've come to see?'

'Naturally. Have you heard from your mother?'

'Not today.'

'In that case, you won't know that the funeral is fixed for tomorrow morning. Leaving the Quai de la Mégisserie at a quarter to ten. The memorial service will be held at Notre-Dame-des-Blancs-Manteaux, and the burial at the Montparnasse cemetery.'

'Great-uncle Antoine was buried at Ivry, I seem to remember.'

'So he was, but your aunt expressed a wish to be buried beside her first husband.'

'We'll be playing again in a few minutes. How do we sound to you?'

'I'm sorry to say I'm no judge. There's just one thing I wanted to ask you. Do you happen to know if your aunt had a revolver?'

'Yes, she did.'

At last, a straight answer to a straight question!

'Did she tell you herself?'

'It was quite some time ago, at least a year or two. I hadn't a bean. I'd been to see her in the hope of making a touch, and I'd noticed that she kept several hundred-franc notes in the chest of drawers.

'A hundred francs is nothing to some people, but to others, including myself at times, it's a fortune.

'I remarked quite casually:

'"Don't you ever feel nervous?"

'"Who is there to be afraid of? You?"

'"No. But you live alone, and people know it. Someone might break in. . . ."'

He broke off to mouth a message to his companions that he would not keep them waiting much longer.

'She said she had taken precautions against that, and she took me into her bedroom and opened her bedside table drawer.

'"And don't think for one moment I'd hesitate to use it." '

Now there was something more to go on than a grease-stain. Someone had actually seen the gun.

'Was it a revolver or an automatic?'

'What's the difference?'

'A revolver has a barrel. An automatic is flat.'

'In that case, as far as I can remember, it was a revolver.'

'How big?'

'I really couldn't say. I just had a glimpse of it. About the size of my hand, I should say.'

'Did you mention it to anyone?'

'No, not a soul.'

'Not even your mother?'

'I'm not in the habit of running to her with every bit of tittle-tattle. We're not that close.'

The young man returned to his companions, and the music

started up again. He seemed genuinely carried away by the rhythm of his guitar, counterpointed by the beat of the drums.

'He's a good kid, that one,' remarked the proprietor, leaning across the bar counter. 'They're a decent lot altogether. Not one of them touches drugs, which is more than I can say for some of my customers.'

Maigret paid for his drink, and went out. He had some difficulty in finding a taxi to take him home.

Next morning, he went upstairs to the Examining Magistrates' floor, and knocked on Judge Libart's door.

'I'd be grateful if you'd make out a search warrant for me, in the name of Angèle Louette, spinster. Occupation: Masseuse. Address: Rue Saint-André-des-Arts.'

The clerk duly wrote out the warrant.

'Does this mean that you'll be making an early arrest?'

'To tell you the truth, I haven't the least idea. I'm groping about in the dark.'

'Isn't she the old lady's niece?'

'Quite.'

'And her sole heir? I must say that does seem rather surprising.'

This Maigret had anticipated. One's first reaction was bound to be one of scepticism. Angèle Louette was secure in the knowledge that sooner or later—and in view of her aunt's great age, it would probably be sooner—she would inherit the old lady's money. Why then should she risk life imprisonment for the sake of a legacy which was as good as hers already?

'Oh well, never mind. You must do as you think fit, and the best of luck.'

At a quarter to ten, Maigret, driven by Lapointe, drew up in one of the little black cars at the entrance to the flats in the Quai de la Mégisserie. There were no black draperies over the door, and not a single interested spectator.

The hearse had only just arrived, and two hefty undertaker's men were on their way upstairs to fetch the coffin. There were no flowers, not even a wreath. At several of the windows, the curtains twitched. The concierge followed the coffin as far as the door, and crossed herself.

The old man with the birds ventured out of his dark shop for a moment, to join his son on the pavement.

That was all.

Angèle Louette, alone, stepped into the black car provided by the undertaker. The church was deserted, except for two women waiting for the confessional. Everyone seemed in a hurry to get it over and done with, not only the undertaker's men, but the priest as well.

Maigret had sat at the back of the church, to be joined by Lapointe after he had parked the car.

'Somehow it wasn't even sad,' remarked the young inspector.

He was right. The aisle was bathed in sunlight. The door had been left open, and a babble of street noises was clearly to be heard.

Et ne nos inducat in tentationem. . . .

Amen. . . .

The coffin, probably lighter than most, was carried out. Less than a quarter of an hour later, they were in the Cemetery of Montparnasse. The small procession stopped at the end of a tree-lined avenue, and the coffin was lowered into a newly dug grave, beside a flat stone of pink marble.

'I told you no one would come,' whispered the masseuse, as the old woman was being laid to rest.

She went on:

'There wasn't time to have the stone engraved. She wanted her name put next to her first husband's. The stonemasons will be attending to it next week.'

She was wearing a very plain black outfit, which made her seem more forbidding than ever. She looked more like a governess or a headmistress than anything else.

'We'll go back to your flat now,' murmured Maigret.

'We?'

'We, yes, that's what I said.'

'What is it you want from me now?'

It was even more cheerful in the cemetery than in the church, with the sunlight dancing among the leaves of the trees, and the birds singing.

'One moment, I'll have to tip all these people, I suppose.
I don't need to keep the car, do I?'

'There's room for you in ours.'

They forgathered at the gate. Angèle got into the back of
the car. Maigret took his usual seat beside Lapointe.

'The Rue Saint-André-des-Arts.'

Bitterly, the old lady's niece remarked:

'I was prepared for a certain amount of gossip. There are
always people ready to talk behind one's back, and, if they
have nothing to go on, to invent lies. But that the C.I.D., in the
person of Chief Superintendent Maigret, should make my life
a misery . . .'

'I'm truly sorry, but I'm only doing my job.'

'What possible reason could I have for sneaking into my
aunt's flat?'

'What possible reason could anyone have had?'

'Do you really think me capable of murdering an old
woman?'

'I don't think anything. I'm only trying to get at the truth.
Join us upstairs, Lapointe, as soon as you've parked the car.'

Upstairs in the flat, she took off her hat and gloves, and
the jacket of her suit, under which she was wearing a white
shirt. For the first time, Maigret noticed that, in spite of her
mannish appearance, she had quite a good figure, and was
astonishingly well preserved for her age.

'Now will you kindly tell me, once and for all, what you
want from me?'

He took the Examining Magistrate's warrant out of his
pocket.

'Read it for yourself.'

'Does this mean that you're going to rummage among my
things, and turn everything upside down?'

'There's no fear of that. We know our job. Two experts
from Criminal Records will be here shortly, and they will see
that everything is put back exactly as it was.'

'I still don't understand.'

'I noticed that your son wasn't at the funeral.'

'I must confess that, after everything that happened yesterday, I forgot to let him know. I haven't even got his exact address, I only know what you told me.'

'You didn't let him know, but I did, which is why I was surprised not to see him there. He struck me as a thoroughly good sort.'

'Provided he always gets his own way.'

'And provided no one tries to make an osteopath of him.'

'He told you about that, did he?'

'He was a great deal more forthcoming than you are, and I didn't have to ask him the same questions ten times before getting straight answers . . .'

'He hasn't had to go through what I've been through! I don't know about you, but I need a drink.'

It was not wine she needed, apparently, but whisky, which she got from a cupboard in the living room, crammed with bottles of various sorts.

'Will you join me? Or would you prefer a glass of wine? Red? White?'

'Nothing for the moment, thanks.'

The men from Criminal Records arrived before Lapointe, who, no doubt, had had to go miles to find a parking place.

'Right, lads, you'd better get started. Everything must be gone through with a fine toothcomb. You know what we're looking for, but you may find something else of interest as well. All I ask is that you should put everything back, exactly as you found it.'

She lit a cigarette, and went and sat in an armchair near the window, which commanded an extensive view of the rooftops of Paris, and from which a corner of the Eiffel Tower could also be seen.

When Lapointe finally arrived, Maigret said:

'You stay here with them. I have another call to make in the district.'

Once out in the street, he made off in the direction of the Rue Mouffetard, but not until he had gulped down a glass of white wine, in a little local bistro with a bowl of hard-boiled eggs on the bar counter.

CHAPTER FIVE

THE HOTEL was tall and narrow, and permeated with a mixture of pungent smells. Maigret, having inquired at the desk and received a grudging answer, went up to the fourth floor, and knocked at the appropriate door.

A sleepy voice called out:

'Come in.'

The shutters were closed, and the room was in darkness.

'I thought it must be you.'

The redhead got out of bed, stark naked, and hastily tied a towel around his middle. In the bed, Maigret could just make out the contours of a girl. She was lying with her face to the wall, and all that could be seen distinctly was her dark hair spread out on the pillow.

'What time is it?'

'Much too late for you to attend the funeral.'

'I suppose you want to know why I wasn't there? Hang on a minute, while I swill out my mouth. It feels like the bottom of a birdcage.'

He filled the tooth mug under the running tap, and rinsed his mouth.

'It's a pity you left so early last night. You missed all the fun. It went like a bomb. Three guys from England turned up with their guitars, and we all got together and improvized for two hours or more. And they had a smashing girl with them. That's her over there.

'I just hadn't the courage to get up this morning, to go to the old girl's funeral. I feel very badly about it, but, to tell you the truth, I wasn't madly keen to meet my mother.

'By the way, has she got hold of the loot yet?'

'What loot?'

'My great-aunt's savings. She must have had a tidy bit put by. She spent almost nothing on herself. And her second

94

husband was a saver too. It looks as though my mother will soon get the little house she's always longed for.'

He opened the shutters a crack, letting a strip of sunlight into the room. The girl groaned and turned over, revealing a naked breast.

'Was your mother planning to buy a house?'

'A small house in the country, to use at weekends at first, and eventually to retire to. She's dreamt of nothing else for years. She tried to get the old girl to lend her the money, but it didn't work out. I'm sorry, I can't offer you anything.'

'I just happened to be passing.'

'Have you found the revolver yet?'

'No. By the way, Le Grand Marcel has taken himself off.'

'You don't say! My mother must be hopping mad!'

'She was the one who showed him the door. He's gone to Toulon, where he has friends.'

'She'll need to find someone else. I doubt if she could get along for three days without a man. Unless she takes to the bottle again—but that has its problems, and it's a lot more expensive.'

There was no malice in his cynicism. Indeed, there was a sort of wistfulness about him, perhaps because of the family life he had never known.

So he covered it up with a swagger.

'Don't leave Paris without letting me know. I'm nowhere near the end of this case, and I may still need your help.'

The young man jerked his chin towards the bed.

'As you see, I have plenty to keep me occupied here.'

Maigret returned to the Rue Saint-André-des-Arts. The men from Criminal Records were still there, waiting for him.

'We're through here, Chief. There's nothing much to report. Clothes, mostly in dark colours, underwear, stockings and shoes. She must have a thing about shoes, because we found no less than eight pairs.'

Angèle Louette was still sitting in the armchair by the window. She appeared completely unmoved.

'The refrigerator is well stocked. For a woman living on her own, she does herself very well. Photographs, mainly photographs of herself, when much younger, and a little boy. An account book recording the names of clients and payments received.'

'You've forgotten the most important thing,' broke in the second man.

The other man shrugged.

'For what it's worth! The top of the wardrobe is very dusty, and mixed in with the dust we found particles of oil or grease, almost certainly gun-grease.'

Angèle interrupted:

'There's never been a gun in this flat.'

'Be that as it may, it's fresh grease. In the kitchen bin, I found some grease-stained paper which had been used as wrapping for a revolver.'

'If so, it must have been Marcel's, and no doubt he took it away with him.'

Maigret climbed on to a chair to see the stain for himself.

'I'd be obliged if you would attend at the Quai des Orfèvres at three o'clock this afternoon.'

'What about my appointments? I'm a professional woman, not a lady of leisure.'

'I'm afraid I shall have to make it an official summons.'

He took a yellow form from his pocket, and filled in the details.

'I said three o'clock, remember.'

Lapointe had been waiting patiently. They walked together to the little black car, which was parked some way off. Moers's men left at the same time.

'Is she on the telephone?'

'Yes.'

'She was probably only waiting to get rid of us before ringing Toulon. Among the photographs were there any of the old lady?'

'Three or four, taken a long time ago. There were also several of a man with a moustache, who she said was old Antoine.'

Maigret went home to lunch. His wife was still being tactful. She asked no questions, except about the funeral.

'Were there many people?'

'No one except the niece and ourselves, Lapointe and me. The memorial prayer was gabbled at top speed. You'd have thought they couldn't get rid of her fast enough.'

When he got back to his office, Janvier was waiting for him with a message.

'Superintendent Marella has been on from Toulon. He wants you to ring him back.'

'Get him for me, will you?'

A few minutes later, he was through to him.

'Marella?'

'Yes. I rang on the off-chance of finding you in. Your friend Marcel got here late last night, and made straight for the Bar de l'Amiral. He spotted me at once, and said, "Good evening," before taking a seat at the bar. He and Bob had their heads together for some time, but I couldn't hear a word they were saying, because the juke-box was going full blast.'

'Was there anyone else with them?'

'No. At one point, Bob went and shut himself up in the telephone box, and made a call. He seemed very pleased with himself when he came back, and gave Marcel the thumbs up sign.'

'Was that all?'

'No. Your friend Marcel has booked himself in at the Hôtel des Cinq Continents, in the Avenue de la République. He was up at nine this morning, and set off by car for Sanary. Does that ring a bell?'

'No.'

'It's where Pepito, the elder of the Giovanni brothers, lives.'

For years the Giovannis had been responsible for most of the crime on the Riviera. Marco, the younger of the two, lived near Paris. Pepito had built himself a luxury villa at Sanary, and now lived there quietly in retirement.

They had been arrested ten or a dozen times, but there had never been enough evidence to make the charges stick.

Now that they were getting on in years, they lived the life of rich, elderly, retired gentlemen.

'How long did Marcel stay at the villa?'

'Nearly an hour. Afterwards he went back to l'Amiral, and then he had lunch at an Italian restaurant in the old town.'

'Had he any previous connection with the Giovannis?'

'Not that I know of.'

'Better have Pepito watched. I'd like to know where, if anywhere, he goes in the next day or two, and also whether any of his old associates start turning up at the villa.'

'I'll see to it. I daresay you'll do as much for me some day. How's your case going?'

'I'm beginning to see a glimmer of light, but there's a long way to go yet. When it's over, I've half a mind to get away for a change of scene and a bit of sun. I might even look you up.'

'I should be delighted. How long is it since we last met?'

'Ten years? Twelve years? It was over that business at Porquerolles.'

'I remember. So long, Maigret.'

They had signed on together at the Quai des Orfèvres, and for more than two years had pounded the same beat until their promotion, after which they had first patrolled the railway stations, and then been assigned to detective work in the large department stores. They had both been young bachelors then.

Old Joseph came to the door, bearing the summons that Maigret had served on Angèle earlier in the day.

'Bring her in.'

She was paler and more tense than usual. Perhaps she was just overawed by the portentous atmosphere of Police Headquarters.

'Take a seat.'

He pointed to a straight-backed chair facing his desk, and opened the communicating door to the Inspectors' Duty Room.

'Come in, will you, Lapointe, and bring your shorthand book.'

Young Lapointe often did duty as a shorthand writer. He sat down at one end of the desk, with pencil poised.

'As you see, you have been summoned here for an official interrogation. Everything you say will be taken down, and at the end you will be required to read and sign the transcript. I may have to repeat some questions that I have already put to you, but this time your answers will be on record.'

'In other words, I'm suspect number one, is that it?'

'You're a suspect, that's all. Numbers don't come into it. You had not the slightest affection for your aunt. Isn't that so?'

'When I told her I was pregnant, the best she could do for me was to hand me a hundred-franc note.'

'And you resented what you regarded as her meanness?'

'She was thoroughly selfish. She never gave a thought to others. And I'm quite sure in my own mind that the only reason she married again was because of the money that was there.'

'Was she a deprived child?'

'She didn't even have that excuse. Her father was a man of property, as they used to say. The family lived near the Luxembourg Gardens, and the two girls, my mother and my aunt, went to a very good school. It wasn't until my grandfather was well advanced in years that he began to speculate recklessly, and eventually lost all he possessed.'

'Was it then that she married Caramé?'

'Yes. He was a frequent visitor at my grandparents. Everyone thought at first that it was my mother he was interested in. I fancy she thought so, too. But it was my aunt who got him in the end.'

'And your mother?'

'She married a bank clerk. He was in poor health, and he died young. She went to work for a business firm in the Rue Paradis.'

'So life was none too easy for the two of you?'

'That's right.'

'Didn't your aunt offer to help?'

'No. I don't quite know what made me decide to become a masseuse. Unless it was that one of our neighbours was a masseuse, and I used to see her drive off in her car to visit her clients.'

'Have you a car?'

'A Mini.'

'To drive you down to your country house, when you get it?'

She frowned.

'Who told you that?'

'Never mind. I gather you've always had this dream of owning a little house, not too far out of town, where you could go for weekends.'

'Well, what's wrong with that? It's what lots of people want. It was my mother's dearest wish as well, only she died before it came true.'

'How much do you hope to get from your aunt's estate?'

'Forty to fifty thousand francs, perhaps. I don't know. I'm only going on what she told me. She may have had other investments that she didn't mention.'

'In other words, you went on seeing her because of what you were hoping to get?'

'You can put it that way if you like. At the same time, she was my only living relative. Have you ever had to live alone, Monsieur Maigret?'

'What about your son?'

'I hardly ever see him, except when he's short of money. I mean nothing to him.'

'Before I put my next question to you, I must remind you that everything you say is being taken down, and urge you to think carefully before you speak. Did you often go to your aunt's flat while she was out?'

It seemed to him that she had turned a shade paler, but her self-possession was unshaken.

'Do you mind if I smoke?'

'Please do, but I'm afraid I haven't any cigarettes to offer you.'

On his desk there were pipes only, six pipes arranged in sizes, side by side in a rack.

'I asked you a question.'

'I'd be grateful if you would repeat it.'

He did so, slowly and clearly, and without hesitation.

'It depends what you mean by going to her flat. Sometimes

I called at the Quai de la Mégisserie, and found her out. On those occasions, I waited until she got back.'

'In the flat?'

'No. Outside on the landing.'

'Did you often have to wait a long time?'

'When she was a long time coming, I used to go for a walk along the Quai, or more often just look at the birds.'

'Did it never occur to your aunt to give you a key to the flat?'

'No.'

'Supposing she had been taken ill suddenly?'

'She'd made up her mind that it couldn't happen to her. She never had so much as a fainting fit in the whole of her life.'

'Did she ever leave the door open?'

'No.'

'Not even when she was at home?'

'No. She always took good care to see that it was shut.'

'Was there someone in particular she didn't trust?'

'She didn't trust anyone.'

'Not even you?'

'I don't know.'

'Was her manner towards you affectionate?'

'It was completely matter-of-fact. She'd tell me to sit down. Then she'd make me coffee, and serve it up to me with some dry biscuits out of a tin.'

'Did she never ask after your son?'

'No. I imagine she saw him quite as often as I did, if not more.'

'Did she ever threaten to disinherit you?'

'Why ever should she do that?'

'To get back to the front door, I've had a look at the lock. There's nothing very special about it. Anyone could have taken a wax impression of it.'

'What for?'

'No matter. Allow me to put my question another way: Were you never, on any occasion, alone in the flat?'

'Never.'

'Think carefully.'

'I have thought very carefully.'

'Did it never happen that, while you were there, your aunt had to slip out to get something from the shops, such as a fresh supply of biscuits, for instance?'

'No.'

'So you never got a chance to go through her drawers?'

'No.'

'And you never saw her Post Office Savings book?'

'I caught a glimpse of it once, when she was getting something out of the drawer, but I don't know what was in it.'

'What about her bank book?'

'I haven't the slightest idea how much she had in the bank. As a matter of fact, I didn't even know she had a bank account.'

'But you knew she had money?'

'I was pretty sure of it.'

'I don't mean just her savings.'

'I don't know what you're talking about. What do you mean?'

'Never mind. Did you ever try and borrow money from her?'

'Just the once, as I told you. That time when I was pregnant, and she gave me a hundred francs.'

'More recently than that, I mean. You wanted to buy a country cottage. Did you never ask her to help you towards that?'

'No. You don't know what she was like.'

'I did meet her.'

'And you were taken in, just like everyone else. You took her for a sweet old lady, with a gentle smile and a shy manner, whereas, in actual fact, she was as hard as nails.'

'Do you own a red striped or check scarf?'

'No.'

'Do you remember the red-striped cushion on the couch in your aunt's sitting room?'

'Vaguely, yes, I think I do.'

'You had a row with your friend Marcel yesterday morning. What was that about?'

'He was becoming impossible.'

'What do you mean by that?'

'Naturally, when I take up with a man, I don't ask for references. But Marcel went too far. He didn't even bother to look for work. He could have got a job as a barman ten times over. But he preferred to sponge on me.'

'Did he know your aunt?'

'I'd hardly be likely to introduce him to her, would I?'

'Did he know of her existence?'

'I may have mentioned her.'

'And told him, I daresay, that she had a nice little nest-egg tucked away?'

'I would hardly have put it quite like that.'

'Be that as it may, he knew where she lived and that, to say the least, she had a tidy bit put by.'

'Yes, I suppose he did.'

'Did you ever see him going into the flats at the Quai de la Mégisserie?'

'Never.'

'And yet there are at least two witnesses who saw him there.'

'Well, it's more than I ever did.'

'Did you ever consider marrying him?'

'Certainly not. Since my son was born, I've never once thought of marriage. I get what I want from a man when I want it, and that's about all there is to it. Do I make myself clear?'

'Perfectly, Now, about the revolver.'

'What, again?'

'It must be somewhere, and I'm determined to find it. For some considerable time, your aunt kept it in the drawer of her bedside table. According to you, your aunt was terrified of firearms, and you find it hard to credit that she ever owned a gun.'

'That's right.'

'Nevertheless, she did own a gun, and she always kept it handy, which, incidentally, rather suggests that she was more concerned for her safety than you led me to suppose.'

'What's all this leading up to?'

Maigret, with great deliberation, refilled his pipe.

'This morning, at your flat, we found evidence that your aunt's gun had, at some time, been concealed on top of your wardrobe.'

'That's what you say.'

'I'm having tests done to confirm it. One of two people must have put the gun there, you or your lover.'

'I object to that term.'

'Does it embarrass you?'

'It's inaccurate. There was no love in our relationship.'

'Let's suppose, for the sake of argument, that he did go to the Quai de la Mégisserie.'

'To murder my aunt?'

'To look for her nice little nest-egg, to use the expression you objected to just now. The old lady came back, and found herself face to face with him. And he snatched up a cushion from the couch, and smothered her with it.'

'Where does the revolver come into it? Why should he have taken it? Why should he have hidden it on top of my wardrobe, and why, when he left for Toulon, should he have taken it with him?'

'So you think he took it with him?'

'If it really exists, it must, as you say yourself, be somewhere. For myself, I assure you that I was nowhere near my aunt's flat on the afternoon of her death. And I don't believe for a moment that Marcel was either. He may be a bad lot, as they say, but he's not a killer. Any more questions?'

'Have you done anything about claiming your inheritance?'

'Not yet. I have an appointment later today with a solicitor, the husband of one of my clients. If it hadn't been for him, I shouldn't have known where to turn.'

She stood up, with every appearance of relief.

'When will you want my signature?'

'On your statement, do you mean? How long will it take you to type it, Lapointe?'

'It'll be ready in half an hour.'

'In half an hour. I suggest you make yourself comfortable in the waiting room meanwhile.'

'Can't I come back some other time?'

'No. I want to get it over and done with. You can see your solicitor later, and by tonight you'll be some tens of thousands of francs the richer. Incidentally, do you intend to move into your aunt's flat?'

'No. My own suits me perfectly well.'

Holding herself stiffly erect, she went to the door and without another word left the room.

He caught the night train, and was fortunate enough to get a sleeping compartment to himself. He awoke at dawn, as he always did when travelling south, just as the train drew into Montélimar.

To him, Montélimar had always been the frontier town of Provence. From there on, he couldn't bear to miss an inch of the terrain. He loved everything about it, the trees and flowers, the countryside, the pale pink and lavender blue houses, with their sun-baked tiled roofs, the villages with their avenues of plane trees and their little bars, where people were already assembling.

At Marseilles, while the train was shunting in the Gare Saint-Charles, he listened with relish to the sing-song voices of the locals.

It was a long time since he and his wife had last been to the Riviera. Why should they not spend their next holiday there? But it would be the height of the season by then, and the whole area would be swarming with tourists.

A few more miles, and there was the sea, as blue as in any postcard, dotted with boats, with motionless fishermen aboard.

Superintendent Marella was waiting for him on the station platform and waving enthusiastically.

'Why don't you come more often? How many years is it since you were last in Toulon?'

'About ten, as I told you on the telephone. I hope you don't mind me trespassing on your territory like this?'

Maigret was outside his own territory. Here Marella was the boss. He was, needless to say, very dark. Though not above medium height, he was extremely ebullient. Since their last meeting, he had developed something of a paunch, which somehow lent him an air of respectability.

In the old days, he had looked more like a gangster than a police officer. Gangsters are no less prone to middle-aged spread than anyone else, but they usually retire before it overtakes them.

'Would you care for a coffee?'

'I'd love one. I had a cup on the train, but it tasted foul.'

'Right then, let's go. There's quite a decent little place across the square.'

The square was shimmering in the heat. They went into a café-restaurant and sat down at the bar.

'Come on then. Tell us all about it.'

'There's nothing to tell. It's a queer business. I can't make any sense of it. I'm just floundering. Where is Marcel at the moment?'

'In his bed. He spent half the night whooping it up with his buddies in the Restaurant Victor, opposite the Port-Marchand. A lot of layabouts, they are. Later, they were joined by some girls.'

'Did you ever come across him when he lived here?'

'He was never in Toulon for very long. His longest stay was two years. I should tell you that none of the villains hereabouts takes him very seriously. He's looked on as a bit of an amateur.'

'Who's this fellow Bob, that he uses as an accommodation address?'

'The barman at l'Amiral. He's up to every trick. At any rate, none of us here has ever been able to pin anything on him.'

'And the Giovanni brothers?'

'Only one of them lives here, Pepito, the older of the two. The other, I'm told, has a place just outside Paris. Pepito owns a magnificent villa, which he bought from a rich old American, who decided she wanted to go home and lay her bones in the old country. It's the finest property in Sanary, with its own private anchorage, in which he keeps his motor launch.

'He's practically a recluse, and scarcely ever sees any of his old cronies. Out of sight, out of mind, appears to be his motto.

All the same, I've been keeping an eye on him. And, what's more, he knows it, and whenever we pass in the street, he greets me most cordially.'

'I wonder what on earth Marcel could possibly have had to say to him.'

'Me too. Especially as Marcel was never one of his boys.'

'Where is he staying?'

'At the Hôtel des Cinq Continents, in the Avenue de la République. It's almost next door to the Harbour-master's Office.'

It was still only eight o'clock.

'Would you mind coming with me? It will help put you in the picture. He'll be livid at being woken up at this time of the morning.'

Maigret did not book into a hotel, as he was hoping to be able to leave that same evening. Marella inquired at the desk for the number of Marcel's room, and they went up together and knocked loudly on his door. It was some time before a sleepy voice called out:

'Who's there?'

'Police.'

It was Marella who had spoken. Marcel, in crumpled pyjamas, and barefooted, stumbled across to the door and opened it.

'Good Lord! Not you again!' he grumbled, catching sight of Maigret. 'Oh well, as you're with Superintendent Marella . . .'

He pulled back the curtains, lit a cigarette, and hastily removed a pair of trousers which were thrown on a chair.

'What have I done now?' he asked.

'Nothing new, as far as I know.'

'As a matter of fact,' broke in Marella, addressing Marcel, 'there was one thing. Yesterday afternoon you went to see La Belle Maria. Don't you know that, for months now, she's been Scarface's girl?'

'I also know that he's in the nick.'

'True enough. I brought him in last week, and this time it's on a very serious charge, trafficking in drugs, no less. All the same, he's got friends on the outside, and you're on foreign soil here.'

'Thanks for the tip. But she's a very old friend. But what about you, Monsieur Maigret? What brings you all this way, only two days after our last meeting?'

'Maybe I've come to take you back to Paris.'

'What? You must be joking!'

'First of all, there's that little matter of the key.'

'What key?'

'The key to the old lady's flat. Who took the wax impression? Angéle couldn't have managed that on her own.'

Marcel didn't bat an eyelid.

'All right! Save your answers for your official statement, which will be taken down and which you will be required to sign.'

'Heavens above! Do you never listen? I know nothing whatever about that filthy business, I tell you! O.K., I was living with the Sergeant-Major, though only, I may say, until I found something better, and I was only too glad to be shot of her.'

'There are at least two witnesses who can remember seeing you.'

'How did they identify me?'

'From a photograph on our files, or rather on the Vice Squad files.'

'And who, pray, are these two witnesses?'

'The owner of the pet-shop on the ground floor, and the tenant who lives in the flat across the landing from the old lady. You actually bumped into her on the stairs, because you weren't looking where you were going, and you apologized.'

'They must both be mad.'

'You were wearing the same check suit that you had on the day before yesterday.'

'I bought it in one of the big department stores. There must be thousands like it in Paris.'

'So, you had no key. Did you pick the lock?'

'How much longer is this going on?'

'I couldn't say. Why?'

'Because if you intend to stay, I'd like to order myself some breakfast.'

'Go ahead.'

He rang for the floor waiter, and ordered coffee and croissants.

'And if you were expecting me to order anything for you, you're in for a disappointment. I've never picked a lock in my life. I wouldn't know how.'

'When did she first tell you about the revolver?'

'Who?'

'You know very well who. Angèle. You're not suggesting, are you, that you guessed the old lady kept a revolver in her flat?'

'I didn't even know of the old girl's existence.'

'That's a lie. Angèle has admitted, in her signed statement, that she pointed to the windows of her aunt's flat, and told you that she was her heir.'

'And you believe her? She'd lie as soon as look at you, that one.'

'And you wouldn't, I suppose?'

'I'm telling you the truth. You won't trip me up, just because you've got your nasty, suspicious eye on me. Take that photograph you got from the Vice Squad. When was it taken, I'd like to know? I have no recollection of it.'

The waiter came in with the coffee and croissants, which filled the room with an appetizing smell. He put the tray down on a small pedestal table. Marcel, still in his pyjamas and barefooted, drew up a chair, and began to eat.

Marella glanced at Maigret with eyebrows raised, as though seeking permission to intervene.

'What were you talking to Bob about?'

'The night before last, soon after I got here? I told him all my news, and he told me his. We're old friends, and it's ages since we last met.'

'And what else?'

'I don't know what you mean.'

'Which of the two of you thought of Giovanni?'

'I think I did. I knew him too, back in the old days, when he lived in Montmartre. I was only a kid then.'

'Why, in that case, didn't you ring him yourself?'

'What on earth for?'

'To make an appointment to see him. As Bob did on your behalf. What was it you wanted to talk to him about?'

'I don't know what you mean.'

'Don't be an idiot. As you very well know, one can't just turn up on Giovanni's doorstep, especially if one happens to be nothing more than a miserable, down-and-out little pimp. But the fact remains that you did go and see him yesterday, and you were with him for nearly an hour.'

'I just went along for a chat, that's all.'

'And what, may I ask, did you chat about?'

Marcel was beginning to show signs of nervousness. He was not at all happy with this particular line of inquiry.

'Let's say I went along to ask him for a job. He has a great many irons in the fire, all on the level. I thought he could probably use a man he could trust.'

'Did he take you on?'

'He wanted time to think it over. He said he'd let me know in a day or two.'

Once more, Marella glanced at Maigret, to indicate that he had finished.

'You heard what my colleague, Marella, said just now. He will be giving the necessary instructions to his staff. You will therefore oblige us by calling at his office, and repeating all you have said to us. This will be taken down by a shorthand writer, and in due course you will be required to sign the transcript.

'Be sure you leave nothing out, especially where Bob and Giovanni are concerned.'

'Do I have to bring him in?'

'Have you told the truth?'

'Yes. But he wouldn't like it if he knew I'd been discussing him with the cops.'

'I'm afraid you have no choice. And don't attempt to leave Toulon until we give you the word.'

'Whatever you say, but if I don't manage to find a job, will you pay my hotel bill?'

'Maybe we can arrange to put you up somewhere else,' interposed Marella. 'It's nice and cool in there, at any rate.'

The two men went out into the avenue.

'I hope you didn't think I was taking too much on myself?' said Marella, a little anxiously.

'Far from it. You were most helpful. I'd be very grateful if you'd do the same for me with Bob.'

The Bar de l'Amiral was just on the other side of the avenue, on the corner of the quay and a narrow cul-de-sac. Out on the pavement, there were four tables, covered with cloths of a small check pattern. Outside, the sunshine, reflected on the shimmering expanse of water, was dazzling.

In contrast, the interior of the bar was dark and pleasantly cool.

A barman, with the broken nose and cauliflower ears of a boxer, was busy washing glasses. It was too early in the day for customers, and the room was deserted, except for a waiter who was laying the tables.

'Good morning, Superintendent. What can I get you?'

He spoke to Marella, whom he knew. Maigret was a stranger to him.

'Have you a good local wine?' asked Maigret.

'A carafe of rosé?'

'Two glasses, or a carafe, as you wish.'

Both men were in high good humour. Only Bob appeared uneasy.

'You had a visitor last night, I noticed, Bob.'

'We're never short of visitors here, you know.'

'I don't mean a customer. I'm referring to someone who came all the way from Paris expressly to see you.'

'To see me, me in particular?'

'Well, let's say to ask you a favour.'

'I can't imagine what.'

'Have you known him long?'

'Seven or eight years.'

'Is he on the level?'

'He's never done time, if that's what you mean. He hasn't got a record.'

'And what about you?'

'You know the answer to that. I haven't got a perfectly clean sheet.'

'What was it he wanted?'

'He happened to be passing, and he just dropped in for a chat.'

'He asked you to make a telephone call for him.'

'Oh?'

'Don't play the fool with me. One of my men was in here at the time. You left your friend at the bar, and shut yourself up in the telephone box, and made a call. It was a long call. Your friend was very jumpy. When you got back, you talked to him at some length in an undertone, after which he looked a good deal relieved.'

'I dare say it was about his ex-girl friend, Maria. He'd been to see her.'

'Is she living at Sanary now?'

'You must be joking!'

'It's not in your interest to hold out on me, Bob. The person you spoke to on the telephone was Pepito Giovanni. You worked for him once upon a time, before he went straight. You persuaded him to see your mate Marcel. Quite a feat that, because Giovanni won't see any Tom, Dick or Harry, especially in his own house. How did you manage it?'

'I just told Giovanni that I had a friend with me, who was looking for a job.'

'No!'

'Why do you say no?'

'Because you know as well as I do that it's not true. Giovanni will laugh his head off when I tell him.'

'I told him that Marcel had an interesting proposition to put to him. And nothing illegal about it either.'

'Did he show you the prototype?'

'No.'

'Do you know what it is?'

'Marcel didn't tell me. All he would say was that it **was** something very, very big, with international potential, and likely to be of special interest to the Americans.'

'That's a bit more like it. Maybe we're getting to the truth at last. Was Giovanni interested?'

'He agreed to see Marcel yesterday afternoon at three.'

'Anything else?'

'He said to be sure and see that no one went with him, and to tell him not to forget the prototype.'

The vin rosé was fruity in flavour and perfectly chilled. Maigret listened to the interchange, smiling a little to himself. He had always had a great affection for Marella, and it occurred to him that, had he stayed in Paris, he might well now be sitting in his, Maigret's, seat at the Quai des Orfèvres. But he was more in his element in Toulon. He had been born in Nice, and knew every delinquent and prostitute from Menton to Marseilles.

'Is there anything you want to ask him, Maigret?'

Bob frowned.

'Do you mean to say that's Chief Superintendent Maigret with you?'

'None other. And, if you don't watch out, he's the one you may find yourself up against.'

'Forgive me, I didn't recognize you.'

And, as Maigret was opening his wallet:

'No, no. It's on the house.'

'I'm sorry, I can't agree to that.'

He laid a ten-franc note on the table.

'I presume that, the minute we've left, you'll be on the phone to Giovanni?'

'Not if you don't want me to. I've no wish to get on the wrong side of you. Nor of Superintendent Marella, for that matter.'

They stood for a moment in the sunlit square, watching the sailors go by, with their navy blue collars and red pompons.

'Do you want me to come with you to see Giovanni? Or would you rather go alone?'

'I wouldn't dream of going without you.'

'In that case, let's go back to Police Headquarters, and collect my car.'

They crossed the Seyne, where they saw a ship being broken up, and were soon in sight of Sanary Point, on the very end of which stood an imposing villa in its own grounds.

'That's the house. Even if Bob has kept his word, Marcel will have been in touch with him, so he'll be expecting us. It won't be quite such plain sailing with him.'

CHAPTER SIX

HE CAME TOWARDS THEM, hand outstretched, across a huge drawing room which was bathed in sunlight. He was wearing a cream shantung suit.

'Good-day to you, Marella,' he said, then pretending to notice Maigret for the first time:

'Chief Superintendent Maigret, of all people! This is an unexpected honour.'

He was a fine-looking man, powerfully built, but without an ounce of surplus fat on him. Maigret knew that he must be over sixty, but, at first glance at least, he looked nearer fifty.

The drawing room was furnished with great taste, probably by an interior decorator, and there was a hint of the theatre about it, owing to its lofty proportions.

'Where would you prefer to sit, here or on the terrace?'

He led the way out, and installed them in comfortable lounging chairs under a beach umbrella.

The butler, in a white jacket, had followed them out and stood, a watchful figure, awaiting orders.

'What would you like to drink? May I suggest a Tom Collins? I know of nothing more refreshing at this time of day.'

Maigret and Marella indicated their approval.

'Two Tom Collinses, Georges, and the usual for me.'

He was close-shaven, with well-kept hands and manicured nails. His manner was easy and relaxed.

'Have you only just got here?' he asked Maigret, by way of making polite conversation.

The terrace looked out on to the sea, which seemed to extend to infinity. A motor-launch rocked gently in the little private anchorage.

'I came on the night train.'

'Don't tell me you came all this way just to see me!'

115

'I had no idea, when I arrived, that I should be coming to see you at all.'

'All the same, I'm flattered.'

Beneath his genial manner he was a hard man, however much he tried to conceal it by a display of affability.

'At any rate, you're not on home territory now, Chief Superintendent.'

'True enough, but my good friend Marella here is.'

'Marella and I understand one another perfectly. Don't we, Marella?'

'Just so long as you keep on the right side of the law.'

'I lead such a very quiet life, you know that. I hardly ever go out. You could almost say that my whole world is bounded by these four walls. I never see a soul, except for a friend occasionally, or a pretty girl from time to time.'

'Do you number Le Grand Marcel among your friends?'

He looked shocked.

'That seedy little runt who came to see me yesterday morning?'

'Be that as it may, you did agree to see him.'

'It's a point of principle with me never to refuse a helping hand. There have been times in the past when I too was in need of help.'

'And did you help him?'

The butler reappeared with a tray, on which there were two tall frosted glasses and a smaller glass that was full of tomato juice.

'Please forgive me. I never touch wine or spirits. Cheers! But I interrupted you. What was it you were saying?'

'I asked you if you had been able to help him.'

'Unfortunately not. I couldn't see my way to fitting him in anywhere.

'You see, Monsieur Maigret, a lot of water has flowed under the Pont-Neuf since last we met. Nowadays I'm a highly respected business tycoon, if I may say so.

'I own a dozen cinemas up and down the Côte d'Azur, two in Marseilles, one in Nice, one in Antibes, and three in Cannes, not to mention the one in Aix-en-Provence.

'I am also the proprietor of a night club in Marseilles, and of three hotels, one of them in Menton.

'And all perfectly respectable, I assure you. Isn't that so, Marella?'

'Quite correct.'

'I also own a restaurant in Paris, on the Avenue de la Grande-Armée. My brother manages it for me. It's an extremely smart place, and the food is superb. You'll be welcome there as my guest any time.'

Maigret was watching him extremely closely, his expression inscrutable.

'You must see, Chief Superintendent, that in my kind of set-up, there's no room for a petty little pimp like Marcel.'

'Did he leave the prototype with you?'

Giovanni, for all his self-assurance, was visibly shaken.

'Prototype? What are you talking about? You must be making a mistake.'

'You agreed to see Marcel because Bob told you on the telephone that he was on to something big, something with almost unlimited potential.'

'I don't understand. It sounds like a fairy tale to me. Surely you didn't get it from Bob?'

'I understand that it was likely to be of particular interest to the Americans.'

'But I have no American business connections.'

'I'm going to tell you a little story, Giovanni, and I hope you may learn something from it. Once upon a time, there lived in Paris a dear little old lady who got it into her head that someone was sneaking into her flat while she was out and moving her things, so that, when she got back, everything was very slightly out of place.'

'I don't see what . . .'

'Let me finish. This same old lady came to Police Head-quarters to ask for protection, but I'm sorry to say we all thought she was mad, to begin with at least. All the same, I had intended to go and see her, if only to reassure her.'

'I seem to remember reading something about it in the newspapers.'

'It was referred to briefly, but the press had no idea what it was really all about.'

'Would you care for a cigar?'

'Thanks all the same, but I prefer my pipe.'

'What about you, Marella?'

'With pleasure.'

There was a box of Havana cigars on the table. Giovanni and Marella each took one.

'Forgive me. I shouldn't have interrupted you. You went to call on the old lady. . . .'

'There's a lot more before we get to that.'

'Please go on.'

'She had an elderly niece with a marked predilection for men much younger than herself. For the past six months, for instance, she's had Marcel living with her, that same Marcel who came to see you yesterday.'

Giovanni was now listening with interest.

'The old lady was murdered before I had a chance to go and see her as I had promised.'

'How was she killed?'

'She was suffocated with a cushion. She couldn't, at her age, put up very much of a fight.'

'I still don't understand what all this has to do with me.'

'As I told you, Le Grand Marcel and the old lady's niece were lovers. There are two witnesses who are prepared to swear that they saw him in the house where the old lady lived on at least one occasion.'

'Do you suspect him of the murder?'

'Either him or the niece. It comes to the same thing, more or less.'

'What were they after?'

'The prototype.'

'What do you mean?'

'Whatever it was that Marcel came to sell you.'

'And what might that be?'

'You should know better than I do, since, unless I'm very much mistaken, it is now in your possession.'

'I still don't know what you're talking about.'

'I'm talking about a revolver. I may as well admit right away that I don't know what sort of revolver, or what there is about it that makes it so special.'

'I've never carried a gun in my life, as you very well know. Even in the very early days, when I was just a young delinquent, I was often stopped and searched by the police, but they were never once able to charge me with being in illegal possession of a firearm.'

'I know.'

'That being so, what possible inducement do you suppose there could be for me to take a revolver from a sleazy little pimp like Marcel?'

'Have no fear, I'm not going to ask my friend Marella to rummage through your house from cellar to attic. You're far too wily a customer to leave the article in question in any place where we could hope to find it.'

'You flatter me. How about another Tom Collins?'

'One is quite enough, thanks all the same.'

Marella had never seen Maigret so circumspect. He spoke very quietly, as though what he was saying mattered very little, and yet somehow every word struck home.

'It was more than I could expect, that you should admit the real purpose of Le Grand Marcel's visit. I came simply to warn you. You certainly won't have learnt from him that the revolver in question is a vital clue in a murder case.

'The murder itself was unpremeditated. The old lady, who used to spend the greater part of every afternoon sitting on a bench in the Tuileries must, for some reason, have returned home earlier than usual. The intruder, man or woman . . .'

'Do you mean the niece?'

'The niece, yes. He or she snatched up a cushion from the couch, and held it over the old lady's face for as long as was necessary.

'I'm sure I need not labour the point, but you must realize that any international deal you may have in mind could have unhealthy repercussions affecting your legitimate business interests, your hotels and restaurants and so forth.'

Maigret fell silent. His expression was bland.

Giovanni was looking a little uneasy, and doing his best to conceal it.

'Thanks for the warning. I can assure you that if the fellow turns up here again, he won't get past the door.'

'He won't come back until you give him the word, and I know you won't do that.'

'Did you know about this, Marella?'

'Not until yesterday.'

'I trust you have put your colleague Maigret in the picture. Doesn't he know that I am now a highly-respected business man, and that I'm on the very best of terms with all those in authority, from the Prefect downwards?'

'I did tell him, yes.'

'Then it only remains for me to repeat that I am in no way involved in this sordid little affair.'

Maigret stood up with a sigh.

'Thanks for the Tom Collins.'

Marella also got to his feet, and the two men, accompanied by Giovanni, crossed the vast drawing room, and stood for a moment in the doorway at the top of the broad flight of marble steps that led down to the garden.

'You'll always be welcome here at any time, gentlemen.'

They got into Marella's car.

When they were outside the main gates, Maigret said:

'There must be some little pub or other in the neighbourhood, from which we can see the villa. If you know of one, stop there.'

They found a little bistro, painted blue, in Sanary itself. Outside there were four men playing bowls.

'What will you have?'

'A glass of rosé. That Tom Collins left a nasty taste in my mouth.'

'I couldn't make out what you were up to,' murmured Marella. 'You didn't press home your advantage. I almost got the impression that you wanted him to think you believed him.'

'Well, for one thing, he's not the man to give anything away.'

'That's true.'

'And anyway, what have I got to go on? Following a telephone call from Bob the Barman, he agreed to see our shady little friend. I haven't even got an accurate description of the revolver.'

'So there really is a revolver?'

'There most certainly is. That was what the intruders were looking for when they disturbed the old lady's ornaments.

'And even if you were able to spare every man you've got for the search, what hope would we have of finding it in that great barracks of a place? You don't imagine, do you, that Giovanni just slipped it into his bedside table drawer?

'Anyway, we shall soon see whether I'm right.'

And a quarter of an hour later, they did see. A man in a yachting cap appeared, boarded the little motor launch, and started up the engine.

A few seconds later, Giovanni followed him down the steps to the landing stage, and climbed aboard.

'Don't you see, it's too hot for him to handle. He can't wait to get rid of it. At any rate, the deal is off.'

The launch nosed out of the anchorage, and headed for the open sea in a swathe of spray.

'In a few minutes, the revolver will be heaven knows how many fathoms deep on the ocean bed. It will never be found.'

'I see.'

'At any rate, there's nothing more for me to do here in Toulon.'

'I hope you'll stay and dine with us. We've got a spare room now.'

'I'm going back on the night train.'

'Must you?'

'I'm afraid so. I've got a very busy day ahead of me tomorrow.'

'The niece?'

'Among others. Le Grand Marcel will still need watching, and if you take my advice, you'll keep an eye on that fellow Bob. It strikes me he has a good deal too much influence for a mere barman. Do you really believe Giovanni is as straight as he makes out?'

'I've been trying to catch him for years. Men of his sort, even when they have bought their passport to respectability, like to keep discreetly in touch with their old chums in the underworld. You've just seen for yourself.'

The white launch, having described a wide arc in the sea, was now returning to the anchorage.

'I daresay he's feeling mighty relieved, now that he's got rid of his precious prototype.'

'What do you plan to do between now and catching your train?'

'I'd like another word with Le Grand Marcel. Do you think I might find him at Maria's?'

'I very much doubt it. After what I told him about her boy friend, he'll be sure to keep well away from her. He may act tough but it's only an act. He's not the sort to stick his neck out.'

'What about l'Amiral?'

'He's sure to look in there sometime.'

It was five o'clock by the time they got to l'Amiral. The bar, once again, was deserted, and Bob was sitting at a table with Le Grand Marcel, who, on catching sight of the two police officers, burst out:

'What, again!'

'Yes, here we are again. Would you bring us a carafe of rosé, Bob?'

'How many times do I have to tell you that I didn't kill the old girl?'

'Be that as it may, you did go to her flat in the Quai de la Mégisserie.'

Maigret, looking very benign, had used the familiar *tu*.

'I'd like to see you prove it. I'd also be obliged if you'd tell me what I was supposed to be doing there.'

'Looking for the prototype.'

'I don't know what you're talking about.'

'I've just come from seeing someone else who said exactly the same thing, someone a lot tougher than you are. But, in spite of what he said, he knew well enough.'

'You've been to see Giovanni?'

Marcel had gone very white. Bob came up to the table with a carafe of wine and two glasses on a tray.

'What did he tell you?'

'A good prospect on the international market, did you say, and likely to be of particular interest to the Americans?'

'I still don't know what you're talking about.'

'No matter. Only I'm warning you that if you have it in mind to go back to the villa in Sanary in the hope of raking in a tidy sum, you'd better think again.'

Bob, resuming his seat at the table, asked:

'Have you seen Giovanni?'

'We've just come from there.'

'Did he tell you Marcel had been to see him?'

'And that you had rung to make the appointment.'

He savoured the local wine, sipping it with discernment. In two hours' time he would be in the train, on his way back to Paris.

Then he turned his attention once more to Marcel.

'If it really wasn't you who killed the old lady, you'd be well advised to tell me the whole truth, and come back with me to Paris.'

Nervously, the man clenched his long fingers.

'What have you to say about it, Bob?'

'It's no concern of mine. I'm ready to give a helping hand to a friend when I can, but that's as far as it goes. I know nothing about this business.'

'What should I go back to Paris for?' asked Marcel.

'To get yourself safely locked up in prison.'

'But I've already told you . . .'

'I know, I know. You didn't kill the old lady. It was her niece who did it. That won't prevent your being charged as an accessory.'

'And so you're advising me to leave Toulon, just so as you can arrest me?'

'I have a feeling you'd be safer there than here.'

A look of cunning spread over Marcel's features.

'Oh no, Chief Superintendent. I wasn't born yesterday. If you have a warrant for my arrest, show it to me and I'll come

123

quietly. But, as you very well know, you can't arrest me without proof, and all you've got is a couple of lousy witnesses, who claim to have seen someone wearing a check suit like mine.'

'It's up to you.'

'So that's my reward for keeping my nose clean for years!'

'It's a pity you couldn't keep it up.'

This time, it was Marella who paid for the drinks. Then, glancing at his watch, he said:

'You'll just have time to come and say hello to my wife, and see over our new house.'

It was a little way out of the town, on a hill. It was quite a small villa, but pleasant and colourful, with a very attractive outlook.

A boy of fifteen was mowing the lawn. The motor buzzed like a gigantic blue bottle.

'You know my son Alain.'

'He was a baby when I saw him last.'

'As you can see, the baby has grown somewhat.'

They went into the sitting room, which was really more of a spacious living room. Madame Marella emerged from the kitchen carrying a rolling pin.

'Oh sorry! I didn't realize we had a visitor.'

Maigret kissed her on both cheeks. Her name was Claudine, and he had never seen her without a smile.

'You'll stay for dinner, I hope. I'm just in the middle of making a strawberry tart.'

'He's got to catch the night train back to Paris.'

'Have you been here long, Maigret?'

'I arrived this morning.'

'Do you really have to go back so soon?'

'Thanks to your husband's invaluable help, I've done what I came to do.'

'What can I give you? You seem to like our local wines. I've got much better stuff in the cellar than anything they stock at l'Amiral.'

For nearly an hour they sat talking of this and that. Alain, the fifteen-year-old son, came in to shake the Chief Superintendent by the hand.

'Why aren't you at school?'

'It's Saturday. Had you forgotten?'

So it was. Maigret had forgotten.

In the confusion of the past week he had lost all track of time.

'What form are you in?'

'Classical Third.'

'Will you be following in your father's footsteps?'

'Oh no! Just think of the hours! And even when one's in bed, there's no guarantee one won't be called out again. Father never knows when the telephone may ring.'

Maigret felt sad. He had always longed for a son of his own, even a son who didn't want to be a policeman.

'I must be on my way. It wouldn't do to miss my train.'

'I'll drive you to the station.'

A few minutes later they were in the car, and Claudine was waving good-bye from the top of the steps.

The Boulevard Richard-Lenoir, as always on a Sunday morning, was almost deserted. The sound of a taxi door slamming was enough to bring Madame Maigret running to the window.

She was waiting for him on the landing.

'I thought you'd be spending the night in Toulon. Why didn't you ring and let me know you were coming?'

'I thought I'd give you a surprise.'

She was doing the housework, with her head tied up in a scarf.

'You didn't overtire yourself, I hope?'

'Not in the least. I had a very good night's sleep.'

'Shall I run you a bath?'

'Yes, that would be lovely.'

He had shaved on the train, as he always did when returning to Paris.

'Everything work out all right?'

'More or less. Incidentally, Marella and Claudine sent you their kindest regards. They've built themselves a very pretty little house on the outskirts of the town.'

'Claudine was as cheerful as ever, I suppose?'

'She hasn't changed. The only one who has is their son. He's a hulking great lad now, with a very deep voice.'

'Are you free for the rest of the day?'

'Almost, though I shall have to go out for a little while later.'

While his bath was running, he rang Police Headquarters. Once again it was dear old Lucas who was on duty.

'Anything been happening while I've been away?'

'Nothing special, chief.'

'Who have you got there with you?'

'Neveu, Janin, Loutrie. . . .'

'Hold it! I don't need all that many. Tell them I want a twenty-four hour watch kept on the flat of the masseuse Angèle Louette in the Rue Saint-André-des-Arts. They can arrange a rota to suit themselves. There's no need for them to keep out of sight. Oh, and one other thing. Warn them that she's got a car.'

He lay soaking for a long time in the soapy water, while his wife made fresh coffee for him. At about half-past nine, he went down into the street, hailed a taxi, and asked the driver to take him to the corner of the Rue Saint-André-des-Arts. Janin was on duty at the door. The Chief Superintendent shook him by the hand.

'I'm going up to see her now, and it's possible that what I have to say to her may send her running for cover.'

'Don't worry. I'll keep my eyes skinned. Neveu and I have got it all worked out. Neither of us particularly wanted to do a long stint, so we're taking turn and turn about every three hours, and tomorrow night Loutrie will give us a hand.'

Maigret went upstairs and rang the bell. The door was opened almost at once.

Angèle Louette, still wearing her black suit, was just putting on a hat.

'You again!' she muttered sullenly. 'Can't you leave me alone even for one day?'

'Are you going out?'

'What do you think? I'm not in the habit of doing my house-work with a hat on.'

'I've just got back from Toulon.'

'What's that got to do with me?'

'A great deal, I assure you. Your boy friend drove there in his car. I saw him there.'

'It's all over between us.'

'Oh no, it's not! He was the one who undertook to negotiate with Giovanni, remember?'

Involuntarily, she gave a start.

'I may as well tell you right away that he didn't pull it off. Your aunt died for nothing. Would you like to know where the revolver is now? It's at the bottom of the Mediterranean, buried heaven knows how many hundreds of fathoms deep. Didn't Marcel ring and tell you?'

'If he'd rung to tell me you were coming, I'd have made it my business not to be at home.'

'Where are you going now?'

'To Mass, if you must know. And if that surprises you, it's just too bad.'

'Kindly listen to me. You are required to attend for interrogation in my office at nine o'clock tomorrow morning. This is an official summons, so please don't be late. I advise you to bring a suitcase with such personal effects as you think you may need, including a change of underwear. In other words, we may be obliged to detain you for a time.'

'You mean I'm to be arrested?'

'It's a possibility you have to face, although the decision rests not with me but with the examining magistrate. Just one more thing, and then you can go. An hour ago, I gave instructions that you were to be kept under supervision for twenty-four hours a day, and this will continue until you arrive at my office tomorrow morning.'

'I hate you!'

'That doesn't surprise me.'

All the way down the stairs, Maigret could hear her pacing up and down the living room, swearing like a trooper.

'Do you know what she looks like?' he asked Janin.

'No.'

'She'll be down in a moment. I'll point her out to you.'

Some ten minutes later, she appeared. As she came out and caught sight of the two men standing on the pavement opposite, she gave a violent start.

'You oughtn't to have any difficulty in keeping her in sight. If she ever took up boxing, she'd be in the heavyweight class.'

He walked home, enjoying the sunshine in the quiet of a Sunday morning. How would they spend the afternoon? he wondered. Sometimes they went out in the car, with Madame Maigret at the wheel, but on the whole she preferred not to drive on a Sunday, especially on the busy roads out of Paris.

Not that it mattered what they did. Even if they only strolled side by side through the streets, they were never bored.

'Your friend Marella telephoned. You just missed him by five minutes. He wants you to ring him back at his house as soon as possible. He says he gave you his number.'

She looked inquiringly at her husband.

'You don't seem surprised that he should be ringing you on a Sunday morning, when you only saw him last night.'

'I was half expecting it.'

He put through a call to Toulon. Within a few minutes, Marella was on the line.

'Did you have a good journey?'

'Thanks to your local wine, I slept like a baby.'

'I daresay you can guess what I rang you about.'

'What's happened to him?'

'At seven o'clock this morning, he was fished out of the harbour.'

'Knifed?'

'No. A .38 bullet right between the eyes.'

A silence followed, both men thinking their own thoughts.

'You did your best by advising him to go with you to Paris. But he was too clever by half. He thought you were lying, and that there was still something in it for him.'

'No hope of pinning it on Giovanni, I suppose?'

'You can bet your life he's covered his tracks. Probably the killer didn't even know who he was working for. No doubt he got his instructions from some intermediary, whom Giovanni knew he could trust.'

'Any ideas?'

'Too many. There are at least twenty men in this area who could have done it. Very likely, he got someone from Nice or Cannes or Marseilles. And I bet you anything you like he isn't in Toulon now. He wouldn't be likely to hang around waiting to be recognized.'

Marella paused, apparently lost in thought.

'Mind you, we'll catch up with him eventually, but it will probably be in four or five years' time, and for something quite different.'

'You don't need to tell me. We have the same problems here. Thanks for letting me know, anyway. Were you there when they emptied his pockets?'

'Yes. Nothing of much interest. Two thousand francs in his wallet, along with his identity card and driving licence. His road-fund licence was in the glove compartment of his car, which was left all night outside the Hôtel des Cinq Continents.

'And there was also some small change and a key.'

'I'd be grateful if you'd let me have the key.'

'I'll post it to you as soon as I can. I'll take it to the railway station myself. Apart from the items I mentioned, there was also a handkerchief, some cigarettes and a packet of chewing gum.'

'Have you been through his suitcase?'

'A black and white check suit. Some underwear. No papers. Nothing else, in fact, but a cheap paperback novel with a lurid cover.'

'Not even a notebook with telephone numbers?'

'No. But someone may have got to it before me. According to the Police Surgeon, he died somewhere around one in the morning. That's only a provisional estimate, of course. We won't know for sure until later today, after the autopsy.'

'I hope Claudine won't hold it against me?'

'Hold what against you?'

'Well, it's because of me that your Sunday morning has been ruined.'

'She's in the kitchen. Hold on! She's saying something. She wants to be remembered to you both. As far as I'm concerned, this is now no more than a routine inquiry, which I shall leave in the hands of my deputy.'

'Have you seen Bob again?'

'No. I hope he won't go the same way. I'd be sorry because he's always played straight with me.'

'Surely he's too valuable to Giovanni?'

'So you've been thinking along the same lines as I have! There has to be a linkman between Giovanni and his chums in the underworld.'

'And who better than Bob, wouldn't you say?'

'Good day to you!'

'The same to you! And many thanks for all your help.'

Maigret replaced the receiver.

'Bad news?' asked Madame Maigret, noting his worried expression.

'From the professional angle, I suppose I should call it very good news. A petty crook has been murdered in Toulon, thus saving the state an expensive trial. He's been known to us for a long time as a pimp, and of late he's been living on a woman of fifty-five. If he wasn't a murderer himself, he was certainly an accomplice.'

'Are you talking about the old lady?'

The old lady in the white hat and gloves, yes. He could still see her, suddenly stepping into his path on the pavement of the Quai des Orfèvres, and looking up at him, her eyes glowing with admiration and hope.

She was dead. And now Le Grand Marcel was dead too, and the object for which the couple had searched so long, the precious revolver, which had been in the bedside table drawer all the time, was lost and gone for ever.

'What are we having for lunch?'

'*Blanquette* of veal.'

They sat around until half-past twelve. Maigret even went so far as to turn on the radio for the news, though, as he had expected, there was no reference to the murder in Toulon.

'Don't think about her. It's such a lovely day.'

'Too lovely to stay shut up indoors, don't you think?'

'Have you anything particular in mind?'

'We can talk about that as we go.'

As always, she took his arm, and they walked towards the Quais. On the Quai de la Mégisserie they went past the bird shop, which today had the shutters up, and stopped for a moment outside the building where the old lady had lived.

'What floor?'

'First.'

'That's going to make someone very happy.'

'What do you mean?'

'The people who take her flat. They'll have one of the finest views in Paris.'

They walked on, and before very long they were in the Tuileries Gardens.

'Let's sit down for a few minutes,' he suggested.

And thus he fulfilled a wish that had been growing on him ever since the previous night. As far as he could remember, this was the first time he had ever sat on a bench in a public park.

He had always thought of park benches as serving no useful purpose, unless it were to provide resting places for tramps and lovers.

It took them some time to find an unoccupied bench. All the others were taken, and not only by elderly people. There were a great many young mothers watching their children at play. A man in his thirties was reading a book on biology.

'It's very pleasant here, isn't it?'

Little toy boats with white sails skimmed over the glassy surface of the pond.

'You'll get wet if you don't watch out, Hubert! If you lean over any further, you'll fall in!'

How restful it was. Seen from here, life seemed very simple and uneventful.

The old lady came here every day of her life, weather permitting. Perhaps, like that other old lady whom they could see over there, she scattered breadcrumbs for the birds, which flocked round her in ever growing numbers.

'Was it because of her that you brought me here?'

He admitted that it was.

131

'Besides, I wanted for once in my life to see what it felt like to sit on a park bench.'

With some warmth, he added, 'Especially with you.'

'You haven't got a very good memory!'

'Have we ever sat on a public bench together, then?'

'When we were engaged. It was in the gardens of the Place des Vosges. That was when you kissed me for the first time, as a matter of fact.'

'You're absolutely right. My memory must be going. I wouldn't mind kissing you now, but there are really too many people about.'

'We're a bit old for that sort of thing, don't you think?'

They decided not to go home for dinner. They went to a restaurant in the Place des Victoires. They liked the food and the atmosphere, and enjoyed going there from time to time.

'Shall we dine on the terrace?'

'I wouldn't advise it,' interposed the head waiter. 'The nights are still quite cold. It's really too early in the year to dine out of doors.'

They had sweetbreads, which were delicious, followed by tiny lamb cutlets and, to end with, strawberry shortcake.

'It's such a rare treat,' murmured Madame Maigret.

'What is?'

'Having you to myself for practically the whole day. I bet you anything you like that tomorrow I shall get a message to say you won't be in for lunch.'

'Very likely. Almost certainly, in fact. Tomorrow, I shall be having a battle of wits with the "Sergeant-Major".'

'Is that what you call that poor woman?'

'That poor woman, as you call her, in all probability murdered her aunt.'

'It wasn't premeditated, was it?'

'No.'

'I suppose, being discovered like that, she completely lost her head?'

'Are you trying to defend her?'

'No, but I can't help thinking about her. Didn't you say she was ugly?'

'A woman entirely devoid of charm, at any rate.'

'And presumably devoid of charm even as a young girl?'

'Almost certainly, I should think.'

'So, as no man would give her a second look, she had to go about things in a rather different way.'

'You would have made a good advocate.'

'Fifty-five! You did say she was fifty-five, didn't you? I daresay she thought she'd never get another after Marcel, so she clung on to him with all her might.'

'She's still clinging. She doesn't know yet what's happened to him.'

'Don't you think she'll try and make a run for it?'

'I'm having her watched twenty-four hours a day.'

'I shouldn't care to be in her place tomorrow morning.'

'I'm not exactly looking forward to it myself.'

But it was his job. And Angèle Louette was not the sort to inspire much compassion.

Madame Maigret had no difficulty in following her husband's train of thought, when he murmured:

'It's a fact that Marella's son has absolutely set his face against joining the force.'

If he himself had had a son, what advice would he have given him?

Arm in arm, they walked back to the Boulevard Richard-Lenoir, and for a long time neither spoke a word.

CHAPTER SEVEN

WHEN, ON THE DOT OF NINE, old Joseph ushered her in, Maigret found himself looking at her in rather a different light. He felt, in her presence, a degree of embarrassment that he had not felt hitherto. Perhaps it was because of what his wife had said the night before.

He even went so far as to get up to greet her, and as he did so it struck him that she looked a little pathetic, with her small overnight bag in her hand.

She was pale, but when had he ever seen her with colour in her cheeks? She was ugly. Would he have been equally hard on her if she had been an attractive woman?

'Put your case down over there, and take a seat.'

They were all set to begin. Lapointe, sitting at one end of the desk, was ready and waiting to take a shorthand note of the interview.

'It's just on nine, isn't it? I've already had to miss my eight o'clock appointment, and I had another at nine. You realize, don't you, that you're taking the bread out of my mouth?'

He had already had the reports of his inspectors on her movements the previous day. After returning from Mass, she had stayed in for the rest of the day. There had been lights burning in her flat until far into the night.

No one had been to see her. She had spent the long hours of waiting alone.

Was that why she was looking so very grave, why all the fight seemed to have gone out of her?

He picked up the telephone.

'Would you see if Judge Libart is in yet?'

He heard the telephone ringing in an empty room.

'Not yet, Chief Superintendent, and his clerk isn't there either.'

'Thank you.'

He lit his pipe, and said to Angèle Louette:

'Do smoke if you want to.'

'You're very kind. Acceding to the last wish of the condemned woman.'

'The time has come, Mademoiselle, for us to get down to brass tacks. I may have to repeat some of the questions I have already asked you, but I sincerely hope this will be the last time.'

A mood of greyness and sullenness seemed to overhang this confrontation. It was reflected even in the weather. For the past two weeks, the sun had shone unremittingly, but now the sky was overcast, and a fine drizzle was spattering the streets of Paris.

'I take it you don't deny that your aunt was murdered?'

'The medical evidence seems conclusive.'

'Had she, as far as you know, any enemies?'

'No.'

She was calm, in a dull and heavy way, like the weather. Her expression was blank. She was looking composedly at the Chief Superintendent. Whatever her feelings, if any, she was concealing them admirably.

It was as though all those long hours of solitude on Sunday had drained the spirit out of her.

'Any friends?'

'I don't know of any friends either.'

'Were you the only person to visit her at the Quai de la Mégisserie?'

'As far as I know.'

'Used you to call by appointment?'

'My aunt hadn't a telephone. I tried to persuade her to have one installed, but she wouldn't hear of it.'

'Why did you go and see her?'

'Because I was her only relative.'

She was wearing the same black suit, as if to convey the impression that she was in mourning.

'You knew, I presume, when you were likely to find her at home?'

'Yes.'

'In other words, you were familiar with her routine.'

'She was a creature of habit.'

'Every morning she went out to do her shopping locally. Isn't that so?'

'That's right.'

'And after lunch, if I'm not mistaken, she took a nap in her armchair?'

She nodded.

'Later, weather permitting, she walked to the Tuileries Gardens, and stayed an hour or two sitting on a bench.'

'Surely we've been through all this before?'

'I have my reasons for going through it again. You were not fond of your aunt, were you?'

'No.'

'You never forgave her, did you, for palming you off with a hundred-franc note when you went to her for help because you were pregnant?'

'It's not the sort of thing one can easily forget.'

'Still, you went on going to see her. How many times a year, would you say?'

'I don't remember.'

'How many times in a month?'

'Once, sometimes twice.'

'Always at the same time of day?'

'Nearly always. I finish work at six. And she usually got in round about that time in the summer.'

'Used she to offer you a chair?'

'I didn't wait to be asked. After all, she was my aunt.'

'You were her sole heir?'

'Yes.'

'Did you often think about it?'

'I realized it would make things easier for me in my old age. It's harder work being a masseuse than most people realize. It takes a good deal of physical strength. In a few years' time I'll be too old for it.'

'In the meantime, did you ever ask her for money?'

'Occasionally. In my kind of work, there are bound to be slack periods. In the holiday season, for instance, when all my clients are away from Paris, some of them for two or three months.'

'Did you ever quarrel with your aunt?'

'Never.'

'Did you never reproach her for her meanness?'

'No.'

'Did she know how you felt about her?'

'I suppose so, yes.'

'Were you aware that she never kept much money in the flat?'

'I knew that, yes.'

'Who took the wax impression of the lock?'

'I didn't, at any rate.'

'Was it your lover?'

'If so, he never told me.'

'But he did show you the key he'd had cut?'

'I never saw any key.'

'Now you're lying again. Not only did you have a key to the flat, you also had a key to your Uncle Antoine's little cubby hole on the other side of the landing.'

She was sulkily silent, like a scolded child.

'I have some bad news for you, I'm afraid. When you've heard it, you may feel inclined to alter your statement. I was in Toulon the day before yesterday.'

She started violently. So she did not know, as he had suspected, that Le Grand Marcel had gone to Toulon.

'First of all, you may as well admit that there was no quarrel between you, and that you did not, as you claim to have done, turn him out of doors.'

'Think what you like. I can't stop you.'

'All your indignation at his habit of spending half the day in bed was an act, put on for my benefit.'

No reaction.

'I saw him in Toulon. You, needless to say, knew perfectly well what he had gone there for.'

'No.'

'You're lying again. A few miles out of Toulon, there is a villa belonging to a man by the name of Pepito Giovanni.

137

He's a retired gangster. He's been going straight, more or less, for years, and is now the head of a substantial, and quite legitimate, business empire. Marcel, I imagine, must have worked for him at some time or other, though he can never have been more than a very small cog in a large machine.

'Marcel was never anything more than a petty crook. The most he ever had was a walk-on part.'

For an instant, the woman's eyes blazed with fury, but she did not speak.

'Do you go along with me so far?'

'I have nothing to say.'

'Excuse me a moment.'

He picked up the receiver again and, this time, was put through to the examining magistrate.

'Maigret speaking. May I come up and see you for a moment?'

'With pleasure, only make it as soon as you can. I have a witness to see in ten minutes' time.'

Leaving Lapointe in charge of his visitor, he let himself through the communicating door to the Palais de Justice.

'How is it going?'

'I don't want to sound over-optimistic, but I hope today will see the end of it. I went to Toulon on Saturday, as a result of which there have been several developments, but I won't bother you with them now.

'What I need at this moment is a warrant for the arrest of Angèle Louette.'

'Isn't that the niece?'

'Yes.'

'Do you really believe she killed the old lady?'

'I don't know yet, but I will very soon, I hope. Which is why I'm not sure whether or not I shall need to make use of the warrant.'

'You heard what the Chief Superintendent said, Gérard? Make out the warrant, will you?'

When Maigret got back to his office, he found the two occupants stiff and silent, like a couple of wax effigies.

He handed the warrant to Angèle.

'I take it you know what this means, and that you now understand why I asked you to bring a few personal things and a change of underwear with you?'

She neither stirred nor spoke.

'First, let's talk about Marcel. I found him in a bar in Toulon, the Bar de l'Amiral. It was an old haunt of his when he lived in the South. The barman, Bob, was a close friend of his. Did he ever speak of him?'

Dryly, she answered, 'No.'

But she was now very much on the alert, and waiting apprehensively for what was to follow.

'A man of Giovanni's standing wouldn't normally have any dealings with small fry like Marcel. An intermediary was required, and that was where Bob came in. I don't know what he said to Giovanni exactly, but it was to the effect that Marcel had something to sell, something very big. It had to be, since the former boss of the underworld agreed to see him the next morning. Do you follow me?'

'Yes.'

'You do understand that I'm talking about the revolver?'

'As I've said time and again, I've never seen the revolver to which you refer.'

'And each time you were lying. Giovanni was interested, so much so that he kept the prototype. I went to see him shortly afterwards, and we had a most interesting talk. Among other things, I told him where the revolver came from, and also how deeply Marcel was implicated in the murder of your aunt.

'Now if there's one person more touchy than another about getting mixed up in anything dirty, it's an underworld boss who has made a fortune and virtually retired from criminal activity.

'Giovanni had learnt from me that, as long as he was in possession of the gun, he was in grave danger, and I was scarcely through the gates of his house, when he boarded his motor launch and roared out to sea.

'And as a result, your uncle's precious revolver is now lying many fathoms deep on the ocean bed.'

Maigret tapped the ashes out of his pipe and filled another.

'But that's not all that happened in Toulon. There were further developments after I left. A colleague of mine there rang me soon after I left you yesterday. But before I go into that, are you prepared to repeat your statement that everything was over between you and Marcel, and that you told him, once and for all, that you never wanted to see him again?'

'I'm waiting to hear the rest of your story.'

'Marcel himself had become something of a menace. As they say in the profession, dead men tell no tales.'

'Is he dead?'

She looked absolutely stricken. Even her voice was scarcely recognizable.

'It's no longer any concern of yours, is it?'

'What happened exactly?'

'He was shot between the eyes in the middle of the night. With a .38 calibre gun, which no one but a professional would use. The body was found yesterday morning, floating in the old dock.'

'Is this a trap?'

'No.'

'Will you swear by everything you hold sacred?'

'I swear.'

And then the tears began to roll down her cheeks. She opened her handbag to get out a handkerchief.

CHAPTER EIGHT

HE CROSSED OVER to the window, to give her time to recover. The light spring rain was still falling, and glistening umbrellas were to be seen all along the Quai.

He heard her blow her nose and, when he returned to his seat, she was dabbing a little rouge on to her cheeks.

'So you see, although your aunt paid with her life, it all came to nothing.'

She was still snuffling as she got a cigarette from her bag and lit it with a trembling hand.

'All that remains for me to discover is whether it was you or Marcel who smothered the old lady.'

Contrary to his expectations, she did not seize the opportunity of putting all the blame on her lover, who was no longer there to defend himself.

'As far as he is concerned, naturally, the case is closed. But that doesn't apply to you.'

'Why do you hate me so?'

'I don't hate you. I'm only doing my job, as humanely as possible, I hope, in the circumstances. You have persistently lied to me, right from the very first. That being so, how else could you expect me to react?'

'You know perfectly well that I loved him.'

'I'll go further than that, I believe you still love him, even now he's dead.'

'You're right, I do.'

'Why pretend you'd quarrelled and parted for ever?'

'That was his idea, to put you off the scent.'

'Did you know why he'd gone to Toulon?'

For the first time she looked him straight in the face, without attempting to lie or evade the question.

'Yes.'

'How long have you known of the existence of the revolver?'

'Thirteen or fourteen years. I got on very well with my Uncle Antoine. He was a thoroughly good sort, but rather a lonely man in a way. I don't think my aunt could give him the companionship he'd hoped for. So he spent most of his time shut up in his little cubby hole.'

'And you kept him company?'

'Quite often. He had this overriding passion for gadgets. Scarcely a year went by without his submitting an invention for the Lépine Prize.'

'Is that how you knew about the revolver?'

'I watched him at work on it for the best part of two years.

'"There's just one problem I don't seem to be able to overcome," he told me in confidence. "If I ever do manage it, it will go off with quite a bang."

'And then he burst out laughing.

'"I don't mean that literally. Quite the reverse, in fact. Do you know what a silencer is?"

'"I've seen them on television and in films. It's a thing you fit on to the end of a gun, to prevent it from making a noise when it's fired."

'"That's it, more or less. Of course you can't just go into a shop and buy one. It's against the law. But suppose you could do away with the silencer as a separate piece of equipment, by incorporating it into the design of the gun itself?"

'He sounded tremendously excited.

'"I'm very nearly there. There are just one or two small adjustments to be made. Then I'll register the patent, and in a few years all firearms, including those of the armed forces and the police, will be silent."'

She sat musing for a little while, and then said:

'A few days after that, he died. I know nothing about firearms, and I forgot all about his precious revolver.'

'When did you mention it to Marcel?'

'About a month ago. No, less than that, three weeks ago. We were walking on the Pont-Neuf, and I pointed out my aunt's flat in the Quai de la Mégisserie. I mentioned that I would be inheriting some money from her one of these days.'

'What made you say that?'

She flushed and looked away.

'I didn't want to lose him.'

She cherished no illusions.

'A few minutes later, we stopped for a drink at an open air café, when I suddenly remembered about the revolver. I told him the story, and to my amazement he seemed terrifically excited about it.

'"Did you ever see the gun after your uncle died?"

'"No. I've never even been in his workshop since."

'"Did your aunt know about it?"

'"He may have mentioned it to her, but I doubt if she'll have given it a second thought, any more than I did. I'll ask her."

'"No, don't do that. Don't even mention it."

'This may surprise you, but we never used the familiar *tu* with one another. Except on very rare occasions,' she added, clearly embarrassed.

'"Have you a key to the flat?"

'"No."

'"And this room you call the cubby hole, does it have a separate key?"

'"Yes, but I don't know where my aunt keeps it. In her bag, I should think."

'It was several days before he mentioned the matter again. One evening, when I got home, he was standing there with two keys in his hand.

'"What are you going to do?"

'"Find the revolver."

'"What for?"

'"Don't you realize, it's worth a fortune. I want you to go to your aunt's sometime when you know she's out, and search every room in the flat, and the workshop."

'"What's the point? It will all come to me eventually in any case."

'"Women of that sort have a very strong grip on life. You may have to spend another ten years massaging women, all over Paris, before you see a penny."'

She looked at Maigret, and sighed.

'Now do you understand? At first, I refused to have anything to do with it, but he just wouldn't let it drop, and I was afraid of losing him. In the end, I agreed. One afternoon, I took the keys and went to the Quai de la Mégisserie. I saw my aunt set off for the Tuileries, and I knew she wouldn't be back before six.

'First, I searched the flat. I went through every drawer, and looked in every possible place where I thought it might be hidden. And then I put everything carefully back as it was before.'

'Not quite carefully enough, though. She knew someone had been there.'

'Two days later, I searched the workroom. In all, I went to the Quai de la Mégisserie four times.'

'And Marcel?'

'Just the once.'

'When was that?'

Once more, she turned her head away.

'On the afternoon of my aunt's death.'

'What did he say when he got back to your flat?'

'I wasn't there. I had an appointment with a client at half-past five. She kept me waiting. The client is someone I've been giving massage to for the best part of twenty years. She's Madame de la Roche, of 61 Boulevard Saint-Germain.'

'What time did you get home?'

'At seven. As usual, she kept me gossiping.'

'Why didn't you tell me you had an alibi?'

'That would have been as good as to accuse Marcel.'

'And you preferred to let me go on suspecting you?'

'As long as you didn't know which of us it was . . .'

'So the gun was hidden, for a time, on top of your wardrobe?'

'Yes.'

'And it was your lover who found it in the bedside table drawer?'

'Yes. It's the last place I'd have thought of looking for it. My aunt was scared stiff of firearms.'

'Have you got all that, Lapointe? Just ring and check with

Madame de la Roche, of the Boulevard Saint-Germain, and then you can start typing.'

Left alone with her in his office, Maigret felt oppressed. He got up and went over to the window.

'As far as Marcel is concerned,' he mumbled, 'the case is closed. You can't prosecute a dead man. You, on the other hand, are very much alive. It's true that you had no hand in the death of the old lady, assuming your alibi is confirmed.'

She was no longer the same woman, sitting there at his desk facing his empty chair. All the stiffening had gone out of her. Her face was crumpled in misery, her shoulders drooping.

Five long minutes of silence passed before Lapointe came back into the room.

'The lady confirms her story,' was all he said.

'Thanks.'

'Do you realize the position you're in at this moment?'

'You showed me the warrant, I realize what it means.'

'When I had the warrant drawn up, I didn't know whether it was you or Marcel who had smothered your aunt.'

'Well, you know now.'

'You were not present at the time. It was an unpremeditated crime, so you couldn't possibly have foreseen that it was going to happen. In other words, you are not implicated in the murder itself. Where you did wrong was in shielding your lover, and in concealing on your premises a stolen firearm.'

She looked at him blankly. It was as though she had lost all interest in life. She seemed to be miles away, in Toulon perhaps with Marcel?

Maigret went across and opened the door of the Inspectors' Duty Room. Fat Torrence happened to be the one nearest to him.

'Come into my office a minute, will you? Stay here till I get back, and don't let the lady go.'

'Right, Chief.'

Once more he climbed the stairs to the Examining Magistrates' floor. Judge Libart was interviewing a witness, but he sent him out for a few minutes, so that Maigret could have a word with him in private.

'Did she do it?'

'No. She's got an alibi as solid as a rock.'

Maigret told him the whole story as briefly as possible. All the same, it took him quite some time.

'There doesn't seem much point in going after Giovanni,' he murmured, in conclusion.

'It wouldn't do any good.'

'If you consider the matter carefully, she's no more guilty than he is.'

'You mean . . . ?'

The judge scratched his head.

'That is what you have in mind, isn't it? To let her go scot-free?'

It would never do to admit that it was Madame Maigret who, indirectly at least, had put the idea into his head.

'First of all, we've got to prove that she was a party to the theft. And that won't be easy, especially now that the revolver has disappeared.'

'I see your point.'

It was another quarter of an hour before Maigret got back to his office, because, in the meantime, the Examining Magistrate had carted him off to see the Public Prosecutor.

The Chief Superintendent could not help being a little shocked at finding Torrence seated behind his desk in his own personal armchair.

'She hasn't moved a muscle, Chief.'

'Did she say anything?'

'She never opened her mouth. Can I go now?'

Angèle looked at Maigret without interest. She seemed to be resigned to her fate.

'How old are you exactly?'

'Fifty-six. I don't proclaim it to all and sundry, mind you, because some of my clients might begin to think I was past it.'

'Which of the two flats do you intend to live in, yours or your aunt's?'

She stared at him in amazement.

'Have I any choice in the matter?'

Deliberately, he picked up the warrant, and tore it across.

146

'You're free to go,' he said simply.

She did not get to her feet immediately. For a moment, it seemed as though she had not the strength. Tears rolled down her cheeks, but she made no attempt to wipe them away.

'I don't . . . I have no words . . .'

'There's nothing more to be said. I'd be obliged if you'd call back some time this afternoon to sign your statement.'

She got up, hesitated for a moment, then went slowly towards the door.

He called after her:

'Your suitcase!'

'Yes, of course. I'd forgotten all about it.'

But there was so much that she would never forget.

Epalinges, May 7th, 1970

MAIGRET
AND THE KILLER

*

*Translated from
the French by*
LYN MOIR

CHAPTER ONE

FOR THE FIRST TIME since they had started dining once a month at the Pardons', Maigret would take away an unpleasant memory of the evening in the Boulevard Voltaire.

It had begun in the Boulevard Richard-Lenoir. His wife had phoned for a taxi because it had been raining for three days, harder, according to the radio, than it had rained for thirty-five years. The rain was bucketing down, icy cold, slapping one's face and hands, plastering the wet clothes to one's body.

On stairs, in lifts and offices, feet left muddy marks and people were in a filthy mood.

They had gone downstairs and had waited almost half an hour at the door of the building, getting more and more chilled, for the taxi to arrive. Even then he had to argue to get the driver to take such a short fare.

'Do forgive us. We're late.'

'Everyone is late on days like this. I hope you won't mind sitting down to dinner straight away.'

The flat was warm, friendly, and felt even cosier with the wind banging the shutters. Madame Pardon had made a *boeuf bourgignon* in the way that only she could, and this dish, delicate and satisfying at the same time, had taken up most of the conversation.

Then they had talked about provincial cooking, cassoulet, *potée lorraine*, *tripes à la mode de Caen*, bouillabaisse . . .

'After all, most of these recipes grew out of necessity—if we had had refrigerators right from the Middle Ages . . .'

What else had they talked about? The two women, as usual, had ended up by installing themselves in a corner of the room, where they talked in low tones. Pardon had taken Maigret into his surgery to show him a rare book which had been presented to him by one of his patients. They had sat down without thinking and Madame Pardon had taken their coffee and calvados in to them.

Pardon was tired. For quite some time his features had been drawn and sometimes there was an expression of something like resignation in his eyes. He still worked a fifteen-hour day, at least, never complaining or moaning, spending the mornings in his surgery, part of the afternoons dragging his heavy bag from street to street, then back home again to a waiting room which was always full.

'If I had a son and he told me he wanted to be a doctor, I think I'd try to dissuade him.'

Maigret almost turned his face away out of sheer embarrassment. It was the most unexpected thing to hear from Pardon's lips, for he was in love with his profession and one couldn't imagine him doing anything else.

This time he was discouraged, pessimistic and, what was more, he went so far as to put his pessimism into words.

'They're trying to turn us into clerks and turn medicine into a vast computer giving out more or less adequate cures.'

Maigret, lighting his pipe, watched him.

'Not only into clerks,' went on the doctor, 'but bad clerks, for we can't give the necessary time to every patient. Sometimes I'm almost ashamed as I see them to the door, almost shoving them out. I see the look in their eyes—worried, imploring even. I know that they expect something else of me, questions, words, in fact time that I can devote to their case alone. . . .'

He lifted his glass.

'Your good health.'

He forced a smile, a mechanical smile which did not suit him.

'Do you know how many patients I've seen today? Eighty-two. And that's nothing out of the ordinary. After which I am obliged to fill up various forms. That takes up my evenings. I'm sorry to bore you with this. You must have your own problems at the Quai des Orfèvres.'

What had they talked about after that? Nothing memorable. Pardon sat at his desk, smoking a cigarette, Maigret in the upright chair used by the patients. A particular smell pervaded the room, one which the superintendent knew well, for he smelt it on each of his visits. A smell which somehow brought to mind that of a police station. The smell of poverty.

Pardon's patients were local people, almost all of low income.

The door opened. Eugénie, the maid, who had worked so long in the household in the Boulevard Voltaire that she was almost part of the family, announced:

'It's the Italian, doctor.'

'Which Italian? Pagliati?'

'Yes, doctor. He's in a terrible state. He says it's very urgent.'

It was half past ten. Pardon got up, opened the door into the dismal waiting room with magazines scattered over a table.

'What's wrong, Gino?'

'It's not me, doctor. Nor my wife. There's a man lying wounded on the pavement, he must be dying.'

'Where?'

'In the Rue Popincourt, a hundred yards away.'

'Were you the first to find him?'

Pardon was already in the hall, putting on his black overcoat, looking for his bag, and Maigret instinctively put his coat on too. The doctor opened the dining-room door.

'We'll be right back. There's a wounded man in the Rue Popincourt.'

'Take your umbrella.'

He didn't take it. He would have felt ridiculous holding an umbrella and leaning over a man dying in the middle of the street with the rain pattering all around.

Gino was a Neapolitan. He had a small grocery store at the corner of the Rue du Chemin-Vert and the Rue Popincourt. Or, more exactly, it was his wife, Lucia, who kept the shop while he made fresh noodles, ravioli, tortellini. The couple were well-liked in the district. Pardon had treated Gino for high blood-pressure.

The noodle-maker was a short man, stockily-built, heavy, with a ruddy complexion.

'We were coming back from my brother-in-law's in the Rue de Charonne. My sister-in-law's going to have a baby and he's expecting to take her to the maternity hospital at any moment. . . . We were walking home in the rain when I saw . . .'

Half of his words were lost in the storm. The gutters had become rushing rivers which had to be jumped over, and the few passing cars threw up sprays of dirty water for several yards.

The sight which greeted them in the Rue Popincourt was unexpected. There wasn't anyone walking, from one end of the street to the other, and only a few windows, apart from those of a little café, were still lit.

About fifty yards from the café a stoutish woman was standing motionless under an umbrella shaken by the wind. A street lamp showed up the shape of a body lying at her feet.

That brought back old memories to Maigret. Long before he was head of the Criminal Division, while he was only a detective, he often happened to be the first at the scene of a brawl, of a settling-up, of an armed attack.

The man was young. He looked hardly twenty, wore a suede jacket and had fairly long hair. He had fallen on his face and the back of his jacket was caked with blood.

'Have you informed the police?'

Pardon, bent close over the wounded man, interrupted:

'Get them to send an ambulance.'

That meant that the unknown man was alive and Maigret went towards the light which he saw fifty yards away. On the faintly-lit shop front were the words 'Chez Jules'. He pushed open the glass door which had a cream-coloured curtain stretched over it and went in to an atmosphere so calm that it seemed unreal. It might have been a *genre* painting.

It was an old-fashioned bar, with sawdust on the floor and a strong smell of wine and spirits. Four oldish men, three of them fat and red-faced, were playing cards.

'May I use the telephone?'

In amazement they watched him go over to the wall telephone which was near the zinc counter and the rows of bottles.

'Hello. Is that the 11th *Arrondissement* police station?'

It was a stone's throw away, in the Place Léon-Blum, which used to be called the Place Voltaire.

'Hello. This is Maigret. There's a man lying wounded in the Rue Popincourt. Near the Rue du Chemin-Vert. Send an ambulance.'

The four men came to life as if they were actors on a stage. They kept their cards in their hands.

'What's that?' asked the one in shirt-sleeves, who must have been the proprietor. 'Who's wounded?'

'A young man.'

Maigret put the money on the counter and went towards the door.

'A tall thin chap in a suede jacket?'

'Yes.'

'He was in here a quarter of an hour ago.'

'Alone?'

'Yes.'

'Did he seem nervous?'

The proprietor, obviously Jules, gave the others a questioning look.

'No, not especially.'

'Did he stay long?'

'About twenty minutes.'

When Maigret went out again he saw two policemen with bicycles, the rain pouring down their capes, standing beside the wounded man.

Pardon had stood up again.

'There's nothing I can do. He has been stabbed several times. The heart has not been touched. No artery has been cut either, as far as I can see, or there would have been more blood.'

'Will he regain consciousness?'

'I don't know. I don't dare move him. We can only see once we get him to hospital.'

The two vehicles, the police car and the ambulance, arrived at almost the same time. The card-players, rather than get wet, stood in the doorway of the little café and watched from a distance. Only the proprietor came forward, wearing a sack over his head and shoulders. He recognized the jacket straight away.

'It's definitely him.'

'Didn't he say anything to you?'

'No. Only ordered a brandy. . . .'

Pardon was giving instructions to the ambulance men carrying their stretcher.

'What's that?' asked one of the policemen, pointing to a black object which looked rather like a camera.

The wounded man was carrying it on a strap round his neck. It was not a camera but a cassette tape-recorder. The rain was soaking it, and when they slid the man on to the stretcher, Maigret took advantage of the situation to undo the strap.

'To Saint-Antoine Hospital.'

Pardon got into the back of the ambulance with one of the men while the other drove.

'What are you?' the driver asked Maigret.

'Police.'

'Come up here with me.'

The streets were deserted, and less than five minutes later the ambulance, followed by one of the police cars, arrived at Saint-Antoine Hospital.

Here too Maigret found old memories surging back—the light shining over the door open day and night, the long, badly-lit corridor where two or three uncomplaining people waited silently on the benches, leaping up each time a door opened and closed again, each time a man or woman in white went from one place to another.

'Do you have his name and address?' asked a sister enclosed in a glass cage with a small opening.

'Not yet.'

A houseman, alerted by a bell, came from the end of the corridor, regretfully stubbing out a cigarette. Pardon introduced himself.

'You've done nothing?'

The wounded man, stretched out on a trolley, was pushed into a lift and Pardon, following him, signalled vaguely to Maigret from a distance, as if saying: 'I'll be right back.'

'Do you know anything, Superintendent?'

'No more than you do. I was dining at a friend's house nearby when someone came to tell my friend, who is a doctor, that there was a wounded man lying on the pavement in the Rue Popincourt.'

The policeman noted this down in his book. Less than ten minutes had passed in an unpleasant silence when Pardon appeared at the end of the corridor. It was a bad sign. The doctor's face was worried.

'Dead?'

'Before he could even be undressed. Haemorrhage in the lung cavity. I feared that when I heard his breathing.'

'Stab wounds?'

'Yes. Several. A fairly thin blade. In a few minutes they'll bring you the contents of his pockets. Then I suppose he'll be sent to the Forensic Institute?'

This Paris was familiar to Maigret. He had lived in it for years and yet he had never grown completely accustomed to it. What was he doing here? A stab wound, several stab wounds, they were none of his business. Such things happened every night and in the morning they were written off in three or four lines in the daily reports.

Chance had had it that this evening he was in the stalls, and suddenly he felt himself a little part of it. The Italian noodle-maker had not had the time to tell him what he had seen. He must have gone home with his wife. They slept on the first floor, above the shop.

A nurse was walking towards the little group, a basket in her hand.

'Who is in charge of the case?'

The plainclothes man looked at Maigret, and it was to him that she spoke:

'Here's what was found in his pockets. You'll have to sign a receipt.'

There was a small wallet, one of those which slip into the hip pocket, a ball-point pen, a pipe, a tobacco pouch with very pale Dutch tobacco in it, a handkerchief, some change and two cassette tapes.

In the wallet an identity card and driving licence in the name of Antoine Batille, twenty-one years old, address Quai d'Anjou, Paris. That was on the Ile Saint-Louis, not far from the Pont-Marie. There was also a student's card.

'Pardon, would you ask my wife to go home without me and go to bed?'

'Are you going there?'

'I have to. He obviously lives with his parents and I must tell them.'

He turned to the policemen.

'You see what information you can get from Pagliati, the Italian grocer in the Rue Popincourt, and the four men who were playing cards in "Chez Jules", if they're still at the café.'

As always, he was sorry not to be able to do everything himself. He would have liked to go back to the Rue Popincourt, push open the door of the café where the smoke gathered around the electric light and where the card-players had probably gone on with their game.

He would have liked, too, to question the Italian and his wife, and possibly a little old woman whom he had only glimpsed at the lighted window on the first floor of one of the houses.

Had she been there when the drama took place?

But first he had to inform the parents. He telephoned the duty-sergeant of the 11th *Arrondissement* and put him in the picture.

'Did he have a great deal of pain?' he asked Pardon.

'I don't think so. He lost consciousness immediately. I couldn't do anything there on the pavement.'

The wallet was of excellent quality crocodile, the ballpoint pen was silver, the handkerchief bore the hand-embroidered initial 'A'.

'Would you be so kind as to call me a taxi, Madame?'

She did it, in her cage, without any kindness. It was true that it couldn't be very pleasant to spend all one's nights in such a dismal place waiting for the tragedies of the district to come to an end at the hospital.

By a miracle, the taxi arrived less than three minutes later.

'I'll drop you off, Pardon.'

'Don't wait for me.'

'You know how it is, with news like mine. . . .'

He knew the Ile Saint-Louis fairly well since he used to live in the Place des Vosges, and at that time they often walked arm in arm around the island in the evening.

He rang at a green-painted door. Cars were parked all along the sides of the road, most of them very expensive. A narrow door cut into the big one opened.

'Which is Monsieur Batille's residence, please?' he asked, stopping at an opening in the wall.

The sleepy voice of a woman answered simply.

'Second floor on the left.'

He took the lift and some of the rain which had soaked right through his overcoat and trousers made a puddle at his feet. The building, like most of those on the island, had been restored. The walls were of white stone, the lighting by bronze candelabra. On the marble landing, the doormat had a large red letter 'B'.

He rang and heard an electric bell far in the distance, but it was a long time before the door opened silently.

A young maid in a smart uniform looked at him with some curiosity.

'I would like to speak to Monsieur Batille.'

'Father or son?'

'The father.'

'Monsieur and Madame are not back yet and I don't know when they will return.'

He showed his police identity badge.

'What is it about?' she asked.

'I am Superintendent Maigret, of the Police Judiciaire.'

'And you have come to see Monsieur at this time of night? Is he expecting you?'

'No.'

'Is it very urgent?'

'It is important.'

'It's almost midnight. Monsieur and Madame went to the theatre.'

'In that case, they are likely to be returning soon.'

'Unless they go to have supper with friends afterwards, as they often do.'

'Did young Monsieur Batille not go with them?'

'He never goes anywhere with them.'

He could feel that she was embarrassed. She did not know what to make of him, and he must be a terrible sight, dripping with water.

He glimpsed a huge hall, the floor covered completely with a pale blue carpet with a hint of green in it.

'If it is really urgent . . .'

She resigned herself to letting him in.

'Give me your hat and coat.'

She gave his shoes a worried look. She could not, however, ask him to take them off.

'This way.'

She hung the coat in a cloakroom and hesitated before showing Maigret into the large drawing room which opened on the left.

'You won't mind waiting in here?'

He understood very well what she meant. The luxurious appearance of the flat was almost too refined, rather feminine. The armchairs in the drawing room were white and the pictures on the walls Picasso's blue period, Renoirs and Marie Laurencins.

The maid, who was young and pretty, was visibly wondering if she ought to leave him alone or keep an eye on him, as if she were not too sure of the badge he had shown her.

'Is Monsieur Batille in business?'

'Don't you know him?'

'No.'

'You don't know that he is the owner of Mylène perfumes and beauty aids?'

He knew so little about aids to beauty! And Madame Maigret, who only used a little powder, was not the woman to put him in the picture on such things.

'How old is he?'

'Forty-five? Forty-six? He looks very young.'

She blushed. She must be more or less in love with her employer.

'And his wife?'

'If you lean forward a little you will see her portrait over the mantelpiece.'

In a blue evening dress. Pale blue and pink seemed to be the colours of the house, as in the Marie Laurencin paintings.

'I think I can hear the lift.'

And, in spite of herself, she heaved a slight sigh of relief.

She spoke to them in a low voice, near the door which she had rushed towards. They were a young couple, elegant, with no apparent cares, returning home after an evening at the theatre. First one and then the other looked from a distance at the intruder with soaking trousers and shoes who had risen awkwardly from his chair and who was wondering what expression to put on.

The man took off his grey coat under which he wore a dinner jacket. His wife, under her leopard-skin coat, was wearing a cocktail dress made of delicate links of silver.

They had about ten yards to walk, perhaps less. Batille walked in front, his steps quick and nervous. His wife followed him.

'I'm told you are Superintendent Maigret,' he murmured, frowning.

'That is correct.'

'If I am not mistaken, you are the head of the Criminal Division.'

There was a short, rather unpleasant silence during which Madame Batille was trying to guess what had happened. She was no longer in the same gay mood in which she had entered a few moments earlier.

'It's odd that you should come at this time of night. Would it be about my son, by any chance?'

'Were you expecting to hear bad news about him?'

'Not at all. We won't stay here. Let's go into my study.'

It was the end room, opening off the drawing room. Batille's real office must be somewhere else, in the Mylène

Products building, which Maigret had often noticed in the Avenue Matignon.

The bookcases were of pale wood, lemon-wood or maple, and the walls were lined with books. The leather armchairs were a soft biege, as were the desk fittings. On the desk were photographs in a silver frame—Madame Batille, and the heads of two children, a boy and a girl.

'Sit down. Have you been waiting long?'

'Only ten minutes or so.'

'Will you have something to drink?'

'No, thank you.'

It seemed now as if the man was putting off hearing what the superintendent had to say to him.

'You have had no problems with your son?'

He appeared to reflect for a moment.

'No. He's a quiet boy, and reserved. Perhaps too quiet and reserved.'

'What do you think of his friends?'

'He has hardly any friends. He's quite the opposite of his sister, who is only eighteen and makes friends easily. He has no close friends, no friends at all. Has anything happened to him?'

'Yes.'

'Has he had an accident?'

'You might call it that. He was attacked this evening, in the dark, in the Rue Popincourt.'

'Was he wounded?'

'Yes.'

'Badly?'

'He is dead.'

Maigret would have preferred not to see them, not to be present at this sudden disintegration. The society couple, full of self-assurance and ease, disappeared. Their clothes no longer looked as if they came from a couturier or a high-class tailor. The flat itself lost its elegance and charm.

All that remained was a man and a woman, shattered with grief, who were still battling not to believe the news they had just been given.

'Are you sure it is my . . .'

'He is Antoine Batille, isn't he?'

Maigret held out the still sodden wallet.

'Yes, that is his.'

Batille lit a cigarette mechanically. His hands were trembling. His lips too.

'How did it happen?'

'He had just left a small local bar. He had gone about fifty yards in the pouring rain and someone stabbed him several times, from behind.'

The woman grimaced as if she had been the one to be stabbed and her husband put his arm around her shoulders. He tried to speak but could not, at first. What was there to say, anyway? The things that were passing through his head, even if they were not what he was really worried about?

'Have they caught the . . .'

'No.'

'Did he die immediately?'

'As soon as he got to Saint-Antoine Hospital.'

'Can we go to see him?'

'I would advise you not to go there tonight but to wait until the morning.'

'Was he in pain?'

'The doctor says he wasn't.'

'Go to bed, Martine. Lie down on your bed, at least.'

He led her away gently but firmly.

'I shall be with you in a moment, Superintendent.'

Batille was away for almost a quarter of an hour and when he returned he was very pale, his face drawn and his eyes expressionless.

'Do sit down.'

He was a small man, thin and nervous. One got the impression that Maigret's vast, heavy bulk upset him.

'Are you sure you won't have anything to drink?'

He opened a little cocktail cabinet and took out a bottle and two glasses. 'I must admit I need one.'

He poured himself a whisky and poured some into the second glass.

'Much soda?'

And, immediately:

'I don't understand. I just can't understand it. Antoine was a boy who didn't keep anything from me, and, besides, there was nothing in his life to hide. He was . . . It's hard for me to speak of him in the past tense, but I must get used to it. He was a student. He was reading for an Arts degree at the Sorbonne. He didn't belong to any particular group. He wasn't interested, not even slightly, in politics.'

He gazed at the brown carpet, his arms hanging loosely, and spoke to himself.

'Somebody killed my boy. . . . Why? . . . But why?'

'That's what I'm here to try to find out.'

Batille looked at Maigret as if seeing him for the first time.

'Why have you come in person? As far as the police are concerned, it's just an everyday occurrence, isn't it?'

'As luck would have it, I was almost on the spot.'

'Did you see anything?'

'No.'

'Did nobody see anything?'

'An Italian grocer, who was on his way home with his wife. I have brought you the things which were found in your son's pockets, but I forgot his tape-recorder.'

The father seemed not to understand straight away, then he murmured:

'Oh! Yes. . . .'

He gave a half-smile.

'It was his passion. You'll probably laugh. His sister and I teased him too. Some people are mad about photography and go on the hunt for picturesque faces, even under the bridges. Antoine collected human voices. He often spent whole evenings at it. He would go into cafés, into stations, any public place, and switch on his tape-recorder. He wore it on his chest and many people thought it was a camera. He had a miniature microphone hidden in his hand.'

Maigret had something to get hold of at last.

'Did he ever have any trouble?'

'Only once. It was in a bar somewhere near Les Ternes.

Two men were leaning at the counter. Antoine was standing beside them and recording surreptitiously.

'"Here, boy," one of them said suddenly. He took the tape recorder away from him and removed the cassette.

'"I don't know what you're playing at, but if I see you round here again, make sure you don't have that thing with you."'

Gérard Batille took a drink and spoke again.

'Do you think that . . .'

'Anything is possible. We can't risk making any hypotheses. Did he often go out hunting voices?'

'Two or three times a week.'

'Always on his own?'

'I've already told you he didn't have any friends. He called these recordings human documents.'

'Are there a lot of them?'

'Maybe a hundred, maybe more. He listened to them from time to time and erased the ones which weren't so good. What time tomorrow, do you think?'

'I'll tell the hospital you are coming. Not before eight o'clock, in any case.'

'Shall I be able to bring the body home?'

'Not straight away.'

The father understood and his face grew even greyer as he imagined the autopsy.

'Forgive me, Superintendent, but I . . .'

He could take no more. He needed to be alone, or perhaps to rejoin his wife, perhaps to weep or cry out endlessly in silence.

He said, as if to himself, 'I don't know when Minou will come in.'

'Who is that?'

'His sister. She is only eighteen, but she lives her own life. I expect you had a coat?'

The maid appeared just as they reached the cloakroom and helped Maigret into his sodden coat and handed him his hat.

He went downstairs, then opened the little door and waited

a full minute in the doorway, watching the rain fall. The wind seemed to have dropped a little, the squalls of rain to be less fierce. He had not dared ask permission to telephone for a taxi.

Shoulders hunched, he crossed the Pont-Marie, went down the narrow Rue Saint-Paul and finally found a taxi in a rank near the Saint-Paul metro station.

'Boulevard Richard-Lenoir.'

'Right, chief.'

A driver who knew him and who didn't complain that the distance was too short. Raising his head when he got out of the car, he saw the lighted windows of his flat. As he climbed the last flight of stairs, the door opened.

'You haven't caught a cold?'

'I don't think so.'

'I have the water boiling to make you a toddy. Sit down. Let me take your shoes off.'

His socks were wringing wet. She went to find his slippers.

'Pardon told his wife and me what had happened. How did his parents react? Why was it you who . . .'

'I don't know.'

He had become involved in this case mechanically, because he had almost fallen over it, because it reminded him of many years spent in the streets of Paris at night.

'They didn't take it in straight away. It's only now that they must both be feeling the strain.'

'Are they young?'

'The man must be a bit more than forty-five, but I think he's less than fifty. As for his wife, she hardly looks forty and she's very pretty. You know Mylène perfumes?'

'Of course. Everyone does.'

'Well, then, that's who they are.'

'They're very rich. They have a château in Sologne, a yacht at Cannes and they give fabulous parties.'

'How do you know?'

'Are you forgetting that I have to spend a lot of time waiting for you and I sometimes read the gossip columns in the papers?'

She poured some rum into a glass, and some icing sugar, left the spoon in so that the glass wouldn't crack and poured in some boiling water.

'A slice of lemon?'

'No.'

The room around him was small, narrow. He looked at the décor like someone just returned from a long trip.

'What are you thinking about?'

'As you said, they're very rich. They have one of the most luxurious flats I've ever seen. They were coming back from the theatre, still in high spirits. . . . They saw me sitting at the end of the hall. . . . The maid whispered to them who I was. . . .'

'Get undressed.'

After all, wasn't it better here? He put on his pyjamas, brushed his teeth, and a quarter of an hour later, his head a bit light after the toddy, he was lying in bed beside Madame Maigret.

'Goodnight,' she said, putting her face close to his.

He kissed her as he had done for many years and murmured 'Goodnight'.

'As usual?'

That meant 'Shall I wake you at half past seven as usual with a cup of coffee?'

His grunted 'Yes' was already indistinguishable, for sleep came upon him suddenly. He did not dream. Or, if he did, he didn't remember it. And all at once it was morning.

While he sat in bed drinking his coffee and his wife opened the curtains, he tried to see through the net half-curtains.

'Is it still raining?'

'No. But from the way people are walking with their hands in their pockets, it isn't spring yet, whatever the calendar may say.'

It was the 19th of March. His first task, when he had put on his dressing-gown, was to ring Saint-Antoine Hospital, and he had enormous difficulty getting put through to anyone in administration.

'Yes. . . . I want him to be put in a private room. . . . I

know perfectly well he is dead. . . . That's no reason why the parents should have to see him in the basement. . . . They'll be there in an hour or two. . . . After they have gone, his body will be taken to the Forensic Institute. . . . Yes. . . . Don't worry . . . the family will pay. . . . Yes, of course. . . . They will fill up all the forms you like. . . .'

He sat down opposite his wife and ate two croissants while drinking another cup of coffee and staring mechanically at the street. Low-lying clouds still scudded across the sky, but they were not the same unhealthy colour as on the previous day. The wind, still strong, shook the branches of the trees.

'Do you have any idea . . . ?'

'You know very well I never have any ideas.'

'And if you do, you don't talk about them. Didn't you think Pardon looked ill?'

'Did you find that too? He's not just tired, he has become a pessimist. Yesterday he spoke to me about his profession in a way he has never done before.'

At nine o'clock he was in his office ringing the 11th *Arrondissement* police station. 'Maigret here. Is that you, Louvelle?'

He had recognized his voice.

'I expect you're ringing about the tape-recorder.'

'Yes. Do you have it?'

'Demarie picked it up and brought it here. I was afraid that the rain might have ruined it, but I got it to work. I wonder why the boy recorded those conversations.'

'Can you send me the tape-recorder this morning?'

'When I send the report, which will be typed in a few minutes.'

The mail. Paperwork. He had not told Pardon the previous evening that he too was snowed under with administrative bumph.

Then he went to the briefing, in the director's office. He gave a summary of what had happened the night before since the case was likely to get a lot of publicity because of who Gérard Batille was.

In fact, when he returned to his office he ran into a crowd of newspapermen and photographers.

'Is it true that you almost witnessed the murder?'

'I only arrived on the scene so quickly because I was nearby at the time.'

'This boy, Antoine Batille, is he really the son of Batille the perfume manufacturer?'

How had the press found out? Had the leak come from the police station?

'The concierge says . . .'

'What concierge?'

'The one at the house in the Quai d'Anjou.'

He hadn't even seen her. He hadn't given his name, or his rank. The maid must have told her.

'It was you who broke the news to the parents, wasn't it?'

'Yes.'

'What was their reaction?'

'The same as that of any man and woman who are told that their son has been killed.'

'Have they any idea who did it?'

'No.'

'You don't think it could be a political killing?'

'Certainly not.'

'Something to do with a love affair, then?'

'I don't think so.'

'He wasn't robbed, was he?'

'No.'

'Well, then?'

'Well nothing, gentlemen. The investigation is only beginning and when it brings in some results I'll pass you the information.'

'Have you seen the daughter?'

'Who?'

'Minou. The Batille's daughter. She seems to be well known in certain interesting circles.'

'No, I haven't seen her.'

'She has some very strange friends.'

'Thank you for telling me, but I'm not investigating her.'

'One never knows, does one?'

He pushed them to one side, opened the door of his office

and shut it behind him. He stood in front of the window while he filled his pipe, then he went into the inspectors' room. They were not all there. Some of them were telephoning, others working at their typewriters.

'Are you busy, Janvier?'

'Ten more lines to type, chief, and I'll have finished my report.'

'Come and see me then.'

While he waited, he rang the forensic surgeon who had succeeded his old friend Doctor Paul.

'He'll be sent over to you later in the morning. It is an urgent case, not because of what I expect to hear from the autopsy, but because of the parents' impatience. . . . Mess him about as little as possible. . . . Yes. . . . That's right. . . . I can see you understand. Most of Parisian society will be paying its respects to the body. . . . There are already newspapermen outside in the corridor here.'

The first thing he had to do was to go to the Rue Popincourt. Gino Pagliati hadn't had time to say much the previous evening and his wife had practically not opened her mouth at all. Then there was the man called Jules and the three other card players. Finally, Maigret had not forgotten the silhouette of the old woman he had seen at the window.

'What are we doing, chief?' asked Janvier as he came into the office.

'Is there a free car in the car park?'

'I hope so.'

'Drive me to the Rue Popincourt. Not far from the Rue du Chemin-Vert. I'll tell you when to stop.'

His wife was right, he realized while he waited in the middle of the courtyard for the car: it was cold enough for December.

CHAPTER TWO

MAIGRET REALIZED that even Janvier was a little surprised at the importance given to this case. Every night there
are a certain number of stabbings recorded in some part or
other of Paris, particularly in the poorer districts, and normally the papers would only have given a few lines to the
tragedy in the Rue Popincourt, under the heading of 'News
in Brief'.

Stabbing

A young man, Antoine B . . . , twenty-one years old,
student, was stabbed several times as he walked along the
Rue Popincourt at about 10.30 on Tuesday evening. It
appears that it was an attempted robbery but the arrival
of a man and his wife, local shopkeepers, on the scene
stopped the man from stripping his victim. Antoine B . . .
died on arrival at Saint-Antoine Hospital.

But Antoine B . . . was called Antoine Batille and lived in
the Quai d'Anjou. His father was a well-known man, a
prominent figure in society, and everyone had heard of
Mylène perfumes.

The little black car from the Police Judiciaire crossed the
Place de la République and Maigret found himself in his own
district, a network of narrow streets, heavily populated,
bounded by the Boulevard Voltaire on one side and the Boulevard Richard-Lenoir on the other.

Madame Maigret and he walked along these little streets
each time they went to the Pardons for dinner, and Madame
Maigret often did her shopping in the Rue du Chemin-Vert.

It was at Gino's, as it was called by the locals, that she
bought not only pasta but mortadella, Parma ham and olive
oil in large, golden-coloured cans. The shops were narrow,

deep and badly lit. Today, because of the lowering sky, the street-lights were on almost everywhere, making a false daylight which gave people's faces a waxy appearance.

Lots of old women. Many old men, too, alone, a shopping-basket in their hands. Resignation on their faces. Some stopped from time to time and put their hand to their heart, waiting for a spasm to stop.

Women of all nationalities, carrying young children, a slightly older boy or girl hanging on to their dresses.

'Park here and come with me.'

He began with the Pagliatis. There were three customers in the shop and Lucia was very busy.

'My husband's in the back. Just push open the little door.'

Gino was busy making ravioli on a long marble-topped table covered with flour.

'Oh! Superintendent . . . I thought you would be coming.'

He had a deep voice, a naturally smiling face.

'Is it true that the poor boy is dead?'

That piece of information was not yet in the newspapers.

'Who told you that?'

'A reporter who was here ten minutes ago. He photographed me and I'm going to have my picture in the paper.'

'I'd like you to tell me once again what you told me last night, with as much detail as possible. You were coming back from your brother- and sister-in-law's . . .'

'Yes, the one who's expecting a baby. In the Rue de Charonne. We had only taken one umbrella because when we're walking in town Lucia always takes my arm.

'You remember it was raining hard, a real storm. Several times I thought the umbrella was going to turn inside out and I had to hold it in front of us like a shield.

'That explains why I didn't see him sooner. . . .'

'Who?'

'The murderer. He must have been walking a little way in front of us, but I was only concerned with keeping the rain off us and not stepping in the puddles. Or he might have been standing in a doorway. . . .'

'When you saw him . . . ?'

'He was farther on than the café, Chez Jules, which was still lit up.'

'Could you see how he was dressed?'

'I talked that over with my wife yesterday evening. We both think he was wearing a light-coloured raincoat, with a belt. He walked with an easy step, very quickly.'

'Did he look as if he were following the young man in the jacket?'

'He was walking quicker than the young man was, as if he wanted to catch up with him, or to pass him.'

'How far were you from the two men?'

'A hundred yards, perhaps. I could show you.'

'Did the man in front turn round?'

'No. The other man caught up with him. I saw his arm rise and fall. I didn't see the knife. He struck three or four times and the young man in the jacket fell on his face on the pavement. The killer took several steps towards the Rue du Chemin-Vert, then he turned back. He must have seen us, because we were then only about sixty yards away. But even so he bent over and struck again two or three times. . . .'

'You didn't run after him?'

'Well, you see, I'm rather fat and I have high blood-pressure. I can't run easily.'

He had reddened, embarrassed.

'We walked more quickly, and he went round the corner this time.'

'You didn't hear a car start up?'

'I don't think so. . . . I didn't think of that.'

Mechanically, without Maigret's having had to tell him, Janvier was taking the interview down in shorthand.

'When you got up to the wounded man, what then?'

'You saw him exactly as I left him. His jacket was torn in several places and the blood was pouring out. I thought at once of getting a doctor and I ran to Monsieur Pardon's, telling Lucia to stay there.'

'Why?'

'I don't know. I felt he shouldn't be left alone.'

'Did your wife have anything to tell you when you got back?'

'No one had come by, almost as if it were on purpose.'

'The wounded man didn't speak?'

'No. He was having trouble breathing, gurgling in his chest. Lucia will tell you the same. It's her busy time, just now.'

'Is there any other detail which springs to mind?'

'No, none. I've told you everything I know.'

'Thank you, Gino.'

'How is Madame Maigret?'

'Very well, thank you.'

A passage at the side led to a little courtyard where a welder was working in his glass-fronted workshop. There were courtyards and cul-de-sacs like that scattered throughout the district. There were craftsmen in all of them.

They crossed the street and a little farther on Maigret pushed open the door of 'Chez Jules'. In the daylight the little café was almost as dark as it was at night, and the opaque white globe was lit. A heavily-built man with his shirt sticking out between his trousers and his waistcoat was standing at the counter. He had a red face, a thick neck and a double chin which looked like a goitre.

'What can I get you, Monsieur Maigret? A little glass of Sancerre? My cousin sends it. He . . .'

'Two glasses,' Maigret said, standing at the counter himself.

'You're not the first today.'

'There was a reporter, I know.'

'He took my picture, just as I am just now, holding a bottle. You know Lebon. He worked on the roads for thirty years. Then he had an accident and now gets a pension plus a small compensation for his eye. He was here yesterday evening.'

'There were four of you playing cards, weren't there?'

'Auction *manille*. Always the same players, every evening except Sunday. I close on Sundays.'

'Are you married?'

'My wife is upstairs, She's an invalid.'

'What time did the young man come in?'

'It must have been ten o'clock.'

Maigret glanced at the clock, complete with advertisement, which hung on the wall.

'Don't pay any attention to that. It's twenty minutes fast.
. . . First he pushed the door open a few inches, as if he wanted
to see what kind of place it was. The card game was noisy—
the butcher was winning and when he wins he gets insulting,
as if he were the only one who could play. . . .'

'He came in. And then what?'

'I asked him from my place at the card-table what he
wanted to drink. He hesitated a bit, then mumbled, "Do you
have any cognac?"'

'I waited until I'd played the four cards I had left in my
hand and went behind the counter. While I was serving him
I noticed the triangular black box he was wearing on his chest,
hanging from a strap round his neck, and I thought it must
be a camera. Some tourists do get lost round here, but not
very often.

'I went back to my place at the table. Baboeuf had dealt
the cards. The young man didn't seem in a hurry. He wasn't
interested in the game either. . . .'

'Did he seem preoccupied?'

'No.'

'He wasn't standing facing the door as if he was waiting
for someone?'

'I didn't notice anything.'

'Or as if he were afraid someone might come in?'

'No. He stood there, one elbow on the counter, and from
time to time he touched his lips to the glass.'

'What did you think of him?'

'Well, he was soaking, you know. He looked just like a lot
of young people these days, with his jacket and his long hair.

'We went on playing cards as if he weren't there. Baboeuf
got more and more excited because he kept on getting all the
good cards.

'"You'd better go home and see what your wife's up to,"
Lebon joked.

'"You go and check on yours. She's a bit too young for you,
she . . ."

'I thought for a moment they were going to hit each other.
Then it calmed down, as usual. Baboeuf played the ace.

175

'"What do you say to that?"'

'Then Lebon, who was sitting beside me on the bench, gave me a dig in the ribs with his elbow and I looked at the customer standing at the bar. I looked at him but I didn't understand. He looked as if he were laughing at a private joke, isn't that so, François? I wondered what you were trying to show me. You whispered "I'll tell you later".'

And the man with the blind eye took up the story.

'I had noticed a movement of his hand on the machine. I have a nephew who had a thing like that for Christmas and he amuses himself by recording what his parents say. He looked so angelic, standing there with his drink, but he was listening to everything we were saying, and it was all going on the tape.'

'I wonder what he hoped to gain by that,' grumbled Jules.

'Nothing. Like my nephew. . . . He records for the fun of recording, then forgets all about it. Once he let his parents hear one of their rows and my brother almost broke the tape-recorder:

'"If I catch you at it again, you little bastard . . ."'

'Baboeuf would have been furious too if he'd heard the things he said last night.'

'How long did the boy stay?'

'A bit less than half an hour.'

'Did he only have one drink?'

'Yes. He even left a little cognac in the bottom of his glass.'

'He went out and you didn't hear anything after that?'

'Not a thing. Only the wind, and the water coming out of the drainpipe on to the pavement.'

'No other customer came in before him?'

'You see, I only stay open in the evenings for the card game, because only the regulars come. There's never a lot of people except in the morning for their coffee and croissants, or an indigestion tablet. About ten o'clock or ten-thirty workmen come in for a break, when there's some work going on anywhere nearby. I'm busiest when people come to have a drink before lunch or before dinner.'

'Thank you.'

Here too Janvier had taken the interview down in shorthand and the proprietor had kept on looking at him as he did it.

'He has told me nothing new,' Maigret sighed. 'He has only confirmed what I knew already.'

They got into the car again. Some women were watching them, for their identity was known already.

'Where to, chief?'

'Back to the office first.'

His two visits in the Rue Popincourt had not been useless. Above all, he had the story of the attack, from the Neopolitan. Antoine Batille's assailant had first stabbed him several times. He had begun to move away when, for some unknown reason, he had turned back on his tracks, in spite of the couple a short distance away on the pavement. Was it in order to finish off his victim that he had stabbed again before running off?

He had been wearing a light-coloured, belted raincoat, that was all anyone knew about him. As soon as he arrived back at the Quai des Orfèvres, Maigret, in his office which was pleasantly warm, rang the Pagliati's shop.

'May I speak to your husband for a moment? This is Maigret speaking.'

'I'll call him, Superintendent.'

And Gino's voice:

'Hello, what is it?'

'Tell me, there's one thing I forgot to ask you. . . . Was the killer wearing a hat?'

'A reporter has just asked me the same thing. He's the third since this morning. I had to ask my wife. She can't swear to it, but she's almost sure he was wearing a dark-coloured hat. It happened so quickly, you see. . . .'

The light-coloured, belted raincoat seemed to point to a fairly young man, while the hat would probably mean he was a few years older. In fact, few young people wear a hat these days.

'Tell me, Janvier, do you understand tape-recorders?'

Maigret knew nothing about them, nor did he know anything about photography or about cars, which was why it was his wife who drove. It took all his mechanical knowledge to turn the television from one channel to another in the evenings.

'My son has one just like that.'

'Take care not to erase the recording.'

'Don't worry, chief.'

Janvier smiled and pressed some buttons. They could hear a confused noise, the sound of forks and plates and indistinct voices in the distance.

'And what will Madame have?'

'Do you have any silverside?'

'Of course, Madame.'

'I'll have that with plenty of onions and gherkins.'

'Remember what the doctor told you. No vinegar.'

'A minute steak and a silverside with plenty of onions and gherkins. Would you like the salad served with it?'

The recording was far from perfect and there was a continuous background noise which made it impossible to distinguish the words clearly.

A silence, then a sigh, very distinct.

'You'll always be irresponsible. You're going to have to get up tonight too to take bicarbonate of soda.'

'It's me who gets up and not you. Anyway, since you go on snoring whatever happens . . .'

'I don't snore.'

'You do snore, particularly when you've drunk too much Beaujolais, as you're about to do now. . . .'

'One steak done to a turn. I'll bring the silverside in one moment.'

'You hardly touch the stuff at home.'

'We aren't at home.'

There was a gurgling sound. A voice called:

'Waiter! Waiter! When you decide to pay some attention to us . . .'

Then silence, as if the tape had been cut off. Then a toneless voice spoke very clearly, since this time it must have been speaking directly into the microphone. 'The Brasserie Lorraine, in the Boulevard Beaumarchais.'

Almost certainly the voice of Antoine Batille, noting in that way where the recording had been made. He had obviously had dinner in the Boulevard Beaumarchais and had switched on his tape-recorder. The waiter would probably remember him. It was easy to check.

'You can go over there in a minute,' Maigret said. 'Turn the thing on again.'

Some curious sounds at first, street noises, because they could hear the cars going by. Maigret wondered for a time what the boy had been trying to record and it took him a while to realize that it was the noises of water in the drains and gutters. The sound was difficult to identify, but it changed suddenly and they were once more in a public place, a café or a bar, where there was quite a bit of noise.

'What did he tell you?'

'That it was O.K.'

The voices were thick, but still quite clear.

'Did you go there, Mimile?'

'Lucien and Gouvion are taking turns. In this weather . . .'

'What kind of car is it?'

'Same as usual.'

'Don't you think it's a bit too close?'

'Too close to what?'

'Too close to Paris.'

'Seeing he only goes there on Fridays. . . .'

The sound of glasses, of cups, of more voices. Silence.

'Recorded at the Café des Amis, Place de la Bastille.'

It was not far from the Boulevard Beaumarchais, not far from the Rue Popincourt either. Batille didn't hang around, doubtless so as not to be noticed, and he set off in the rain for a new place.

'And what about your own wife? It's easy to talk about others, but you'd do well to keep an eye on what goes on in your own home.'

That must be the butcher, the game of cards in Chez Jules.

'Don't you worry about my affairs, I'm giving you some good advice. It's not because you're winning. . . .'

'I'm winning because I don't throw away my trumps like a fool.'

'Stop it, you two.'

'He started it. . . .'

If the voices had been shriller, one would have thought it was a children's quarrel.

'Shall we get on with the game?'

'I don't play with anyone who . . .'

'He was just talking off the top of his head. He didn't mean anyone in particular.'

'Let him say so, then, if that's how it was.'

A silence.

'You see, he's careful to keep his mouth shut.'

'I'm keeping it shut because this is so stupid. And here, I'm leading my ace. That fixes you, doesn't it?'

The sound was poor. The people were too far away from the microphone and Janvier had to play that piece of tape three times. Each time they made out one or two more words.

Batille finally said 'Chez Jules, a small local bistro, Rue Popincourt.'

'Is that all?'

'That's all.'

The rest of the tape was blank. Batille must have spoken the last words on the pavement a few seconds before being attacked by an unknown man.

'What about the other two cassettes?'

'They are blank. They are still in their original wrappings. He intended to use them later in the evening, I expect.'

'Did anything strike you as odd?'

'The voices in the Place de la Bastille?'

'Yes. Play that bit again.'

Janvier took it down in shorthand. Then he replayed the few bits of dialogue which seemed, the more they heard them, to take on a more and more particular meaning.

'I would say there were at least three of them.'

'Yes.'

'Plus the two they talked about, Gouvion and Lucien. A little more than half an hour after that was recorded, Antoine was attacked in the Rue Popincourt.'

'But the man didn't take his tape-recorder.'

'Perhaps because the Pagliatis were getting close.'

'I forgot one thing in the Rue Popincourt. Yesterday evening I caught sight of an old woman at a first-floor window, almost opposite the spot where the boy was attacked.'

'I understand, chief. Shall I go there right now?'

Maigret, left on his own, went and stood in front of the window. The Batilles must have been to the hospital and soon the forensic surgeon would have the body.

Maigret had not yet seen the dead boy's sister, the girl the family called Minou, who had, so it seemed, some very odd friends.

Strings of barges glided slowly along the grey Seine and the tugs lowered their funnels as they passed under the Pont Saint-Michel.

Throughout the cold season the terrace was protected by glass screens and heated by two braziers. The room, around the wrought-iron bar, was fairly big, the tables tiny, the chairs the type which could be stacked at night.

Maigret sat down near a pillar and, when one of the waiters came by, ordered a beer. He gazed at the faces around him with an absent expression. The clientele was mixed. At the bar, for example, there were mainly men in blue work-clothes or old men from the surrounding district who came in for their glass of red wine.

As for the others, those who were sitting down, they were of all kinds: a woman in black surrounded by her two children and a large suitcase, as if she were in a station waiting-room; a couple holding hands and gazing rapturously into each other's eyes; some very long-haired boys who sniggered as they followed the waitress with their eyes and teased her every time she passed near them.

For, apart from the two waiters, there was a waitress with a particularly unpleasant face. In her black dress and white apron she was thin, hunched with tiredness, and it was with difficulty that she managed to direct vague smiles at the customers.

Some men and women were quite well-dressed, others less

so. Some were eating sandwiches and drinking coffee or a glass of beer. Others were having an apéritif.

The proprietor sat at the cash-desk, dressed in black with a white shirt and a black tie, his brown hair carefully plastered over the baldness which it covered with an inadequate network of fine dark lines.

It was his post, one could tell that, and nothing that went on in his establishment escaped him. He watched the two waiters coming and going, at the same time keeping an eye on the *commis* who put the bottles and glasses on the trays. Each time he was given a token he pressed a key on the cash-register and a figure appeared in the little glass aperture.

He had obviously been in the trade a long time, and he had probably begun as a waiter himself. Maigret was to discover later, when he went downstairs to the toilets, that there was another, smaller, low-ceilinged room below, where some customers were eating.

This was not a place where one played cards, or dominoes. It was a place for birds of passage, and there must have been very few regulars. Those who remained seated at the tables for any length of time were waiting to keep an appointment near by.

Maigret finally rose and went over to the cash-desk, under no illusions as to the welcome he would get.

'Excuse me, Monsieur.'

He held his badge out discreetly in the palm of his hand.

'Superintendent Maigret, of the Police Judiciaire.'

The proprietor's eyes kept their distrustful expression, the same look he had for the waiters and for the customers who came and went.

'So what?'

'Were you here yesterday evening at about nine-thirty?'

'I was in bed. My wife does the desk in the evenings.'

'Were the same waiters on duty?'

He continued to keep a watchful eye on them.

'Yes.'

'I'd like to ask them two or three questions about some customers they may have noticed.'

The black eyes stared at him, hardly encouraging.

'We only let respectable people in here and the waiters are very busy just now.'

'I only need a minute with each one. Was the waitress here too?'

'No. There's less of a crowd in the evenings. Jérôme!'

One of the waiters stopped abruptly in front of the desk, tray in hand. The proprietor turned to Maigret.

'Go on. Ask your questions.'

'Did you notice, yesterday evening, about 9.30, a young man, about twenty-one, wearing a brown jacket, with a tape-recorder hanging round his neck?'

The waiter turned towards the proprietor, then towards Maigret, and shook his head.

'Do you know of any regular customer nicknamed Mimile?'

'No.'

When it was the second waiter's turn the results were no more spectacular. They hesitated to answer, as if they were afraid of their boss, and it was difficult to know if they were telling the truth. Maigret, disappointed, returned to his table and ordered another glass of beer. It was at that moment that he went downstairs to the lavatory and discovered a third waiter below, younger than the two upstairs.

He decided to sit down and order a drink.

'Tell me, do you ever work upstairs?'

'Three days out of four. We all take a turn down here.'

'Yesterday evening?'

'I was up above.'

'In the evening, too? About half past nine?'

'Right up till we closed, at eleven. We closed early because, what with the weather, there was hardly anyone here.'

'Did you see a young man with fairly long hair, wearing a suede jacket, with a tape-recorder hanging around his neck?'

'So it was a tape-recorder.'

'You saw it?'

'Yes. It isn't the tourist season yet. I thought it was a camera like the ones Americans wear. Then there was the matter of a customer.'

183

'What customer?'

'There were three of them at the next table. When the young man left, one of them watched him go with a worried, anxious look. He called me over.

'"Tell me, Toto . . ."

'Of course my name isn't Toto, but it's a way of speaking some people have, particularly around here.

'"What did that chap have to drink?"

'"A cognac."

'"You didn't see if he used the thing he was carrying?"

'"I didn't see him take any pictures."

'"Pictures my eye! It was a tape-recorder, idiot. Have you ever seen that chap before?"

'"This is the first time."

'"What about me?"

'"I think I've served you three or four times before."

'"That's all right, then. Give us the same again."'

The waiter moved off, because a customer was tapping his table with a coin to attract his attention. The customer paid. The waiter gave him his change and helped him on with his coat.

Then he came right back to Maigret.

'You said there were three of them.'

'Yes. The one who spoke to me and who seemed the most important is a man of about thirty-five, built like a P.T. instructor, brown hair, dark eyes with bushy eyebrows.'

'Had he really been in only two or three times before?'

'I only noticed him those times.'

'What about the others?'

'One of them, a redhead with a scar, hangs around about here often enough, and he comes in and has a glass of rum at the counter.'

'And the third?'

'I've heard him called Mimile by his mates. I know him by sight and I know where he lives. He's a picture-framer. His shop is in the Faubourg Saint-Antoine, almost at the corner of the Rue Trousseau. That's where I live, the Rue Trousseau.'

'Does he come in here a lot?'

'I've seen him sometimes. Not very often.'

'With the two others?'

'No. With a little blonde who seems to come from round here too, a shop assistant or something like that.'

'Thank you. You can't think of anything else to tell me?'

'No. If I think of anything, or if I see them again . . .'

'In that case, telephone me at the Police Judiciaire. Ask for me, or, if I'm not there, for one of my assistants. What's your name?'

'Julien. Julien Blond. The others call me Blondinet, because I'm the youngest. When I'm as old as they are, I hope I'll have a better job than that.'

Maigret was too near home to go and have lunch at the Brasserie Dauphine. He almost regretted it. He would have liked to take Janvier there and put him in the picture on what he had just found out.

'Have you got anywhere?' his wife asked.

'I don't know if it's anything interesting. I have to look everywhere.'

At two o'clock he gathered together three of his favourite inspectors in his office—Janvier, Lucas and young Lapointe, who would no doubt still be called that when he was fifty.

'Would you play the tape again, Janvier? You two, listen carefully.'

Lucas and Lapointe pricked up their ears, of course, as soon as the piece recorded at the Café des Amis began.

'I went there a little while ago. I know the profession and the address of one of the three men seated round the table speaking in low voices. The one they call Mimile. He's a picture-framer with a shop in the Faubourg Saint-Antoine, two or three houses before you get to the Rue Trousseau.'

Maigret didn't dare feel too pleased. Things had gone a bit too quickly for his liking.

'You two will take up a position near the picture-framer's shop. Arrange for two of your colleagues to relieve you this evening. If Mimile goes out, one of you must follow him, preferably both of you. If he meets someone, one of you tag on to him. The same thing if someone who doesn't look like a customer comes to the shop. In other words, I want to know the people he may be in contact with.'

'That's understood, chief.'

'You, Janvier, will look through the files for men of about thirty-five, well-built, good-looking, brown hair, thick eyebrows and black eyes. There must be several, but it's someone who doesn't hide himself, perhaps someone who has never been sentenced or someone who has done his time.'

When he was alone in his office he rang the Forensic Institute. Doctor Desalle came to the telephone.

'Maigret here. Have you finished the autopsy, Doctor?'

'Half an hour ago. Do you know how many stab wounds that boy had? Seven. All in the back. All about the level of the heart and yet the heart was not touched.'

'What about the knife?'

'I was coming to that. The blade isn't wide, but long and pointed. In my opinion it's one of those Swedish flick-knives where the blade shoots out when a button is pressed.

'Only one of the wounds was fatal, the one which perforated the right lung and caused a fatal haemorrhage.

'Did you notice anything else?'

'The boy was healthy, well built, not very athletic—the type of intellectual who doesn't take enough exercise. All the other organs were in excellent condition. Although his blood contained a certain amount of alcohol, he was not drunk. He had had two or three glasses of what I think must have been cognac.'

'Thank you, Doctor.'

'You'll get my report tomorrow morning.'

There was still the routine work to be done. The Public Prosecutor had appointed an examining magistrate, Monsieur Poiret, with whom Maigret had never worked. Another young man. It seemed to the superintendent that for several years the legal profession had been renewing itself with disconcerting rapidity. Wasn't that impression due to his own age?

He rang the examining magistrate, who asked him to come up at once if he was free. He took with him the transcripts of the tape-recorded conversations which Janvier had typed out.

Poiret only merited one of the old offices as yet. Maigret sat down on an uncomfortable chair.

'I'm pleased to meet you,' the magistrate said pleasantly. He was a tall man with his fair hair *en brosse*.

'And I you, Monsieur. Of course I'm here to talk to you about young Batille.'

The magistrate unfolded an afternoon paper where a three-column headline splashed on the first page. There was a photograph of a young man, his hair not yet grown long, who looked very much a 'boy of good family'.

'I understand you have seen the father and mother.'

'Yes, it was I who broke the news to them. They had just come back from the theatre, both of them in evening dress. I think they were humming a tune as they came through the front door. I have rarely seen two people collapse so completely so quickly.'

'Was he an only child?'

'No, there's a sister, a girl of eighteen, who seems to be a bit of a handful.'

'Have you seen her?'

'Not yet.'

'What is their flat like?'

'Very big, luxurious, but bright and gay. A few antiques, but not many. The whole feeling is modern, but not aggressively so.'

'They must be very rich,' sighed the magistrate.

'I suppose so.'

'The paper has an account of what happened which seems to me to be highly romanticized.'

'Does it mention the tape-recorder?'

'No. Why? Does a tape-recorder play an important part in this case?'

'Perhaps. I'm not sure yet. Antoine Batille had a passion for recording conversations in the street, in restaurants, in cafés. They were, for him, human documents. He led a rather lonely life and he often went out on the hunt like that, particularly in the evenings and especially in the poorer districts.

187

'Last night he began in a restaurant in the Boulevard Beaumarchais, where he recorded snatches of a domestic quarrel.

'Then he went to a café in the Place de la Bastille and here is the text of his recording.'

He held the paper out to the magistrate, who frowned.

'That seems fairly incriminating, doesn't it?'

'It's obviously about a rendezvous for Thursday evening in front of a house near Paris. Certainly a weekend residence, for the owner only comes on Fridays and leaves on Monday mornings.'

'That is indeed what the text says.'

'In order to be sure that the villa is empty, the gang has it watched by two men who relieve each other. I know from another source who Mimile is and I have his address.'

'In that case?'

The magistrate seemed to be saying that it was all tied up, but the superintendent was less optimistic.

'If it's the gang I have in mind . . .' he began. 'In the last two years several important villas have been robbed while their owners were in Paris. In almost every case the stolen objects were pictures and valuable curios. At Tessancourt they left behind two canvases which were only copies, which indicates . . .'

'People who know about art.'

'One person who does, at least.'

'What's worrying you?'

'That these people have never yet killed anyone. It's not their line.'

'But it could happen, in a case like yesterday evening.'

'Let's suppose that they suddenly had suspicions that the tape-recorder was working. It would be easy for two of them, let's say, to follow Antoine Batille. Once he was in a deserted street, like the Rue Popincourt, all they had to do was jump on him and grab his tape-recorder.'

The magistrate sighed regretfully.

'Of course.'

'Thieves like that rarely kill, and when they do it's in desperate circumstances. They have operated for two years without being caught. We haven't the slightest idea how they resell the pictures and objets d'art. That supposes at least one brain behind them, a man who knows about painting, who has contacts, who plans the raids, who may even take part in them himself after he has allotted a specific task to each one.

'That man, who most certainly exists, does not let his accomplices kill.'

'In that case, what do you think?'

'I don't think anything yet. I'm fumbling in the dark. I am following that trail, of course. Two of my inspectors are watching the picture-framing shop kept by the man called Mimile. Yet another is going through the files looking for a man of about thirty-five with dark bushy eyebrows.'

'You'll keep me informed?'

'As soon as I have anything new.'

Could one believe all that Gino Pagliati had said? The Neapolitan had sworn that the killer had struck several times, that he had taken a few steps towards the corner of the street, and that he had come back again and struck three more times.

That did not go with the hypothesis of a semi-professional, either, especially when one took into account the fact that he had not taken away the tape-recorder.

Janvier gave him a report on his visit to the woman seen at a first-floor window.

'Madame Esparbès, a widow of seventy-two. She lives alone in a flat comprising three rooms with kitchen, where she has lived for ten years. Her husband was an officer. She has a pension and lives comfortably but not extravagantly.

'She suffers with her nerves and says that she rarely sleeps any more, and she has the habit of peering out of the window every time she wakes up.

'"It's an old woman's fancy, Inspector."

'"What did you see yesterday evening? Don't be afraid to give details, even if they may seem irrelevant to you."

'"I hadn't yet got ready to go to bed. I listened to the ten o'clock news on the radio as usual. Then I turned off the wireless and went over to look out of the window. I hadn't seen

rain like that for a long time and it brought back memories. . . .
That's not important.

'"At about ten-thirty, or a little before, a young man wearing a jacket came out of the little café opposite and he had what I thought was a rather large camera on his chest. I was a little surprised at that.

'"At almost the same time I saw another young man . . ."

'"You're sure it was a young man?"

'"I thought he was quite young, yes. He was smaller than the first man, and a little broader, but not much. I didn't notice where he came from. In a few swift, and doubtless silent, steps he was behind the other man and he began to strike him several times. I almost opened the window and screamed, but it wouldn't have done any good. The victim was on the ground already. Then the killer bent over him, and lifted up his head by the hair, to look at his face."

'"Are you sure of that?"

'"I'm certain. The street-lamp is not far away, and I myself could vaguely make out his features."

'"And then what?"

'"He went away. Then he came back on his tracks, as if he had forgotten something. The Pagliatis were walking along the pavement about fifty yards away, sheltering under their umbrella. But the man still struck the one on the ground three times more, then he ran away."

'"Did he go round the corner into the Rue du Chemin-Vert?"

'"Yes. The Pagliatis arrived on the scene then. . . . But you know the rest. I recognized Doctor Pardon. I didn't know the man who was with him."

'"Would you recognize the killer?"

'"Not to make a formal identification. Not his face. Only his figure."

'"Are you sure he was young?"

'"In my opinion he is no more than thirty."

'"Long hair?"

'"No."

'"Moustache, sideburns?"

'"No. I would have noticed that."

'"Was he as wet as if he had been walking in the rain, or had he just come out of a house?"

'"They were both soaking. It only needed a few minutes outside to have one's clothes wringing wet."

'"Was he wearing a hat?"

'"Yes. A dark hat. I think it was brown."

'"Thank you."

'"I've told you everything I know, but please see that my name doesn't get into the papers. I have nephews in good jobs and they would be upset if people knew I live here. . . ." '

The telephone rang. Maigret recognized Pardon's voice.

'Is that you, Maigret? I'm not disturbing you? I didn't expect to find you in your office. I thought I'd ring you to see if you have any news.'

'We've got a lead, but I don't know if it's any good. As for the autopsy, it confirms your diagnosis. Only one wound was fatal, the one which entered the right lung.'

'Do you think it was an underworld killing?'

'I don't know. There weren't many prowlers or drunks about in the streets at that time. There was no fight. Young Batille didn't quarrel with anybody in the two places he was in before he went into Jules's café.'

'Thank you. You see, I feel a bit involved in this case. Now, back to work. I have eleven patients in my waiting-room.'

'Best of luck!'

Maigret went over and sat in his armchair, chose a pipe from his desk and filled it, his gaze as vague as the view from the window which was becoming more and more foggy.

CHAPTER THREE

AT ABOUT FIVE-TWENTY there was a telephone call from Lucas.

'I thought you'd like me to make a preliminary report, chief. I'm in a little bar just opposite the picture-framer's shop. In fact, his name is Emile Branchu. He set up shop in the Rue du Faubourg-Saint-Antoine about two years ago.

'He appears to have come from Marseille, but that's not certain. They say, too, that he was married down there but that he's separated from his wife, or divorced.

'He lives alone. An old woman, a local, comes in to clean for him, and he takes most of his meals in a restaurant where most of the customers are regulars.

'He has a car, a green six-horsepower, which he keeps in the courtyard nearest his shop. He goes out a lot in the evenings and comes home in the small hours, often with a pretty girl and always a different one. Not the type of girl one finds round about here or in the night-clubs in the Rue du Lappe. They look like models and wear evening dresses and fur coats.

'Does that interest you?'

'Of course. Go on.'

Of all the men who worked for him, Lucas had done so longest, and Maigret now called him 'tu'. He called Lapointe 'tu' too, because he had been almost a boy when he started and still looked like an overgrown schoolboy.

'There have only been three customers, two men and a woman. The woman bought a mirror with a magnifying mirror on one side—he sells mirrors too. One of the men brought an enlarged photograph for framing and took a long time making his choice.

'The third customer went off with a framed picture under his arm. I was able to see it quite clearly, because he came over to the glass door to look at it. It was a landscape with a river, the work of an amateur.'

'Has he telephoned anyone?'

'I can see the phone very well from where I'm watching. It's on the counter. He hasn't used it. However, when the paper-boy came past, he came to the door and bought two different newspapers.'

'Is Lapointe still there?'

'He's outside at the moment. There's a back door giving on to not only the courtyard but a whole network of alleys, the kind this district's full of. Since there's a car and he might use it, it would be better if Lourtie and Neveu, who are going to relieve us, brought a car with them.'

'I'll see to that. Thank you.'

Janvier had come downstairs again with about fifteen photographs of brown-haired men with bushy eyebrows, about thirty-five years old.

'These are all I can find, chief. Do you need me any more? It's one of the children's birthdays. . . .'

'Wish him a happy birthday from me.'

Maigret went into the inspectors' office, saw Lourtie and told him to take a car when he went to the Rue du Faubourg-Saint-Antoine. 'Where is Neveu?'

'He's somewhere in the building. He'll be right back.'

Maigret had nothing more to do at the Quai and he went down to the courtyard with the photographs in his pocket. He went through the gateway, saluted the man on duty with a wave of the hand and went in the direction of the Boulevard du Palais, where he found a taxi. He was not in a bad temper, but he wasn't very happy either. One might have said that he was leading this investigation without being convinced, as if something had been wrong from the start, and he continually thought of the scene which had taken place in the pouring rain in the Rue Popincourt.

Young Batille, who had come out of the dimly-lit café where the four men were playing cards. The Pagliatis, under their umbrella, still quite far down the street. Madame Esparbès at her window.

And someone, a man of thirty at the most, who suddenly appeared on the scene. No one could say if he had been waiting in a doorway for Antoine Batille, to come out or if he too had been walking along the pavement, following him. He covered several yards quickly, then struck once, twice, four times at least.

He heard the footsteps of the pasta-maker and his wife who were no more than fifty yards away. He went towards the corner of the Rue du Chemin-Vert and, just as he was about to turn the corner, he retraced his steps.

Why did he lean over his victim, and why did he only lift his head?'

He didn't feel his wrist or his chest, to see if Antoine was dead. He looked at his face.

Was it to reassure himself that it was in fact the man he had decided to attack? From that moment, something didn't jell. Why did he strike the man lying on the ground three more times?

It was a film which Maigret ran over and over again in his head, as if he hoped to understand all of a sudden.

'Place de la Bastille,' he said to the taxi-driver.

The proprietor of the Café des Amis was still at the cash-desk, his hair plastered over his bald patch. Their eyes met, and the expression in those of the proprietor was not welcoming. Instead of taking a seat upstairs, Maigret went down to the basement, where he took a seat at a table. There were many more people than in the morning. It was the time for the before-dinner apéritif. When the waiter came to take his order, he was less friendly than before.

'A beer.'

And, holding the packet of photographs out to him:

'See if you recognize any of these men.'

'I haven't got much time.'

'It'll only take a minute.'

The proprietor must have had a word with him when he saw the superintendent come up from the basement after having spent some time there.

The waiter hesitated, then finally took the photographs.

'I'd better take them over in the corner to look at them.'

He came back almost at once and handed the bundle back to Maigret.

'I don't recognize anyone.'

He appeared to be sincere and he went to get the beer Maigret had ordered. There was nothing left for Maigret to do but go home for dinner. He took his time drinking his beer, then climbed the stairs to the street-floor and saw Lapointe sitting alone at a table just opposite him.

Lapointe saw him too, but pretended not to recognize him. Emile Branchu must have been somewhere in the café and the superintendent made an effort not to look too hard at the clientèle.

He had two hundred yards to go to reach home, where there was a pervading aroma of baked mackerel. Madame Maigret cooked them in white wine, in a slow oven, with lots of mustard.

She saw immediately that he was not happy with his case and asked no questions.

Once at table, she remarked:

'Don't you want the television?'

It had become a habit, a mania.

'On the seven o'clock news they talked about Antoine Batille for a long time. They went to the Sorbonne to interview several of his friends.'

'What did they have to say about him?'

'That he was a nice boy, rather retiring, a bit embarrassed to belong to such a well-known family. He had a passion for tape-recorders and he was waiting for a miniature one which can be held in the palm of the hand to arrive from Japan.'

'Is that all?'

'They tried to question his sister. All she said was "I have nothing to say."'

'"Where were you that night?"'

'"At Saint-Germain-des-Prés."'

'"Did you get on well with your brother?"'

'"He left me alone and I left him alone"'

The reporters were all over the place, in the Rue Popincourt, at the Quai d'Anjou, at the Sorbonne. Even the provincial radio stations had got hold of it. They already had a label for the case: the madman of the Rue Popincourt.

They dwelt on the number of stab-wounds—seven! In two groups! The murderer had retraced his steps to strike again, as if he had not reached his quota.

'Does that not suggest the idea of a revenge killing?' one of the reporters insinuated. 'If the seven blows had been struck one after another, one could believe in a kind of mad rage, more or less unconscious. A large number of blows, which always impresses the jury, is almost always the sign that a murderer has lost control of himself. Batille's killer was interrupted, went away, came back on his tracks to strike the last three blows.'

One of the papers finished up with:

'Did the tape-recorder play a part in this case? We believe that the police attach a certain importance to it, but no one at the Quai des Orfèvres is willing to answer questions on the subject.'

At eight-thirty the telephone rang.

'Neveu here, chief. Lucas told me to keep you in the picture.'

'Where are you?'

'In the little bar opposite the picture-framer's shop. Before Lourtie and I arrived, Emile Branchu shut up shop and went to the Place de la Bastille where he had a drink. As he passed by the cash-desk he greeted the proprietor who returned his greeting as if he were a regular.

'The picture-framer didn't speak to anyone. He read the newspapers he had in his pocket. Lapointe was there. . . .'

'I saw him.'

'Good. Did you also know that he went and had his dinner in a little restaurant where his napkin is kept in a pigeon-hole and where they call him Monsieur Emile?'

'I didn't know that.'

'Lapointe says he ate very well there. It seems that the andouillettes . . .'

'What happened after that?'

'Branchu went home, pulled down the shop's shutter and fixed the wooden panel to the glass door. A faint light is showing through the window shutters. Lourtie is watching the courtyard.

'Do you have the car?'

'It's parked a few yards from here.'

The first channel was rife with sob-singers of both sexes. Maigret hated that. There was an old American film with Gary Cooper, which Maigret and his wife watched, on the second channel.

The film finished at a quarter to eleven and Maigret was in shirt-sleeves, brushing his teeth, when the telephone rang again. This time it was Lourtie.

'Where are you?' the superintendent asked him.

'In the Rue Fontaine. The picture-framer went out at about half past ten and got his car from the courtyard. Neveu and I took the police car.'

'Did he notice you following him?'

'I don't think so. He came directly here, as if it were an old habit, and after he had found a parking-place he went into the Pink Rabbit.'

'What is the Pink Rabbit?'

'A strip-tease club. The doorman greeted him as if he knew him. We went in after him, Neveu and I, because two men are less noticeable than one in places like that. Neveu even acted the part of someone a little drunk.'

That was Neveu all over. He loved adding the personal touch. He also liked putting on disguises, which he carried out to the smallest detail.

'Our man is at the bar. He shook hands with the bartender. The proprietor, a small fat man in a dinner-jacket, came over and shook hands too, and two or three of the girls kissed him.'

'The bartender?'

'You've got it. He looks very like the description we were given. Between thirty and forty, handsome, Mediterranean type.'

When he left the Café des Amis Maigret should have given the packet of photographs to Lucas, who was still in the Rue du Faubourg-Saint-Antoine and who would have handed them over to Lourtie. He had thought of it when he left the Quai des Orfèvres, then it had slipped his mind.

'Go back to the Pink Rabbit. I'll be there in about twenty minutes. What's the name of the *bistro* you're ringing from?'

'You can't miss it. It's the *tabac* on the corner. I didn't want to ring from the club in case I was overheard.'

'Be at the *tabac* in twenty minutes.'

Madame Maigret had understood and, sighing, went to get down her husband's hat and coat.

'Shall I call a taxi?'

'Yes, please.'

'Will you be long?'

'Less than an hour.'

In spite of the fact that they had had a car—which Maigret had never driven—for a year, Madame Maigret preferred to use it as little as possible in Paris. They used it mainly on Saturday evenings and Sunday mornings, to get to Meung-sur-Loire, where they had their little cottage.

'When I retire . . .'

Sometimes it seemed as if Maigret, desperate to retire, were counting the days. At others one could sense that he had a feeling of panic at the idea of leaving the Quai des Orfèvres.

Up until three months before, the retiring age for superintendents was sixty-five and he was sixty-three. A new regulation had changed everything and put the retiring age back to sixty-eight.

In some streets the fog was thicker than in others and the cars moved slowly, their headlights having a haloed effect.

'I've driven you before, haven't I?'

'It's very likely.'

'It's funny. I never manage to put a name to your face. I know you're someone well-known. Are you an actor?'

'No.'

'Have you never been in pictures?'

'No.'

'And I haven't seen you on television either?'

Fortunately they reached the Rue Fontaine at that point.

'Try to find a place to park and wait for me.'

'Will you be long?'

'A few minutes.'

'That's all right then, because it's just now that the theatres are coming out, and . . .'

Maigret pushed open the door of the *tabac* and found Lourtie at the counter. He ordered a brandy, since there had been a lot of talk about brandies the previous evening, then he took the photographs out of his pocket and slipped them into the inspector's hand.

'Go into the gents' to look at them, it's safer.'

A few moments later Lourtie returned and gave the photographs back to the superintendent.

'It's the one on top of the pile. I've put a cross on the back.'

'You're absolutely sure?'

'Absolutely. Except that on the photograph he's three or four years younger. He's still a good-looking man.'

'Go back over there.'

'The strip show is about to begin. You know, we've had to order champagne. They don't serve anything else.'

'That's all right. And if anything else of importance happens, particularly if the picture-framer goes out of the city, be sure to ring me.'

Back in the taxi, he looked at the photograph marked with a cross. It was the best-looking man of the lot. There was something impudent, something sarcastic in his expression. A tough, like the members of the Corsican gang or the gang from Marseille.

Maigret slept fitfully and was in his office long before nine o'clock. He sent Janvier to Records.

'It came off, then? I didn't dare hope too much. The description was pretty vague.'

Janvier came down a quarter of an hour later with a card.

'*Mila*, Julien Joseph François, born in Marseille. Bartender by profession. Bachelor. Height . . .'

There followed the various measurements of the said Mila, whose last known domicile was a furnished room in the Rue Notre-Dame-de-Lorette.

Sentenced four years previously to two years imprisonment for armed robbery. That had taken place at the entrance to a factory in Puteaux. The bank messenger had been able to spring the catch on his case, from which a cloud of thick smoke then appeared.

A policeman standing at the corner saw it. A chase. The thieves' car had ended up against a lamp-post.

Mila had got himself out of it rather well, first of all because he had claimed to be only an accomplice, then because the thieves had only used toy guns.

Maigret sighed. He knew professional criminals well, but he had never been very interested in them. For him, they were the routine stuff, a sort of game which had its rules, sometimes also its pretences and trickery.

Could one suppose that a man who had used a toy pistol to stage a hold-up had twice leapt on a young man, for the sole reason that the man might have recorded snatches of an incriminating conversation? And that when the young man was on the ground, the killer would not have taken the trouble to take his tape-recorder away or to break it?

'Hello? . . . Get me Monsieur Poiret, the magistrate, please. . . . Hello, yes. . . . Thank you. . . . Monsieur Poiret? . . . Maigret here. . . . I have some information which raises a few questions and I would like to show it to you. . . . In half an hour? . . . Thank you. . . . I'll be in your office in half an hour.'

The sun broke through suddenly. One could almost believe that spring intended to keep its appointment on the 21st. Maigret, with Mila's photograph in his pocket, went off to the director's office for the briefing.

It was a day of comings and goings, of telephone calls. The little gang, of whom only Mila and the picture-framer, and a third, unidentified person were known, was apparently planning a robbery in a country house near Paris.

But the Police Judiciaire of the Quai des Orfèvres was powerless outside the boundaries of Paris. It was the domain of the Sûreté Nationale, in the Rue des Saussaies, and, in agreement with the magistrate, Maigret telephoned the man whom it was now fashionable to call his homologue.

It was Superintendent Grosjean, a long-serving man of about the same age as Maigret and who, like him, always had a pipe in his mouth. He was a native of the Cantal and had kept the rich accent of that region.

They met a little later in the enormous buildings of the Rue des Saussaies, which the men of the Police Judiciaire called 'the factory.'

After half an hour of work Grosjean got up, grumbling:

'Still, I'll have to make the gesture of referring it to my chief.'

When Maigret got back to his office, everything was fixed. Not necessarily in the way he would have liked, but in the way the Sûreté Nationale were accustomed to work.

'And now what?' Janvier, who had remained in contact with the men on watch in the Rue du Faubourg-Saint-Antoine, asked him.

'A scene from a film!'

'Lucas and Marette are in the Rue du Faubourg-Saint-Antoine. Emile came and took his apéritif in the bar they were in, without paying any attention to them. Then he had dinner in the same restaurant as yesterday evening.

'No comings or going. Two or three customers who looked like genuine ones. There's a little workshop which joins on to the shop and that's where he works.'

At about four o'clock Maigret had to go up to the magistrate's to keep him informed on the plan which had been decided on. When he came down again he was handed a slip of paper on which a name only was written: Monique Batille. The space intended for the purpose of the visit had not been filled in.

How had she got the nickname Minou from Monique? He went towards the waiting room, saw a tall thin girl wearing black trousers and a trench-coat over a transparent blouse.

'You're Superintendent Maigret, aren't you?'

She seemed to be inspecting him from head to foot to reassure herself that he lived up to his reputation.

'Would you care to come with me?'

She went without the slightest embarrassment into the office where so many destinies had been at hazard. She didn't seem to take any notice of the place and remained detached, taking a packet of Gitanes from her pocket.

'May I smoke?'

A little laugh.

'I forgot that you smoke your pipe all day.'

She walked over to the window.

'It's like at home. You can see the Seine. Don't you find it boring?'

Did she want a movable backdrop?

Aah! She let herself sink finally into the armchair while Maigret remained standing by his desk.

'You must be wondering what I have come here for. Don't worry, I'm not here out of idle curiosity. . . . It's true that although I know all kinds of celebrities I've never met any policemen before.'

It wasn't worth trying to stop her. Was it a mannerism she put on to hide a basic shyness?

'Yesterday I waited for you to come and question my parents again, to question me, then the servants, and all that. . . . Isn't that what you usually do? This morning I decided I would come and see you this afternoon. I gave it a lot of thought.'

She saw the flicker of a smile on Maigret's lips and guessed what he was thinking.

'I do think quite a bit, believe me. I only talk in this haphazard way. My brother's body was found in the Rue Popincourt, wasn't it? It isn't a dreadful street, is it?'

'What do you mean by a dreadful street?'

'A street where criminals meet in the bars and plan their crimes, something like that, I don't know.'

'No. It's just an ordinary street where ordinary people live.'

'That's what I thought. Well, my brother went to other places to do his recording, really dangerous places. Once I begged him to take me with him.

'"I can't do it, my child. Where I'm going, you wouldn't be safe. Even I'm not safe there, either."

202

'I asked him "Do you mean there are criminals there?"'

'"Certainly. Do you know how many bodies are fished out of the Canal Saint-Martin every year?"'

'I don't think he was trying to frighten me or to get rid of me. I begged him and begged him. I came back to the subject several times, but he would never take me on any of what he called his expeditions.'

Maigret looked at her, surprised that she had retained such a fresh outlook beneath a deliberately sophisticated exterior. And, come to that, her brother seemed to have been, like her, only an overgrown child.

'Did he keep his recordings?'

'There are dozens of cassettes in his room, carefully numbered, the numbers corresponding to a catalogue which he kept up to date.'

'No one has touched it since . . . since his death?'

'No.'

'Is the body at home?'

'They've turned the small drawing room, which we call mother's drawing room, into a mortuary chapel, with candles. The other drawing room was too big. There are black hangings at the door of the flat, too. It's all too gloomy. They shouldn't do things like that any more these days, should they?'

'What else were you going to tell me?'

'Nothing. That he ran risks. That he met people of all kinds. I don't know if he spoke to them, or if he got to know any of those people. . . .'

'Did he ever carry a gun?'

'It's funny you should ask that.'

'Why?'

'He managed to persuade Daddy to give him one of his revolvers. He kept it in his room. And he said to me, not very long ago,

'"I'll be glad when I'm twenty-one. I shall ask for a permit to carry a gun. Given the type of research I do . . ."'

That lent a new pathos, and an almost unreal character, to the scene in the Rue Popincourt. An overgrown child. He believed that he studied man in the raw because he recorded scraps of conversations in cafés and in restaurants. These findings he docketed carefully, making a catalogue of them.

'I shall have to hear his recordings. Have you ever heard them?'

'He didn't let anyone hear them. Only once, I thought I heard a woman crying in his room. I went to see what was going on. He was alone, listening to one of his tapes. Have you any more questions to ask me?'

'Not just now. I shall probably come to your house sometime during the day tomorrow. I suppose there are a lot of people paying their respects.'

'The doorbell never stops ringing. Oh well, that's that. I had hoped I would have been of some use to you.'

'Perhaps you have been, more than you think. Thank you for coming.'

He took her to the door and shook hands with her. She was thrilled.

'Goodbye, Monsieur Maigret. Don't forget you promised I could hear the recordings with you.'

He had not promised anything of the kind, but he decided not to argue.

What had he been doing when he had found her card in his office? He had just come down from the magistrate's office.

'A scene from a film,' he thought, grumbling.

And he remained in a more or less grumbling mood throughout the evening and a good part of the night. Because it wasn't just like a scene from any old film, but one from a real, riproaring thriller, just the thing the men in the Rue des Saussaies were past masters at organizing.

At seven-thirty, Lucas rang to say that the picture-framer had closed the shutters and put up the wooden panel on the glass door. A little later he had gone to his usual restaurant for dinner. Then he walked around the block, as if he were just taking the air, then went to the Place de la Bastille, where he bought several magazines at a kiosk, then went home.

'What shall we do?'

'Wait.'

As for Maigret and Janvier, they had dinner at the Brasserie Dauphine. It was almost empty. It was mainly at mid-day and before dinner that the two small rooms were crowded.

Maigret rang his wife just to say hello.

'I have no idea what time I'll be back. Certainly it will be very late—unless it falls flat. I'm not in charge of the operation.'

He was in charge of the men only as long as they were in Paris and that was why, at nine o'clock, the car he was in, with Janvier at the wheel and fat Lourtie in the back, stopped in front of, or almost in front of, the picture-framer's shop.

It was a black car with no distinctive marks, but fitted with a radio transmitter and receiver. Another car, exactly like it, equipped in the same way, was parked about fifty yards away. Superintendent Grosjean and three of his inspectors were sitting in it.

Finally, in a cross street, there was a police van belonging to the Sûreté, with about ten plainclothes policemen inside.

Lucas was on watch, also in a car, not far from Mila's room in the Rue Notre-Dame-de-Lorette.

It was he who made the first move.

'Hello? 287? Is that you, chief?'

'Maigret here.'

'Lucas here. Mila has just left in a taxi. We are going through the centre of the city and I think we are about to go over to the Left Bank.'

At the same moment the door of the shop opened and the picture-framer, who was wearing a lightweight biege raincoat, locked it behind him and walked briskly towards the Place de la Bastille.

'Hello, 215,' Maigret called. 'Is that you, Grosjean? Are you receiving me? Hello, 215?'

'215 here.'

'We are about to move slowly towards the Place de la Bastille. He's on foot.'

'Over?'

'Over.'

Maigret shrugged his broad shoulders.

'To think that I'd be playing at cops and robbers!'

Once in the Place de la Bastille, Emile Branchu went towards the Boulevard Beaumarchais and opened the door of a black Citroën DS which moved off immediately.

Maigret could not see who was driving, probably the third man from the Café des Amis, the one who drank rum and had a scar on his face.

Grosjean followed at some distance. From time to time he called on the radio and Maigret, hating himself for being churlish, replied. The van also stayed in radio contact.

The traffic was moving well. The DS was going fast and the driver did not appear to notice that he was being followed. Even less did he imagine that he was at the head of a little procession.

At the Port de Châtillon he stopped for a moment and a tall, dark man standing at the edge of the pavement got into the car as if he did it every day of his life.

Now the three men were together. They too were organized in an almost military manner. They were going faster and Janvier had to adjust his speed so as not to lose them while still remaining unnoticed.

They had taken the road to Versailles and they went through Petit-Clamart hardly slackening their pace.

'Where are you?' Grosjean asked at regular intervals. 'You're keeping them in sight?'

'We're leaving my territory now,' Maigret growled. 'Now it's your turn.'

'When we get wherever we're going.'

They turned left towards Châtenay-Malabry, then right towards Jouy-en-Josas. There were thick clouds, some fairly low, but a good part of the sky was clear and the moon showed through.

The DS slowed down turned to the left again and soon could be heard braking.

'Shall I stop here?' asked Janvier. 'I think they're stopping. . . . Yes, they've stopped.'

Lourtie got out to see. When he came back he announced:

'They've met someone who was waiting for them. They went into a big garden or park, I don't know which. I could see the roof of a villa.'

Grosjean, lost in the country lanes, asked what was going on, and Maigret brought him up to date.

'Where did you say you were?'

And Lourtie whispered:

'Chemin des Acacias. I saw the sign.'

'Chemin des Acacias.'

Lourtie went to take up his post at the corner of the road where Mila and his companions had got out of the car. They had left the DS at the edge of the road. The look-out was still there, but the other three men seemed to have gone into the house.

The Sûreté car finally parked behind Maigret's, then, a few moments later, the impressive van stuffed with policemen joined them.

'Over to you now,' Maigret hissed, filling his pipe.

'Where are they?'

'Almost certainly in the villa whose gate you can see from the corner. The man on the pavement is their look-out.'

'Won't you come with me?'

'I'll stay here.'

Some moments later, Grosjean's car swung into the road on the left so suddenly that the look-out, caught by surprise, had no time to give the alarm. Before he knew what had happened to him, two men had grabbed him and handcuffed him.

Policemen hurtled out of the van into the grounds of the villa which they surrounded hastily, cutting off all exits. It was a modern building, fairly large, and the water which could be seen glinting through the trees was that of the swimming-pool.

All the windows were dark, the shutters closed. Nevertheless footsteps could be heard, and when the men of the Sûreté, with Grosjean at their head, opened the door, they found themselves facing three men in rubber gloves who, having heard strange noises, were trying to get out.

They made no attempt to escape, raised their hands above their heads, and a few seconds later they too were handcuffed.

'Put them in the van. I'll question them when we get back to my office.'

Maigret was walking up and down stretching his legs. From a distance he watched the men being pushed into the van, then saw Grosjean coming towards him.

'Aren't you coming with me to have a look at the inside?'

The first thing they noticed was a marble plaque to the right of the gate which said, in gilded letters, 'The Golden Crown'. A crown, carved in the stone, made Maigret think of something. What was it? He couldn't remember.

There was no corridor. One entered, on the same level, an immense room where hunting trophies and paintings alternated on the white stone walls. One of the pictures had been taken down and was lying upside down on a mahogany table.

'A Cézanne,' murmured Grosjean, who had turned it over.

In a corner there was a Louis XV desk. The leather blotting pad bore the same crown as the plaque at the gate. In a drawer there were writing paper and envelopes with the same crown and below that the name Philippe Lherbier.

'Look at this, Grosjean.'

He showed him the crown on the blotting pad, then the writing paper.

'Have you got it? The famous leather-merchant in the Rue Royale.'

A man of sixty with a thick head of snow-white hair which made his face look fresher and younger.

Not only was his shop the most elegant place to buy leather in Paris, but he owned branches in Cannes, Deauville, London, New York and Miami.

'What shall I do? Telephone him?'

'That's up to you, my friend.'

Grosjean lifted the receiver and dialled the number on the writing paper.

'Hello. . . . Is that Monsieur Lherbier's residence? . . . Yes, Monsieur Philippe Lherbier. . . . He's not at home? . . . Have you any idea where I might reach him? . . . What's

208

that? . . . At the home of Maître Legendre, Boulevard Saint-
Germain. . . . Can you tell me the number?'

He took a pencil from his pocket and scribbled some figures
on the beautiful crown-embossed paper.

Legendre, the lawyer, also belonged to the upper ranks of
Parisian society.

Maigret looked at the paintings. Two more Cézannes, a
Derain, a Sisley. He pushed open a door and found a smaller,
more feminine drawing room, its walls hung with buttercup-
yellow silk. It reminded him of the house in the Quai d'Anjou.
He had landed back in the same world, and undoubtedly the
two men knew each other, if only through meeting in the
places they both frequented.

Philippe Lherbier was often the object of newspaper gossip,
particularly for his marriages and divorces. He was called the
most divorced man in France. Was it five times? Or six?

The strangest thing was that after each divorce he married
again in less than six months. Always to the same kind of
woman! All of them, except one who was an actress, had been
tall, slim models with more or less fixed smiles. One would
have thought that he only married them to be able to dress
them sumptuously and to have them play a purely decorative
rôle.

'Yes. . . . Thank you for getting him. . . . Hello? . . . Is
that Monsieur Lherbier? . . . Superintendent Grosjean of the
Sûreté Nationale here. . . . I'm in your villa at Jouy-en-
Josas. . . . What am I doing here? . . . I have just arrested
three burglars who were making off with your pictures. . . .'

Grosjean put his hand over the mouthpiece and whispered
to Maigret, 'He's laughing. . . .'

Then, in a normal voice.

'What's that? . . . Yours are insured? That's good. . . .
You're not coming this evening. . . . Well, I can't leave the
place open and I have no way of locking it up. That means
that one of my men will have to stay in the villa until you
send someone with, among other things, a locksmith. . . . I
must . . .'

He stood still a moment, listening, his face very red.

'He hung up,' he murmured finally.

He was furious at having been cut off while he was speaking.

'That's the kind of person for whom we . . . we . . .'

He undoubtedly would have added:

'For whom we risk our lives.'

But he realized that in the present situation that seemed to be rather overstating the case.

'I don't know if he was drunk, but he sounded as if he thought the whole thing was a huge joke.'

He detailed one of his men to remain in the villa until further notice.

'Are you coming, Maigret?'

Maigret was not yet ready to leave.

'Cézannes. . . . And . . . it doesn't matter. Hundreds of thousands of francs' worth of pictures in a villa he only uses at weekends.

'He has an even bigger villa at Cap d'Antibes. It's called "The Golden Crown" too. If the papers are to be believed, he has his cigars and cigarettes marked with the same gold crown. His yacht is called "The Golden Crown". . . .'

'Really?' breathed Grosjean, incredulous.

'It appears to be true.'

'Doesn't anyone laugh at him?'

'They're all vying for invitations to one of his houses.'

They found themselves outside again and stopped for a moment to look at the swimming-pool which must have been heated, for a thin cloud of steam rose from it.

'Are you coming to the Rue des Saussaies?'

'No. The robbery is none of my business, as it didn't take place in my jurisdiction. The only thing I would like, tomorrow if possible, is to question them on another matter. Poiret would like to hear what they have to say, too.'

'The Rue Popincourt case?'

'That's how we got on their tracks.'

'That's true. I'd forgotten.'

When they were back at the cars the two men shook hands, each one about as stout as the other, each with the same career behind him, the same experiences.

'I'll be there for the rest of the night. Oh, well . . .'

Maigret got in beside Janvier. Lourtie, sitting behind, was smoking a cigarette which made a small red glow in the dark.

'Well, that's that. Up to now we've only been working for the Sûreté boys. Tomorrow we'll try to do our own work.'

And Janvier, alluding to the lack of cordiality which has always existed between the two branches of the police, asked:

'Do you think they'll let us see them?'

CHAPTER FOUR

IT MUST HAVE BEEN a busy night in the Rue des Saussaies, where the reporters and photographers, alerted as usual God only knows how, were quick to arrive and invade the corridors.

At half past seven, Maigret switched on the wireless automatically, while shaving. It was time for the news and, as if he had been expecting it, they were talking about the villa in Jouy-en-Josas and the well-known millionaire Philippe Lherbier, the man with the six wives and the golden crowns.

'Four men are under lock and key, but Superintendent Grosjean remains convinced that none of them is the real head of the gang, the mastermind. Besides, rumour has it that Superintendent Maigret may intervene, not in the picture-stealing case, but about some other matter the criminals may be involved in. This is being kept a great secret. . . .'

He learned another piece of news from the wireless: the three robbers and the look-out had not been armed.

He was in his office at nine o'clock and immediately after the briefing he rang Grosjean at the Rue des Saussaies.

'Did you get any sleep?'

'Less than three hours. I had to be a bit rough with them. None of them will say anything. One of them, in particular, makes me see red. It's Julien Mila, the bartender, the most intelligent of the three. Whenever you ask him any questions, he gives you a mocking look and says in a soft voice:

' "Unfortunately I have nothing to say".'

'Haven't they asked to see their lawyers?'

'Of course they have. Maître Huet, naturally. He's coming to see me this morning.'

'When can you send them over to me? Poiret, the magistrate, wants to see them too.'

'Some time this afternoon, I hope. I expect you'll have to give them back to me, because I imagine I'll need a long time with them yet. The list of burglaries of the same type which have been committed around Paris in the last two years is a long one—at least twelve, and I'm sure that they are responsible for most of them, if not all. What about you? The Rue Popincourt case?'

'Nothing new.'

'Do you think these characters I've got have anything to do with it?'

'I don't know. One of the thieves, the small, broad-shouldered one with a scar on his face, was wearing a light-coloured, belted raincoat, wasn't he? And a brown hat?'

'Demarle. Yes, he was. We're looking at his record. He seems to be bent and the law has had dealings with him more than once.'

'What about Branchu, the one they call Mimile? The picture-framer?'

'No criminal record. He lived for a long time in Marseille but he comes from Roubaix.'

'See you before long.'

The newspapers published photographs of the handcuffed criminals on the front page, together with a photograph of the leather-merchant at the weigh-in at Longchamps, in tails with a pale grey topper.

Mila was looking at the camera with an ironic smile. Demarle, the scarred sailor, looked completely surprised at what was happening to him, while the picture-framer held his hands over his face. As for the look-out, badly dressed in a suit too big for him, he looked like a straight-man of rather limited intelligence.

'After an investigation which Divisional Superintendent Grosjean of the Sûreté Nationale has been carrying out for nearly two years, a good haul . . .'

Maigret shrugged his shoulders. It wasn't so much about the thieves that he was thinking but, in spite of his efforts to the contrary, of Antoine Batille. He had often said that it was almost always by getting to know the victim that one was led to the murderer.

There was a thin sun. The sky was a very pale blue. The

temperature remained at two or three degrees Centigrade and it was freezing in most of France, except on the west coast.

He put on his coat, picked up his hat and went through the inspectors' office. 'I'm going out for about an hour.'

Alone, for once. He wanted to go alone to the Quai d'Anjou. He walked there along the *quais* as far as the Pont-Marie, which he crossed. He smoked his pipe slowly and kept his hands stuffed in his pockets.

He was going over in his mind the ground the young man with the tape-recorder had covered that night, the night of 18th-19th March, which was to be his last night.

Already, from a good distance away, he could see the black hangings surrounding the doorway with, in silver, an enormous 'B', fringes and teardrops. As he passed by the lodge he saw the concierge who was watching the comings and goings.

She was still young, attractive. Her black dress was brightened up by a white collar and cuffs which gave it the look of a uniform. He wondered whether to go into the lodge, not because he had reason to, but because he was looking in all directions.

He did not go in, but took the lift. The door of the Batille's flat was shut to. He pushed it open and went towards the little drawing room which had been turned into a mortuary chapel. A very dignified old woman was standing by the door and nodded to him. Was she a relation? A friend or a nanny who was representing the family?

Antoine had not yet been put into his coffin, but was laid out in state on the couch, his clasped hands entwined with a rosary.

In the flickering light of the candles his face looked very young. He could have been fifteen years old as easily as twenty. Not only had he been shaved, his hair had been cut, undoubtedly so that those who came to pay their respects did not take him for a hippy.

Maigret too moved his lips, mechanically, without conviction, then went back into the entrance hall, looking for someone he could speak to. He found a valet in a striped waistcoat who was vacuum-cleaning the large drawing room.

'I should like to see Mademoiselle Batille,' he said. 'I am Superintendent Maigret.'

The valet hesitated and finally went off, grumbling, 'If she's up.'

She was, but she obviously wasn't ready, because he had to wait at least ten minutes and when she appeared she was wearing her peignoir, her bare feet stuck into a pair of mules.

'Have you found out something?'

'No. I only wanted to see your brother's room.'

'Do forgive me for receiving you like this, but I slept very badly and anyway I'm not used to getting up early.'

'Is your father in?'

'No. He had to go to the office. Mother's in her room, but I haven't seen her yet this morning.'

They went along the corridor, then along another which cut across the first at right angles. As they passed an open door through which Maigret saw an unmade bed and a breakfast tray, she explained, 'That's my room. Don't look at it. It's very untidy.'

Antoine's room was two doors farther along. It looked out on to the courtyard and at that time of day gathered in the sun's oblique rays. The Scandinavian furniture was simple and harmonious. On a stretch of wall there were shelves full of books, records and, on two shelves, cassette tapes.

On the desk there were books, notebooks, coloured pencils and, on a glass plate, three miniature tortoises swimming in about three-quarters of an inch of water.

'Was your brother fond of animals?'

'He had grown out of it a bit. There was a time when he brought home all kinds of creatures, a crow with a broken wing, for example, hamsters, white mice, a snake more than a yard long. He tried to tame them but he never succeeded.'

There was also an enormous globe on a stand, and a flute lying on a table, and some sheet music.

'Did he play the flute?'

'He had five or six lessons. There must be an electric guitar around somewhere too. He took piano lessons. . . .'

Maigret smiled.

'Not for long, I imagine.'

'His enthusiasms never lasted long.'

'Except for his tape-recorder.'

'That's true. That craze has gone on for nearly a year.'

'Did he have any idea what he was going to do with his future?'

'No. Or if he did he didn't tell anyone. Papa would have liked him to enrol in the Faculty of Science and take a degree in chemistry, so that he could take over the business later.'

'He didn't agree?'

'He hated the business world. I think he was ashamed to be the son of Mylène perfumes.'

'How do you feel about it?'

'I don't care one way or the other.'

One felt at ease in that room, among objects which differed widely, it is true, but one had the feeling that they were well-loved things. Someone had really lived in that room and had made it his kingdom.

Maigret picked out one of the cassettes on the shelves at random but there was only a number on it.

'The exercise book he used as a catalogue should be here,' said Minou. 'Wait a minute.'

She opened and shut drawers, most of them full. Certain objects and papers must have dated from his first years at the lycée.

'Here. I should think it's up to date, because he took it very seriously.'

It was an ordinary exercise book with squared paper. On the cover, Antoine had written 'My Experiences' in ornate lettering, with pencils of various colours.

It began with:

'Cassette 1: The family at table one Sunday.'

'Why a Sunday?' Maigret asked.

'Because my father rarely comes home to lunch on weekdays. And in the evening my mother and he often have dinner in town, or they have guests. . . .'

So he had still reserved his first recording for the family.

'Cassette 2: The Southern motorway one Saturday evening.

'Cassette 3: Forest of Fontainebleau, at night.
'Cassette 4: The Metro at 8 p.m.
'Cassette 5: Noon in the Place de l'Opéra.'

Then there was an interval at the Théâtre de la Gymnase, the sounds of a supermarket in the Rue de Ponthieu, and the drugstore in the Champs-Elysées.

'Cassette 10: A café in Puteaux.'

His curiosity began to cover a wider field and by slow degrees he changed social strata: a factory at knocking-off time, dance-halls in the Rue du Lappe, a bar in the Rue des Gravilliers, the neighbourhood of the Saint-Martin canal, a Bal des Fleurs at La Villette, a café at Saint-Denis.

He was no longer interested in the centre of Paris but in the periphery, and one of the addresses was on the edge of a shanty-town built out of tin cans and boxes.

'Was it really dangerous?'

'More or less. Let's say it wasn't to be recommended, and he was right not to take you with him. The people who frequent such places don't like anyone sticking his nose into their affairs, particularly with a tape-recorder.'

'Do you think that's why . . . ?'

'I don't know. I'm doubtful. To be sure, I'd have to hear all his tapes. From what I can see, that would take hours, if not several days.'

'You're not going to do that?'

'If I could take them away temporarily, I would give one of my detectives the job of . . .'

'I couldn't dare take that responsibility on my own. Since his death, my brother has become sacred and everything which was his has taken on a new value. Do you understand? Before, they treated him rather like an overgrown schoolboy, which made him furious. It's true that in certain respects he had remained very young. . . .'

Maigret's glance slid over the walls, over nude photographs cut out of an American magazine.

'That's very young too,' she interrupted his thoughts. 'I'm sure my brother has never slept with a girl. He went out with two or three of my friends but never went all the way . . .'

'Did he have a car?'

'My parents gave him a little English car for his twentieth birthday. For two months he spent all his time out in the country and he fitted the car out with every imaginable accessory. After that he wasn't interested in it any more and he only took it out when he really needed it.'

'Not for his nocturnal expeditions?'

'Never. I'm going to ask mother if I can let you have the cassettes. I hope she's up.'

It was ten-thirty. The girl was away for quite some time.

'She trusts you,' she announced on her return. 'All she wants is for you to catch the murderer. By the way, my father is even more overwhelmed than she is. It was his only son. Since it happened, he doesn't speak to us and he goes off early to the office. . . . How are we going to wrap that lot up? It needs a suitcase, or a big box. A suitcase would be best. Hold on—I think I know where to find what we need.'

The suitcase she brought in a few moments later bore the golden crown of the leather-merchant in the Rue Royale.

'Do you know Philippe Lherbier?'

'My parents know him. They've been to dinner at his house two or three times, but he's not what you might call a friend. He's the man who's always getting divorced, isn't he?'

'His country house was burgled last night. Didn't you hear on the radio?'

'I only listen to it on the beach, for the music.'

She helped him to stack the cassettes in the suitcase, and she added the exercise book which served as a catalogue.

'Haven't you anything more to ask me? You can come and question me at any time and I promise you I'll answer as frankly as I have up till now.'

She was clearly excited to be helping the police.

'I won't show you out, because I'm not dressed for going past the room where he is. People would take that as a lack of respect. Why must they suddenly respect someone when he's dead, when they didn't pay any attention to him when he was alive?'

Maigret went out, a little embarrassed by his suitcase,

particularly when he passed the concierge. He was lucky enough to see a woman get out of a taxi and pay the driver, so that he didn't have to wait to find one.

'Quai des Orfèvres.'

He wondered whom he would give Antoine Batille's tape-recordings to. It had to be someone who knew the places where the recordings had been made and who was familiar with the people who frequented them.

He ended up by going along to the end of the corridor to find his colleague in the Social Division—a euphemism for the Vice Squad.

Since he was carrying the suitcase, his colleague asked ironically:

'Have you come along to say good-bye before leaving us for good?'

'I have some tape-recordings here, most of them made around the periphery of Paris—dance-halls, cafés, bistros . . .'

'Should I be interested?'

'Perhaps not, but I am, and they may have a connection with a case I have in hand.'

'The Rue Popincourt case?'

'Just between you and me, yes. I would rather no one else knew that. You must have someone amongst your men who knows those places and to whom these recordings might mean something.'

'I'm with you. Nose out a dangerous character, for example. A man who, if he were afraid he'd be incriminated . . .'

'That's it exactly.'

'Old Mangeot. He has almost forty years' service. He knows the animal-life of these places better than anyone.'

Maigret knew him.

'Is he free?'

'I'll fix it so that he is.'

'Does he know how to work these things? I'll go and get the tape-recorder from my office.'

When he came back, a sad-faced man, soft-featured, no sparkle in his eyes, was standing in the office of the Vice Squad chief.

He was one of the little men of the Police Judiciare, one of those who, through the lack of a certain basic education, remain unpromoted all their lives. These men, since they go all over Paris on foot, acquire the walk of maîtres d'hotel and waiters, people who are on their feet all day. One might even say that they become the same dull colour as the poor streets they pace along.

'I know how to work those things,' he said at once. 'Are there a lot of cassettes?'

'About fifty—maybe a few more.'

'At half an hour per cassette. Is it urgent?'

'Fairly urgent.'

'I'll give him an office where he won't be disturbed,' intervened the chief of the erstwhile Vice Squad.

They explained carefully to Mangeot what was expected of him, and he nodded to show that he understood, then went off carrying the suitcase while Maigret's colleague murmured:

'Don't worry. He looks senile. It's true that he has no illusions left, but he's still one of my best men. A sort of bloodhound. You let him get the scent and he's off, head down. . . .'

Maigret went back to his office and ten minutes later the magistrate telephoned him.

'I've tried several times to get you since . . . First of all I must congratulate you on last night's haul.'

'The men from the Rue des Saussaies did it all.'

'I've been to see the public prosecutor, who is delighted. They're bringing me the four rascals at three this afternoon. I'd like you to be in my office, because you know the case better than me. When I've finished with the burglaries you can take them down to your office if you think fit. I know you have your own way of carrying out your interrogations.'

'Thank you. I'll be in your office at three o'clock.'

He pushed open the door of the inspectors' office.

'Are you free for lunch, Janvier?'

'Yes, chief. I just have to finish my report and then . . .'

Always reports and paperwork.

'What about you, Lapointe?'

'You know I'm always free. . . .'

220

For that meant that the three of them were going to have lunch together in the Brasserie Dauphine.

'Meet you at twelve-thirty.'

Maigret remembered to ring his wife and she, as usual, did not fail to ask:

'Do you think you'll be back for dinner? It's a pity about lunch. I'd got *escargots*.'

As if by chance, each time that he did not go home for a meal, the dish which had been prepared was one which he particularly liked.

After all, there might be *escargots* at the Brasserie Dauphine, too.

When, at three o'clock, Maigret entered the long corridor with magistrates' offices opening off it on both sides, photographers' flashguns went off while ten or eleven reporters rushed towards him.

'Have you come to listen to the interrogation of the gang?'

He tried to slip through without answering yes or no.

'Why are you here and not Superintendent Grosjean?'

'For heaven's sake, I don't know. Ask the magistrate.'

'You're in charge of the Rue Popincourt case, aren't you?'

He had no reason to deny it.

'Might there be a connection between the two cases?'

'Gentlemen, I have nothing to say at the moment.'

'But you aren't denying it?'

'You'd be making a mistake to draw any conclusions.'

'You were at Jouy-en-Josas last night, weren't you?'

'I don't deny that.'

'Why?'

'My colleague Grosjean can tell you that better than I.'

'Did your men get on the track of the thieves in Paris?'

The four men arrested the previous night were seated on two benches, one on each side of the magistrate's door, handcuffed and between policemen, and they were watching the scene not without some amusement.

At the far end of the corridor a counsel appeared, a short man, but broad. He was robed and looked as if he were

221

flapping his wings. When he saw the superintendent he walked over to him and shook him by the hand.

'How are you, Maigret?'

A flash. The handshake had been photographed just as if the scene had been rehearsed.

'Why are you here, in fact?'

Maître Huet asked this question in front of the photographers, and he did not do so by chance. He was a clever man, wily even, who was accustomed to defending the big mobsmen. A very cultured man, a lover of music and the theatre, he was at all the first-nights and went to all the big concerts, which had made him a part of fashionable Paris.

'Why are we waiting to go in?'

'I don't know,' replied Maigret not without irony.

And the small, broad-shouldered man knocked at the magistrate's door, pushed it open and signalled the superintendent to go in with him.

'How do you do, my dear magistrate. I hope you aren't too upset at seeing me here. My clients . . .'

The magistrate shook hands with him and then with Maigret.

'Sit down, gentlemen. I'm going to have the prisoners brought in. I assume they won't frighten you and that I can leave the policemen outside?'

He had the handcuffs removed. The office, which was not large, was full. The clerk sat at one end of the table which served as a desk. They had to look for an extra chair in a storeroom. The four men sat on both sides of their lawyer and Maigret sat a little apart, in the background.

'As you know, Maître, I must first establish the identity of the prisoners. Each of you answer when I call out your name. Julien Mila.'

'Here.'

'Your surname, Christian names, place of residence, date and place of birth, profession. . . .'

'Mila with a "t"?' asked the clerk who was taking it all down.

'Just with an "a".'

That took a long time. Demarle, the man with the scar and the muscles of a fairground wrestler, had been born in Quimper. He had been a sailor and was at present on the dole.

'Your address?'

'Sometimes here, sometimes there. I can always find a friend who'll take me in.'

'So in other words, you have no fixed address?'

'Well, with what we get on the dole . . .'

The fourth man, the look-out, was a poor, unhealthy-looking man who said that he was a commissionaire and that he lived in the Rue du Mont-Cenis, in Montmartre.

'How long have you been a member of the gang?'

'Excuse me, Magistrate,' Huet interrupted. 'It must first be established that there is a gang, and . . .'

'I was just about to ask you a question, Maître. Which of these men do you represent?'

'All four of them.'

'Do you not think that in the course of the interrogation there might be a conflict between them due to a divergence of interests?'

'I very much doubt it, and, if it should happen, I would have recourse to a colleague. Does that suit you, gentlemen?'

All four nodded.

'Since we are dealing with preliminary questions, I might have said with questions of ethics,' Huet continued with a smile which boded ill, 'you should know that since this morning there has been a great deal of interest shown in the case by the press. I have had a great number of telephone calls and through them I have obtained information which has surprised, not to say shocked, me.'

He turned his back and lit a cigarette. The magistrate, confronted by such a shining light of the legal profession, could not but be nervous.

'Go on.'

'The arrest, in fact, was not made in the way usual to arrests of this nature. Three radio cars, one of them filled with plain-clothes detectives, arrived on the scene at approximately the same time as my clients, as if the police knew what was going to happen. And, at the head of this procession we find Super-intendent Maigret, whom we have here with us, and two of his colleagues. Is that not so, Superintendent?'

'That is so.'

'I see that my informant was not mistaken.'

Someone from the Rue des Saussaies probably, perhaps a clerk or a typist.

'I believed, I have always believed, that the territory covered by the Police Judiciaire was limited to Paris. Let us say, to Greater Paris, and Jouy-en-Josas does not even belong to that.'

He had got what he wanted. He had forced the direction of the questioning and the magistrate did not know how to silence him.

'Would it not be because the information about this, let us say this attempted burglary, came to the ears of the Police Judiciaire? Have you nothing to say, Maigret?'

'I have nothing to say.'

'Were you not there?'

'I am not here to be questioned.'

'Nevertheless, I am going to ask you another, more important question. Is it not true that while you were dealing with another case, itself a recent one, you chanced on this one?'

Maigret still did not reply.

'Maître, please,' interrupted the magistrate.

'One moment. Detectives of the Police Judiciaire were pointed out to me as having kept watch these past two days opposite Emile Branchu's shop. Superintendent Maigret himself was seen twice the day before yesterday in a café in the Place de la Bastille where my clients meet from time to time, and he questioned the waiters and tried to extract information from the proprietor. Is that not so? Forgive me, Magistrate, but I have to put this case in its true perspective, which is perhaps not that of which you are aware.'

'Have you finished, Maître?'

'For the time being.'

'May I question the first prisoner? Julien Mila, be so good as to tell me who pointed out Philippe Lherbier's villa to you and who told you about the valuable paintings in it.'

'I advise my client not to answer.'

'I shall not answer.'

'You are suspected of having taken part in twenty-one burglaries of villas and châteaux which have occurred under the same conditions in the past two years.'

'I have nothing to say.'

'Particularly,' interrupted the lawyer, 'since you have no proof.'

'I shall repeat my first question, making it more general. Who pointed out these villas and châteaux to you? Who, and it is obviously the same person, took the responsibility of selling the stolen paintings and objets d'art?'

'I don't know a thing about any of that.'

The magistrate, sighing, moved on to the picture-framer, and Mimile was no more talkative. As for Demarle-the-Sailor, he amused himself by being funny.

The only one to have a different attitude was the look-out, the man called Gouvion, who had no fixed address.

'I don't know what I'm doing here. I don't know these men. I was round there looking for a place to sleep which wouldn't be too cold.'

'Is that your point of view, Maître?'

'I am in complete agreement with what he says and I must point out to you that this man has no criminal record.'

'Has no one anything to add?'

'I want to ask one question, at the risk of repeating myself. What part does Superintendent Maigret play in this? And what is going to happen once we leave this office?'

'I do not have to answer you.'

'Does that mean that there is going to be another interrogation, not in the Palais de Justice, but in one of the offices of the Police Judiciaire, where I have no right of entry? In other words, will it be a question not of a burglary but of quite another case?'

'I am sorry, Maître, but I have nothing to say to you. Please ask your clients to sign the provisional report which will be typed, in quadruplicate, by tomorrow.'

'You may sign, gentlemen.'

'Thank you, Maître.'

And, getting up, the magistrate went towards the door, followed closely by the lawyer.

'I have made all my objections.'

'And I have noted them.'

Then, to the policemen:

'Put the handcuffs back on the prisoners and take them to the Police Judiciaire. You may go through the communicating door. Would you wait here a moment, please, Superintendent?'

Maigret sat down again.

'What do you think about that?'

'I think that at this very moment Maître Huet is busy telling the press all about it and making it seem absurdly important, so that by tomorrow, even by tonight in the later editions, it will run to two columns.'

'Does that worry you?'

'I'm not sure. A few moments ago, I would have said yes. My intention was to keep the two cases quite apart from each other and to keep the papers from mixing them up. But now . . .'

He reflected, weighing the pros and cons.

'Perhaps it's better this way. If they stir things up, there's a chance that . . .'

'Do you think that one of those four men . . .'

'I can't say anything for sure. It seems that a Swedish knife like the one used in the Rue Popincourt has been found in the sailor's pocket. The man was wearing a light-coloured, belted raincoat and a brown hat. In any case, probably this evening, I shall let the Pagliatis see him, in the same street, under the same lighting conditions, but it's not conclusive. The old woman from the first floor will be called to identify him too.'

'What are you hoping for?'

'I don't know. The burglaries are the affair of the Rue des Saussaies. What I'm interested in are the seven stab-wounds which took a young man's life.'

When he left the magistrate's office, the reporters had disappeared, but he found them in full strength, more of them even, in the corridor of the Police Judiciaire. The four suspects were not in sight, for they had been taken into an office where they would be out of the public eye.

'What's going on, Superintendent?'

'Nothing out of the ordinary.'

'Why are those four men here instead of being taken back to the Rue des Saussaies?'

He made a sudden decision. Huet had certainly told them that there was a connection between the two cases. Instead of seeing them publish information which was true and false in various degrees, would it not be better to tell them the truth?

'Antoine Batille, gentlemen, had one passion in life: to record what he called "living documents". With his tape-recorder slung over his shoulder, he went into public places, cafés, bars, dance-halls, restaurants, even into the metro, and quietly switched on his toy.

'On Tuesday evening, at about nine-thirty, he was in a café in the Place de la Bastille and, as usual, he had turned his machine on. His neighbours were . . .'

'The thieves?'

'Three of them. The look-out was not there. The recording is not very good. Still, one can hear that a meeting had been arranged for the day after next, and that a certain villa was even then being given the once-over.

'Less than an hour later, in the Rue Popincourt, the young man was attacked from behind and stabbed seven times, one of the wounds being fatal.'

'Do you think it was one of these men?'

'I don't think anything, gentlemen. My job is not to think, but to get proofs or confessions.'

'Did anyone see the assailant?'

'Two passers-by, some distance away, and a lady living right opposite the spot where the murder was committed.'

'Do you think that the thieves realized that their plans had been recorded?'

'Again, I don't think anything. It's a plausible hypothesis.'

'In that case Batille must have been followed by one of them until he was in a quiet enough spot and . . . Did the murderer take the tape-recorder away?'

'No.'

'How do you explain that?'

'I don't explain it.'

'The passers-by you mentioned. I suppose you mean the Pagliati couple. You see, we know more than it appears. Then, when they started to run, did the Pagliatis stop the man from . . .'

'No. He had only struck four times. After going off, he came back on his tracks to strike again three more times. So he could have snatched the tape-recorder from the victim's neck.'

'So you're really nowhere?'

'I am going to question these gentlemen.'

'Together?'

'One by one.'

'Beginning with which one?'

'With Yvon Demarle, the sailor.'

'When will you have finished?'

'I don't know. One of you can stay here . . .'

'And the rest of us go and have a beer! That's a good idea! Thanks, Superintendent.'

Maigret too would gladly have had a beer. He went into his office and called in Lapointe, who could take down shorthand.

'Sit there. Take it all down.'

Then, to Janvier:

'Go and get me Demarle, would you?'

The ex-sailor appeared in front of them, his hands together.

'Take the bracelets off. Sit down, Demarle.'

'What are you going to do to me? Grill me? I might as well tell you straight away that I'm tough and I won't let myself be caught out.'

'Is that all?'

'I just wonder why I was allowed a lawyer with me up there, and here I'm all on my own.'

'Maître Huet will tell you about that when he sees you again. There was a Swedish knife among the objects taken from you. . . .'

'Is that why you've brought me here? I've carried that in my pocket for twenty years. It was a present from my brother,

228

when I was still a fisherman in Quimper, before I went on the liners.'

'How long is it since you've used it?'

'I use it every day to cut up my meat, country style. It's maybe not very elegant, but . . .'

'On Tuesday evening you were in the Café des Amis, in the Place de la Bastille, with your two friends.'

'That's what you say. But I can never remember in the morning what I did the night before. I don't seem to have a very strong head.'

'Mila was there, and the picture-framer, and you. You talked, in more or less guarded words, about the burglary, and you were given the task, among other things, of getting a car. Where did you steal it from?'

'What?'

'The car.'

'What car?'

'I suppose you don't know where the Rue Popincourt is, either?'

'I don't come from Paris.'

'Did none of the three of you notice that a young man at the next table had switched on a tape-recorder?'

'A what?'

'You didn't follow that young man?'

'Why should I? Believe me, I'm not that kind.'

'Your confederates didn't order you to come back with the cassette?'

'That's great! A cassette, now. Is that all?'

'That's all.'

And, to Janvier:

'Take him to an empty office. The same thing.'

Janvier was going to repeat the questions, more or less in the same words and in the same order. When he had finished, another inspector would take over.

Maigret didn't pin his hopes on it, in the circumstances, but it was still the most effective method. It could go on for hours. One interrogation like that had gone on for thirty-six hours before the man concerned, who had come in as a witness, confessed his crime. Three or four times during the interrogation the policemen had been on the point of releasing him, so well did he play the innocent.

Maigret went in to the inspectors' office. 'Go and get Mila for me,' he said to Lourtie.

The bartender knew very well he was a good-looking man, more intelligent, more aware than the others. One would swear that he enjoyed the part he was playing.

'Oh! Isn't my mouthpiece here?'

He pretended to look around for the lawyer.

'Do you think it's in order for you to question me when he isn't here?'

'That's my business.'

'What I mean is, I wouldn't like the whole procedure to be declared irregular because of one little thing.'

'What was the reason for your first conviction?'

'I don't remember. Anyway, it's up there in Records. You see, even if I haven't had anything to do with you personally, I know the place a bit.'

'When did you realize that your conversation was being recorded?'

'What conversation are you talking about, and what recording?'

Maigret was patient enough to ask his questions to the very end, although he knew all the time that there was no point. And Lourtie would repeat them untiringly, just as Janvier was now doing with the sailor.

Then it was the picture-framer's turn.

At first he seemed timid, but he was just as unshakable as the others.

'How long have you been burgling empty houses?'

'I beg your pardon?'

'I said how long . . .'

Maigret was hot and the sweat stuck to his back. The men had agreed among themselves. Each one played his part without letting himself be caught out by any unexpected question.

The commissionaire-tramp held to his story. First, he wasn't at the meeting in the Place de la Bastille. Then, on the Thursday evening, he was looking for a 'crib', as he called it.

'In an empty house?'

'As long as the door is open. . . . In the house or in the garage.'

At six o'clock in the evening the four men went back in a police car to the Rue des Saussaies, where they spent the night.

'Is that you, Grosjean? Thank you for lending them to me. No, I didn't get anything out of them. They're no choirboys.'

'You're telling me! Thursday's burglary, that'll stick, since they were caught in the act. But as for the other burglaries, if we don't get any proof or any witnesses . . .'

'You'll see, when the papers put it out, witnesses will spring up all around.'

'Do you think one of those four did the job in the Rue Popincourt?'

'Not really.'

'Have you any suspicions?'

'No.'

'What are you going to do?'

'Wait.'

And that was true. Already the evening papers were putting out in their final editions the account of what had happened in the corridor outside the magistrate's office and then the statement Maigret had made in the Police Judiciaire.

'*Is this the Rue Popincourt murderer?*'

Below this question was the photograph of Yvon Demarle, handcuffed, by magistrate Poiret's door.

Maigret looked in the telephone directory for the number of the flat in the Quai d'Anjou, and dialled it.

'Hello, who is speaking?'

'This is Monsieur Batille's valet.'

'Is Monsieur Batille at home just now?'

'H⁀ has not come home yet. I think he had an appointment to see his doctor.'

'This is Superintendent Maigret. When is the funeral?'

'Tomorrow at ten.'

'Thank you.'

At last. Maigret's day was over and he rang his wife to say he'd be back for dinner.

'We'll go to the pictures afterwards,' he added.

To get things out of his mind.

CHAPTER FIVE

JUST TO MAKE SURE, Maigret had young Lapointe go with him. They both stood in the crowd, on the embankment side of the street, not opposite the house of the dead boy, but opposite the house next door, for there were so many onlookers that they hadn't been able to get a better place.

There were cars, among them many chauffeur-driven limousines, all along the embankments from the Pont Louis-Philippe to the Pont Sully, and others were parked on the other side of the island on the Quai de Béthune and the Quai d'Orléans.

It was a cold morning, the weather crisp, very clear, very bright, pastel-coloured.

They saw the cars stop in front of the black-draped front door, people go upstairs where they bowed to the coffin before reappearing and waiting outside for the procession to form.

A red-haired photographer, bareheaded, walked about pointing his lens at the rows of spectators. He was not always well-received, and some of them did not hesitate to tell him what they thought of him.

He still went on with his work, unmoved. The people, particularly those who grumbled, would have been very surprised to learn that he did not belong to a newspaper, an agency or a magazine, but that he was there on Maigret's orders.

Maigret had gone up to the Criminal Identity laboratory very early and, with Moers's help, had chosen Van Hamme, the best and, more important, the most resourceful of the available photographers.

'I want photographs of all the onlookers, first outside the house, then outside the church, when the coffin is taken in and again when it comes out, and finally at the cemetery.

'When the pictures are developed, look at them carefully

233

with a magnifying glass. It is possible that one or more people will be at all three places. Those are the ones I'm interested in. You'll need to enlarge them for me, without the surrounding figures.'

In spite of himself Maigret was watching for a light-coloured belted raincoat and a dark hat. There was not much chance that the murderer had kept those clothes, for the morning papers had described them. For the present the two cases, the Rue Popincourt case and the burglary, were definitively intertwined.

In one of the papers, under the picture of Demarle the sailor, in his raincoat and brown hat, was printed:

IS THIS THE MURDERER?

The crowd was a mixture of types. First of all, near the house, were those who had been to pay their last respects to the dead boy and who were waiting to take their place in the procession. On the edge of the pavement it was mainly those who lived on the island, the concierges and the shopkeepers of the Rue Saint-Louis-en-l'Ile.

'Such a nice boy! . . . And so shy! . . . When he came into the shop he always raised his hat. . . .'

'If only he had had his hair cut a little shorter. . . . His parents should have told him. . . . Elegant people like them! . . . It made him look disreputable. . . .'

From time to time Maigret and Lapointe exchanged a look and an absurd idea came into Maigret's head. How excited inwardly Antoine Batille would have been, walking among this crowd with his microphone, had he been alive. Of course, if he had been alive there would not have been any crowd.

The hearse appeared and parked at the kerb, followed by three other cars. Were they going to drive to the church of Saint-Louis-en-l'Ile, only two hundred yards away?

The undertaker's men first brought down the wreaths and sprays. Not only was the roof of the hearse covered, but the flowers filled the three cars.

Among the waiting crowd there was a third category, in little groups, the employees of Mylène perfumes. Lots of girls and young women dressed with an elegance which, in the morning sunlight, had something aggressive about it.

There was a movement in the crowd like a current passing from one end of the rows to the other, and then the coffin, carried by six men, came into view. Once it had been slid into the hearse, the family appeared. At their head, Gérard Batille was framed by his wife and daughter. His features were drawn, his complexion blotchy. He did not look at anyone but seemed surprised to see so many flowers.

One could tell that he was out of touch with reality, that he hardly noticed what was going on around him. Madame Batille showed more composure, even though at intervals she dabbed her eyes through the filmy black veil which covered her face.

Minou, the sister, whom Maigret saw for the first time in black, seemed taller and thinner, and she was the only one to pay any attention to her surroundings.

Other photographers, those of the press, took some photographs. Aunts, uncles and relatives of varying degrees of closeness followed, and also, undoubtedly, the top ranks of the employees of the firm manufacturing perfumes and beauty products.

The hearse moved off, the cars full of flowers and the family fell into place behind, then the friends, students, teachers and finally the local shopkeepers.

A certain number of those who had been standing went in the direction of the Pont-Marie or the Pont-Sully to get back to work, but there were others who went to the church.

Maigret and Lapointe were among the latter. They followed the procession along the street and in the Rue Saint-Louis-en-l'Ile they came upon another crowd of people who had not been present in the Quai d'Anjou. The church was already more than half full. From the street one could hear the solemn murmur of the organ as the coffin was carried as far as the catafalque, half of which was completely covered with flowers.

Many people remained outside. The doors were not closed again and the prayers of intercession for the dead boy began while the sun and fresh air were streaming into the church.

'*Pater noster . . .*'

The priest, a very old man, walked around the catafalque shaking his sprinkler of holy water, then again swinging his censer.

'*Et ne nos inducat in tentationem . . .*'

'*Amen . . .*'

Outside, Van Hamme was still working.

'Which cemetery?' asked Lapointe in a whisper, leaning over Maigret's shoulder.

'Montparnasse. The Batilles have a family vault there.'

'Are we going there?'

'I don't think so.'

Luckily many policemen had come to direct traffic. The immediate family took their seats in the first car. The more distant relatives followed, then came Batille's colleagues, then friends who ran to get their cars and tried to thrust their way through the crowd.

Van Hamme had taken the precaution of being brought by a little black car belonging to the Police Judiciaire which was waiting for him at a strategic point and which took him in at the last moment.

The crowd dispersed little by little. A few groups remained talking on the pavements.

'We can go back,' sighed Maigret.

They crossed the little bridge behind Notre Dame and stopped at a bar on the corner of the Boulevard du Palais.

'What will you have?'

'A white wine. . . . Vouvray.'

Because the word Vouvray was chalked on the windows.

'Me too. Two Vouvrays.'

It was almost noon when Van Hamme came into Maigret's office, holding some prints.

'I haven't finished, but I wanted to show you something now. There are three of us studying the photographs with a strong magnifying glass. This man caught my eye at once.'

The first print, on the Quai d'Anjou, only showed a part of the body and face, for there was a woman pushing from the side, forcing herself through to the front row.

The man undoubtedly wore a light beige raincoat and a dark hat. He was quite young, about thirty. His face was unremarkable and he seemed to be frowning as if there were something near him which offended him.

'Here's a rather better one.'

The same face, enlarged. The mouth was thickish, rather sulky, and the expression was that of a timid man.

'It's on the Quai d'Anjou too. We'll see if he appears in the photographs taken at the church. They're being developed now. I brought these down because of the raincoat.'

'Weren't there any other raincoats?'

'Quite a number, but only three belted ones, one of them a middle-aged man with a beard, and one a man of about forty, hatless and smoking a pipe.'

'Bring me down anything else you find, after lunch.'

In truth, the raincoat did not mean very much. If Batille's murderer had read the morning papers, he knew that they had published his description. Why, then, would he wear the same clothes as he had that evening in the Rue Popincourt? Because he had no others? As an act of defiance?

Maigret had lunch at the Brasserie Dauphine again, with Lapointe only, since Janvier and Lucas were out.

At half past two Maigret had a telephone call which made him relax a little. It seemed that suddenly a lot of his troubles were melting away.

'Hello, Superintendent Maigret? Please hold on. Our editor, Monsieur Frémiet, would like to speak to you.'

'Hello, is that you, Maigret?'

The two men had known each other for many years. Frémiet was the editor of one of the largest morning papers.

'I haven't called to see how your investigation is coming on. I'm taking the liberty of ringing you because we have just received a rather odd communication. Besides, it came by *pneumatique*, which is rare for an anonymous letter.

'You know we published the photographs of the members of the Jouy-en-Josas gang this morning? Under the photograph of the sailor, my writer had them print the phrase "Is this the murderer?"'

'I saw that.'

'What was sent to me was this cutting with one word, written in green ink in capital letters: NO!'

It was at that moment that Maigret's face brightened.

'If you will allow me, I'll send a messenger over for the message. Do you know which *pneumatique* office it was handed in at?'

'The Rue du Faubourg-Montmartre. May I ask you, Superintendent, not to pass the tip on to my rival editors? I can't publish the document until tomorrow morning. It has been photographed already and we're going to make a block . . . unless you want us to keep it secret.'

'No. On the contrary. I would even like you to comment on it. Just a minute. . . . The best thing would be if you could say you were of the opinion that it's a hoax, underlining the fact that the real murderer would not risk compromising himself in such a way.'

'I think I know what you're getting at.'

'Thank you, Frémiet. I'll send someone over for it straight away.'

He went into the inspectors' office, sent one of them over to the Champs-Elysées and asked Lapointe to follow him into his office.

'You look very happy, chief.'

'Only a little! Only a little! There's still a chance I might be wrong.'

He repeated the story of the photograph cut out of the paper and the NO in green ink.

'I even like that green ink.'

'Why?'

'Because the man who stabbed seven times, in two goes, if one can say that, in the pouring rain, while a couple are walking along the street and a woman is looking out of the window, is not quite an ordinary man.

'I've often found that people who use green ink, or red ink, have a great need to make themselves conspicuous. For them it's only one way of doing that.'

'Do you mean he's a nutcase?'

'I wouldn't go quite that far. Many people would say an eccentric. There are all kinds of eccentrics.'

Van Hamme came into the office. This time he carried a thick bundle of photographs, some of which were still wet.

'Have you found the man in the raincoat anywhere else?'

'Apart from the family and their close friends, there are only three people found in all three places, at the Quai d'Anjou, outside the church and, finally, near the tomb in the Montparnasse cemetery.'

'Show me.'

'First this woman.'

A young woman, about twenty-five, with a grief-stricken face. It was obvious that she was upset and troubled. She was wearing a badly-cut black coat and her hair fell untidily down each side of her face.

'You told me only the men, but I thought . . .'

'I understand.'

Maigret looked at her intently, as if to pierce her secret. She looked like a working-class girl who did not pay much attention to her outward appearance.

Why was she as moved as the members of the family, more moved than Minou, for example?

Minou had told him that her brother had probably never slept with a woman. Was she so sure about that? Couldn't she be wrong? And couldn't Antoine have had a mistress?

Given the state of mind which his search for human voices in the lowest quarters of the city revealed, was it not a girl of this type who would be likely to interest him?

'In a moment, Lapointe, when we have finished, go back to the Ile Saint-Louis. I don't know why, but I see her as a shop girl, in a grocer's, or a dairy, perhaps. Maybe a waitress in a café or a restaurant.'

'A second person,' announced Van Hamme, showing an enlargement of a man of about fifty.

If his clothing had been a little more dishevelled, he might have been taken for a tramp. He stared straight in front, with a resigned look, and one wondered what there was in this funeral to interest him.

It wasn't easy to imagine him striking at a young man seven times with a knife and then running away. The murderer had not come into the area in a car, that was an established fact. It was more likely that he had taken the métro at the Voltaire station, close by the place where the crime had been committed. The ticket-collector had only a confused memory of the occasion, for six or seven people had appeared at the entrance to the platforms in the space of one or two minutes. He punched their tickets without raising his head. It was mechanical.

'If I had to look at everyone who went by, I'd be dizzy. Heads, more heads, Faces, almost always bad-tempered.'

Why had this man in the worn-out clothes stood in front of the house, then in front of the church, and why had he then gone to the Montparnasse cemetery?

'The third?' asked Maigret.

'You know him. The one I showed you this morning. You'll notice that he doesn't hide himself. He must have noticed me in all three places. Here, at the path in the cemetery, he is looking at me curiously, as if he were wondering why I was photographing the crowd and not the coffin or the family.'

'That's true. He doesn't look upset or worried. Leave these photographs with me. I'm going to look at them at leisure. Thank you, Van Hamme. Tell Moers I'm very pleased with your work.'

'So,' asked Lapointe, once he was alone with Maigret, 'I go over to the island and show people the photograph of the girl?'

'It's probably a wild goose chase, but it's worth trying. See if Janvier is here.'

He came straight into the office and looked curiously at the pile of photographs.

'Here, Janvier. I want you to go to the Sorbonne. I think you'll have no trouble at the office finding out what courses Antoine Batille went to most often.'

'I'm to question his friends?'

'Exactly. Perhaps he didn't have any real friends, but he must have talked to other students.

'Here's one photograph, of a girl who appeared to be very

upset at the funeral this morning and who went all the way to the cemetery. Maybe someone has seen him with her. . . . Maybe they've only heard him talk about her. . . .'

'Right.'

'This photograph is of a man in a raincoat who was at the Quai d'Anjou, then at the church and finally at the cemetery. Just in case, show it too. I hope there's a lecture this afternoon and that you'll be able to catch them coming out.'

'Will I not question the lecturer?'

'I don't think they have any opportunity to know their students. But here—here's another photo. It probably has nothing to do with the case, but we'd better not forget anything.'

A quarter of an hour later Maigret was brought the newspaper cutting with the word NO written on it in green ink. The word had been written in capital letters almost an inch high and had been underlined with a firm stroke. The exclamation point was a good half inch higher.

It looked like an angry protest. Whoever had written those letters must have been annoyed that anyone could mistake a miserable creature like the ex-sailor for the Rue Popincourt murderer.

Maigret sat still for more than a quarter of an hour in front of the newspaper cutting and the photographs, pulling gently on his pipe. After that, almost unconsciously, he lifted up the telephone receiver.

'Hello, Frémiet? I was afraid you might not still be there. Thank you for the document, which looks very interesting to me. I thought at first I'd put an advertisement in the personal column in tomorrow morning's paper, but he may not read the personal column.

'You'll undoubtedly have an article on the case. . . .'

'Our reporters are studying the previous burglaries. I have them working in a radius of fifty kilometres from Paris, showing photographs of the gang to all the neighbours of the houses which were robbed.'

'Could you put the following lines below the article, or articles?

' "Superintendent Maigret would like to know on what the man who sent the *pneumatique* to the newspaper bases his statement. He begs him to be so good as to get in touch with him, either by letter or by telephone, if he has any interesting information." '

'I understand. Could you repeat that, so that I can be sure I've got every word?'

Maigret repeated it patiently.

'Right. Not only will I print this announcement on the front page, I'll put it in a frame. You must know you'll get letters or phone calls from madmen.'

Maigret smiled.

'I'm used to that. You must be too, of course. Policemen and newspaper editors.'

'Good. Thank you for keeping me up to date.'

And the superintendent immersed himself in the evening papers which had just been brought to him, groaning each time he found a new error. There was an average of one, or at least an exaggeration, per paragraph, and the picture-thieves had become one of the most mysterious and best-organized gangs in Paris.

The final headline:

'*When will they arrest the Brain?*'

Just like the TV serials.

He had sent the article and the photograph of the sailor with the NO in green letters to the criminal anthropometry department so that they could get any fingerprints from it. The answer came back quickly.

'A thumbprint on the photograph, and a very good index finger on the back of the paper. These prints do not tally with any prints in the records.'

That meant, obviously, that Antoine Batille's murderer had never been arrested and, even more, that he had no convictions.

Maigret was not at all surprised and he was just about to start reading the papers again when Lapointe burst in, very excited.

'Some people get it with jam on, chief! I mean, what luck! And you were right. I was going across the footbridge and I found I had no more cigarettes. So I went down the Rue Saint-Louis-en-l'Ile, then into the *café-tabac* on the corner and who did I see?'

'The girl whose picture I gave you.'

'Exactly. She's a waitress there. Wears a black dress and a white apron. There was one table of belote players—the butcher, the grocer, the proprietor and a man who had his back to me. I picked up my cigarettes and went over and sat down.

'When she asked me what I wanted to drink, I ordered a coffee and she went and made me an expresso at the counter.

'"When do you close in the evenings?"

'She looked a bit surprised.

'"That depends on the evening. I finish at seven because it's me who opens in the mornings."

'She gave me my change and went off without paying any more attention to me. I decided not to speak to her in front of her boss. I thought you'd rather do it yourself.'

'You were right.'

'She always seemed on the point of tears. She walked about in a fog and her nose was red.'

Janvier didn't come back to the Quai until six o'clock.

'There was a sociology lecture and it seems he never cut that one. I waited in the courtyard. I watched the students sitting on their benches and then, when the lecture was over, they rushed outside.

'I buttonholed two or three without success.

'"Antoine Batille? The chap the papers are on about? I've seen him, yes, but we never spoke to each other. If you could possibly find a chap called Harteau . . ."

'The third student I collared looked around, called suddenly, turning to a young man who was moving off:

'"Harteau! Harteau! This man wants to talk to you."

'And then said to me:

'"I must go. I have to catch a train."

'Other students were going off on scooters and motor cycles.

243

"'Did you want to speak to me?" asked a tall young man with a pale face and light grey eyes.

"'I understand you were Antoine Batille's friend."

"'Friend is a bit strong. He didn't make friends easily. Let's say I was a friend and we sometimes talked out here in the courtyard and had a beer together from time to time. I only went to his house once and I didn't feel at ease. You see, my mother's a concierge in the Place Denfert-Rochereau. I'm not ashamed of it. But I didn't know how I ought to behave there."

"'Were you at the funeral this morning?"

"'Only at the church. After that I had an important lecture."

"'Do you know if your friend had any enemies?"

"'He certainly didn't have any."

"'Was he well-liked?"

"'He wasn't well-liked either. People didn't pay any attention to him any more than he did to them."

"'What about you? What did you think about him?"

"'He was a nice chap. He was much more sensitive than he let on. I think he was too sensitive and that he closed up very easily."

"'Did he ever talk to you about his tape-recorder?"

"'One day he even asked me to go with him. He was crazy about it. He said that people's voices are more revealing than their photographs. I remember something he said:

"'There are plenty of picture-hunters. I don't know any other sound-hunters."

"'He hoped to get one of the latest miniaturized microphones from Japan for Christmas. You can hold them in the palm of your hand. They aren't available in France yet, but it seems they're waiting for them to come in. He could only have known about them through magazine articles."'

Janvier had not forgotten to ask Harteau if Batille had a mistress.

"'A mistress, no. At least, not as far as I know. He wasn't the type. Besides, he was shy, reserved. And he had fallen in love a few weeks ago.

"'He couldn't help telling me. He had to tell someone, and

244

his sister usually laughed at him and said he was the girl of the family and she was the boy. . . .

"'I never saw the girl, but she works on the Ile Saint-Louis and he saw her every morning at eight o'clock. That's when she was alone in the café. The proprietor was still asleep and his wife was doing the housework upstairs.

"'They were interrupted incessantly by customers, but they still had some time alone together.'"

"'Was it really serious?'"

"'I think so.'"

"'What were his intentions?'"

"'In what way?'"

"'How did he see his future, for example?'"

"'He wanted to take anthropology next year. His dream was to be a teacher in Asia, in Africa, in South America, one after the other, so that he could study the different races. He wanted to prove that they are basically the same, that the differences between them will disappear when living conditions are the same everywhere.'"

"'Did he mean to get married?'"

"'He hadn't spoken about that yet. It had happened too recently. In any case, he didn't want to marry a girl with the same background as his.'"

"'Did he rebel against his parents, against his family?'"

"'Not even that. I remember he once said to me:

"'When I go home, it's like living in 1900.'"

"'Thank you. I'm sorry for taking up so much of your time.' '

And Janvier concluded:

'What do you think, chief? If the girl had a brother? If they'd gone farther than Harteau thinks? If the brother took it into his head that the son of Mylène perfumes would never marry his sister? You see what I mean? . . .'

'Now you're getting a bit 1900, aren't you, Janvier?'

'It still happens, doesn't it?'

'Haven't you read the statistics? So-called crimes of passion have dropped by more than half, so much so that they seem like a delightful anachronism.

245

'In fact, Lapointe has found her and she does work on the Ile Saint-Louis. I'm going to try to talk to her this evening.'

'What do I do now?'

'Nothing. Anything. We're waiting.'

At a quarter past six, Maigret had a drink in the Brasserie Dauphine, where he met two of his colleagues. At the Quai they often went for weeks without seeing each other, each one being almost shut up in his own branch. The Brasserie Dauphine was the neutral territory where everyone saw everyone else at last.

'Well what about the Rue Popincourt murder. Are you working for the Rue des Saussaies now?'

At ten minutes to seven, Maigret walked the short distance to the Rue Saint-Louis-en-l'Ile, and he could see the girl serving the customers in the *café-tabac*.

The proprietor's wife was at the cash-desk, the proprietor serving behind the bar. It was the short rush-hour of the early evening.

At five minutes past seven the girl went through a door and reappeared some moments later wearing the coat which he had seen in the photograph. She said a few words to the proprietor's wife and came out. She turned right in the direction of the Quai d'Anjou without looking around, and Maigret had to quicken his pace to catch up with her.

'Excuse me, Mademoiselle. . . .'

She mistook his intentions and was on the point of running.

'I am Superintendent Maigret. I wanted to talk to you about Antoine.'

She stopped short and looked at him with a sort of anguish.

'What did you say?'

'That I want to talk to you about . . .'

'I heard you. But I don't understand. I don't . . .'

'There's no point in denying it, Mademoiselle.'

'Who told you?'

'Your photograph, or rather your photographs. You were outside the house this morning, holding a handkerchief in your clenched fists. You were at the church when the funeral

246

party went in and when it came out and after that you were at the cemetery.'

'Why was I photographed?'

'If you would spare me a few minutes and walk along with me, I'll explain it to you. We are looking for Antoine Batille's killer. We haven't any real trail to follow, no useful clue. . . .

'In the hope that the murderer would be drawn to the funeral of his victim I had photographs taken of the rows of lookers-on. The photographer then found which people were to be found at the Quai d'Anjou, at the church and at the cemetery.'

She bit her lip. They were walking quite naturally the whole length of the embankment and they passed in front of the Batille's flat. The black hangings with their silver teardrops had disappeared. There were lights on all floors. The house had picked up its normal rhythm of life again.

'What do you want of me?'

'I want you to tell me all you know about Antoine. You are the person who was closest to him.'

She blushed suddenly.

'What makes you say that?'

'He was the one who said it, in a way. He had a friend at the Sorbonne. . . .'

'The concierge's son?'

'Yes.'

'He was his only friend. He didn't feel at ease with the others. He always felt he was different.'

'Well, he led this Harteau to understand that he intended to marry you one day.'

'Are you sure he said that?'

'He didn't say so to you?'

'No. I wouldn't have accepted. We don't belong to the same world. . . .'

'Perhaps he didn't belong to any world except his own.'

'Besides, his family . . .'

'How long had he known you?'

'Ever since I've worked at the *café-tabac*. That's four months. It was winter, I remember. It was snowing the first day I saw

247

him. He was buying a packet of Gitanes. He bought one every day.'

'How long was it before he waited for you coming out?'

'More than a month.'

'Did you become his mistress?'

'Just a week ago today.'

'Have you a brother?'

'I have two. One is in the army, in Germany, the other one works in Lyons.'

'Do you come from Lyons?'

'My father came from there. Now that he is dead, the family has scattered and I am alone in Paris with my mother. We live in the Rue Saint-Paul. I used to work in a department store, but I couldn't stick it. It was too tiring for me. When I learned they were looking for a waitress in the Rue Saint-Louis-en-l'Ile . . .'

'Didn't Antoine have any enemies?'

'Why would he have any enemies?'

'His passion for taking his tape-recorder into certain places with bad reputations.'

'No one paid any attention to him. He sat down in a corner or stood at the bar. He took me with him twice.'

'Did you meet every evening?'

'He came to meet me at the *tabac* and took me home. Once or twice a week we went to the pictures.'

'Will you tell me your name?'

'Mauricette.'

'Mauricette what?'

'Mauricette Gallois.'

They had retraced their steps slowly, crossed the Pont Saint-Marie and they were now in the Rue Saint-Paul.

'This is where I live. Have you anything else to ask me?'

'Not at the moment. Thank you very much, Mauricette. Don't lose heart.'

Maigret sighed, and, outside the Saint-Paul métro station, took a taxi which got him home in a few minutes. He forced himself not to think about his case and, after turning the television set on out of habit, he turned it off for fear that it would still be talking about the Rue Popincourt and the picture-thieves.

'What are you thinking?'

'That we're going out to the pictures and that it's almost warm this evening. We can walk as far as the Grands Boulevards.'

It was one of his most unfailing pleasures. After a few steps, Madame Maigret would take his arm and they would walk along slowly, stopping sometimes to look at a shop window. They didn't keep up a continuous conversation, but chatted about this and that, about a passing face, a dress, the last letter from his sister-in-law.

That evening, Maigret wanted to see a Western and they had to go right to the Porte Saint-Denis to find one. In the interval he treated himself to a glass of calvados and his wife had a *verveine*.

At midnight they put out the lights in their flat. The next day was a Saturday, the 22nd of March. The previous evening it had not occurred to Maigret that it was the first day of spring. It was up to time this year. He saw again in his mind's eye the morning light in the Quai d'Anjou, outside the house where the boy's body lay.

At nine o'clock he had a telephone call from Magistrate Poiret.

'Anything new, Maigret?'

'Not yet, Magistrate. At any rate, nothing definite.'

'You don't think that that sailor, what's his name again? . . . Yvon Demarle . . .'

'I'm sure that although he may be in up to his neck in the picture thefts, he has nothing to do with the Rue Popincourt murder.'

'Have you an idea?'

'It's beginning to get a bit clearer. It's too vague for me to tell you about it, but I'm waiting for certain developments to take place in a very short time.'

'A crime of passion?'

'I don't think so.'

'A sex crime?'

He hated such classifications.

'I don't think so.'

He did not have to wait long before learning something new. The telephone rang half an hour later. It was the chief reporter of one of the evening papers.

'Superintendent Maigret? Jean Rolland here. I'm not disturbing you, am I? Don't worry, I'm not ringing you for information, though of course if you have any it's always welcome.'

Maigret was not on particularly good terms with the editor of that particular paper, precisely because he was always complaining that he was not told about important things before anyone else.

'Our circulation is as big as three other papers put together. It would be only natural . . .'

It wasn't a quarrel between them, more a kind of a strained relationship. That was probably why the chief reporter was ringing and not the editor.

'Did you read our articles yesterday?'

'I looked through them.'

'We tried to analyse the possibility of a connection between the two cases. In the end we found as many points for as against. . . .'

'I know.'

'Well, this article brought us in a letter in this morning's post, which I'm going to read to you. . . .'

'Just a moment. Is the address written in block capitals?'

'That's right. The letter is, too.'

'I suppose it's written on ordinary paper like that sold in packets of six in tobacconists' and grocers'.'

'Right again. Did you get a letter, too?'

'No. Go on.'

'Here goes:

'"Dear Editor,

"I have read carefully the articles printed in the last few days in your worthy paper on the subject of what is called the Rue Popincourt Case and the Paintings Case. Your

250

writer tries, without any success, to establish a link between these two cases.

"I find it naïve on the part of the Press to think that young Batille was attacked in the Rue Popincourt because of a tape-recording. Besides, did the killer take his tape-recorder away?

"As for the sailor Demarle, he has never killed anyone with his Swedish knife.

"These knives are sold in all good ironmongers', and I have one too.

"But mine really did kill Antoine Batille. I am not boasting, believe me. I am not proud of it. But all this fuss tires me. And above all I would not like an innocent man like Demarle to pay for my crime.

"You may publish this letter if you see fit. I guarantee that it is the truth.

"Thank you. Yours very sincerely."'

Of course there was no signature.

'Do you think it's a joke, Superintendent?'

'No.'

'Can it be serious?'

'I'm sure it is. Obviously, I may be wrong, but there is every chance that this letter was written by the murderer. Look at the postmark and tell me where it was posted.'

'Boulevard Saint-Michel.'

'You may have it photographed in case you want to print a copy of it, but I would like it to be handled as little as possible.'

'Do you expect to find fingerprints?'

'I'm almost sure I shall find some.'

'Were there any on the newspaper cutting with the NO written on it in green ink?'

'Yes.'

'I read your appeal. Are you hoping the killer will telephone you?'

'If he's the kind of man I think he is, he will.'

'I suppose there's no point in asking you what kind of man you mean? . . . '

'That's right. At the moment I can say nothing. I shall send someone round to you to collect the letter and I'll give it back to you as soon as the case is over.'

'Fine. Good luck.'

Maigret turned towards the door, astonished. Joseph, the old usher, was framed in the doorway and behind him stood a man in a beige uniform with wide brown stripes down the sides of his trousers. His cap was beige too and bore a coat of arms with a golden crown.

'What is this?' the superintendent asked the intruder.

'I have a message from Monsieur Lherbier.'

'The leather-merchant?'

'Yes.'

'Are you waiting for a reply?'

'I was not told to, but I was ordered to give this parcel into your own hands. Monsieur Lherbier himself told me to do it, late yesterday afternoon.'

Maigret had unwrapped a beige cardboard box marked with the ubiquitous crown, and in this box he discovered a black crocodile wallet the corners of which were reinforced with gold. The crown was gold too.

A visiting-card bore simply the words:

'A token of my gratitude.'

The superintendent put the wallet back into its box.

'One moment,' he said to the man who had brought it. 'You will probably be more efficient than I would at retying the parcel.'

The man stared at him, surprised.

'Don't you like it?'

'Tell your employer that I never accept gifts. You may add, if you wish, that nevertheless I appreciate the gesture.'

'Won't you write to him?'

'No.'

The telephone rang insistently.

'Here, take it. Go and do up the packet in the waiting room. I am very busy.'

And once he was alone at last he picked up the receiver.

CHAPTER SIX

'IT IS SOMEONE who won't give his name, Superintendent. Shall I put him through to you anyway? He says you know who he is.'

'Put him through.'

He heard the click and said hello in a voice which was not quite his normal voice.

And, after a moment of silence, a speaker who seemed very far away repeated, like an echo, 'Hello.'

They were both very nervous, and Maigret made himself a promise that he would avoid saying anything which might frighten away the man he was speaking to.

'Do you know who this is talking to you?'

'Yes.'

'Do you know my name?'

'Your name is of no importance.'

'Aren't you going to try to find out where I'm ringing you from?'

The tone was hesitant. The man lacked assurance and was trying to bolster up his courage.

'No.'

'Why not?'

'Because I'm not interested in that.'

'Don't you believe me?'

'Yes, I do.'

'You believe that I'm the man in the Rue Popincourt?'

'Yes.'

This time there was quite a long silence, then the voice, shy and worried, asked:

'Are you still there?'

'Yes. I'm listening.'

'Has anyone brought you the letter I wrote to the paper yet?'

'No. It was read to me over the telephone.'

'Have you got the cutting with the photograph?'

'Yes.'

'You do believe me? You don't think I'm mad?'

'I've already told you so.'

'What do you think of me?'

'First of all, I know that you have never been convicted of any crime.'

'Because of my fingerprints?'

'Exactly. You are accustomed to leading a quiet, orderly life.'

'How did you guess that?'

Maigret did not say anything and the other man panicked again.

'Don't hang up.'

'Do you have a lot to tell me?'

'I don't know. Perhaps. I have nobody to talk to.'

'You aren't married, are you? No. You live alone. You have taken the day off today, perhaps by ringing your office and telling them you are ill.'

'You're trying to make me say things which will help you to trap me. Are you sure that some of your technicians aren't trying to find out where I'm speaking to you from?'

'I give you my word on that.'

'So you aren't in a hurry to arrest me.'

'I'm like you. I'm glad it's all over.'

'How do you know?'

'You have written to the papers.'

'I didn't want anyone to accuse an innocent man.'

'That wasn't the real reason.'

'Do you imagine that I am trying to be caught?'

'Subconsciously, yes.'

'What else do you think about me?'

'You feel lost.'

'The truth is, I'm afraid.'

'What are you afraid of? Being arrested?'

'No. It doesn't matter. I've already said too much. I wanted to talk to you and to hear your voice. Do you despise me?'

'I don't despise anyone.'

'Not even a criminal?'

'Not even a criminal.'

'You know you'll get me one of these days, don't you?'

'Yes.'

'Do you have any clues to my identity?'

Maigret almost told him, to get it over with, that he already had his photograph, first at the Quai d'Anjou, then in front of the church and finally at the Montparnasse cemetery.

He only had to have those pictures printed in the newspapers for a number of people to tell him the identity of Batille's murderer.

If he did not do it, it was because he had a hazy idea that in this particular case the man would not wait to be arrested and that it would certainly be a dead body which would be found at his home.

It had to come from within himself, slowly.

'There are always clues, but it is difficult to assess their worth.'

'I'm going to hang up soon.'

'What are you going to do today?'

'What do you mean?'

'It's Saturday. Are you going to spend Sunday in the country?'

'Of course not.'

'You don't have a car?'

'No.'

'You work in an office, don't you?'

'That's right. As there are tens of thousands of offices in Paris I can tell you that.'

'Have you any friends?'

'No.'

'A girl-friend?'

'No. When I need one, I make do with what I find. You know what I mean?'

'I think that when tomorrow comes you'll spend the day writing a long letter to the papers.'

'How do you manage to know everything?'

255

'Because you are not the first person to be in this situation.'

'And how did it end up for the others?'

'There have been different endings.'

'Did any of them kill themselves?'

Maigret did not answer and silence reigned once again on the line.

'I do not have a revolver and I know that it is almost impossible to get one now without a special permit.'

'You won't commit suicide.'

'What makes you think that?'

'You would not have telephoned me.'

Maigret wiped his forehead. This conversation, apparently so banal, these flat answers, allowed him none the less to pin down the character of the man more and more.

'I'm going to hang up,' said the voice at the end of the line.

'You can ring me again on Monday.'

'Not tomorrow?'

'Tomorrow's Sunday and I shan't be in my office.'

'Won't you be at home?'

'I'm planning to go out into the country with my wife.'

Each sentence was carefully planned.

'You're lucky.'

'Yes.'

'Are you happy?'

'Relatively so, like most men.'

'I've never been happy.'

He hung up suddenly. Either someone, impatient at seeing him talk for so long, had tried to get into the phone box, or the dialogue had laid his nerves bare.

He wasn't a drinking man. Perhaps he might make an exception, to buck himself up. He had phoned from a café or a bar. People would be elbowing him, looking at him without imagining he was a killer.

Maigret rang his wife.

'What would you say to spending the weekend at Meung-sur-Loire?'

She was so surprised that she could not speak for a moment.

'But . . . you . . . what about your case?'

'It needs to simmer for a bit.'

'When shall we go?'

'After lunch.'

'In the car?'

'Of course.'

She had been driving for a year, but she was not yet at her ease and she always gripped the wheel with an unconquerable apprehension.

'Buy something for this evening's dinner, because we may get there after the shops shut. Get something to make a big breakfast tomorrow morning too. We'll have lunch at the inn.'

He didn't find any of the men he worked most closely with except Janvier, and he invited him for a drink.

'What are you doing tomorrow?'

'You know quite well, chief, that Sunday is the day for my mother-in-law and the children's uncles and aunts.'

'We're going to Meung.'

He and his wife had a quick lunch at home in the Boulevard Richard-Lenoir. Then, when the dishes were done, Madame Maigret went to change.

'Is it cold?'

'A bit cool.'

'So I can't wear my flowered dress?'

'Why not? You're taking a coat, aren't you?'

An hour later they joined the flow of tens of thousands of Parisians who were rushing to find a square of green.

They found the house as clean and tidy as if they had left it the day before, for a local woman came in twice a week to air the house, dust it and do the floors. It was useless to tell her about new housekeeping aids. Everything was done with wax, even the furniture, and a fine smell of caustic pervaded everything.

Her husband did the garden, and Maigret found crocuses on the lawn and, at the foot of the little wall at the end of the garden, in the most sheltered spot, jonquils and tulips.

His first act was to go upstairs and put on an old pair of trousers and a flannel shirt. He always had the feeling that the house, with its bare beams and its dark corners, with the peace which pervaded it, was like a priest's house. That did not displease him, quite the contrary.

Madame Maigret made herself busy in the kitchen.

'Are you very hungry?'

'Just ordinarily hungry.'

They had no television here. After dinner, when the weather was a little warmer, they sat in the garden and watched the evening twilight close in little by little, blotting out the features of the landscape.

That evening they went for a leisurely walk, going as far as the Loire, whose water, after the rains at the beginning of the week, flowed muddily and was carrying tree-branches along with it.

'Are you worried?'

He did not speak for some time.

'Not really. Antoine Batille's killer rang me this morning.'

'Out of cheek? Or defiance?'

'No. He needed reassurance.'

'And he came to you?'

'There wasn't anyone else he could turn to.'

'Are you sure it's the murderer?'

'I said the killer. A murder presupposes premeditation.'

'His act was not premeditated?'

'Not exactly, unless I'm mistaken.'

'Why did he write to the papers?'

'You've read his letter?'

'Yes. I thought at first it was a joke. Do you know who he is?'

'No, but I could find out within twenty-four hours.'

'Don't you want to arrest him?'

'He'll give himself up of his own accord.'

'And if he doesn't give himself up? If he commits another crime?'

'I don't think that . . .'

But the superintendent stopped himself as if in doubt. Had he the right to be so sure of himself? He thought of Antoine Batille who dreamed of going to study tropical man and who wanted to marry young Mauricette.

258

He wasn't yet twenty-one and he had been struck down in a puddle in the Rue Popincourt, never to get up again.

Maigret slept fitfully. He opened his eyes twice, thinking he heard the telephone ring.

'He won't kill again.'

He tried to reassure himself.

'After all, it's himself he's afraid of.'

A real Sunday sun, a sun like those we remember from childhood. The garden, covered with dew, smelled good and the house smelled of bacon and eggs.

The day passed uneventfully. Nevertheless, Maigret's expression was withdrawn. He did not manage to relax completely and his wife sensed it.

They were welcomed at the inn with open arms and they had to have a drink with everyone, for they were considered almost to belong.

'A game of cards this afternoon?'

Why not? They ate rillettes done in the local way, *coq au vin blanc* and, after the goat's cheese, *babas au rhum*.

'About four o'clock?'

'Fine.'

He took his wicker chair to the most sheltered spot in the garden and he fell asleep before long with the sunlight warming his eyelids.

When he woke up, Madame Maigret made him a cup of coffee.

'You were sleeping so soundly it was a real pleasure to watch you.'

He still had a sort of country taste in his mouth and he imagined he could hear flies still buzzing around him.

'Didn't it give you a funny feeling listening to his voice on the telephone?'

They were both thinking about it, in spite of themselves, each one in a different way.

'After forty years in this job, I am always affected when I meet a man who has killed.'

'Why?'

'Because he has crossed the barrier.'

259

He did not explain any more. He knew what he meant. The man who kills cuts himself off, as it were, from human society. From one minute to the next he ceases to be a man like other men.

He wanted to explain himself, to say . . . Quantities of words rose to his lips but he knew there was no point, no one would understand him.

Even the real killers, the professionals. They appeared aggressive, sardonic; it was because they needed to swagger, to make themselves believe that they still existed as men.

'You won't be very late back?'

'I expect to be back before six-thirty.'

He joined his local friends, good men for whom he was not the famous Superintendent Maigret but a neighbour and, moreover, an excellent fisherman. The red cloth was spread out in front of them. The cards, which had seen better days, were a bit sticky. The white local wine was cool and crisp.

'Your call.'

'Diamonds.'

His opponent on the left announced a sequence of three, his partner four queens.

'Trump.'

The afternoon went in dealing cards, in arranging them in fans, in announcing tierces or bellas. It was like a peaceful droning. From time to time the landlord would come over to have a look at each man's hand and would go off again with a knowing smile.

Sunday must be seeming long to the man who had killed Antoine Batille. Maigret hoped he had not stayed at home. Did he have a little flat, with his own furniture, or did he rent a room by the month in a cheap hotel?

It would be better for him not to stay between four walls but to go out and rub shoulders with the crowd or go to the pictures.

On that Tuesday evening in the Rue Popincourt it had been raining so hard that it was like a cataclysm, and elsewhere, in the Channel and in the North Sea, fishing boats had gone down.

Maigret tried not to think about it, to keep his mind on the game.

'Well, Superintendent, what do you say?'

'I pass.'

The white wine was going a little to his head. He wasn't used to it any more. You drank it like water and only felt the effects afterwards.

'I'll have to go soon.'

'We'll stop at five hundred points, all right?'

'Five hundred points is fine.'

He lost and paid for the drinks.

'One can see that you don't play belote in Paris. You're out of practice, aren't you?'

'Yes, a bit.'

'You'll have to come and stay a little longer at Easter.'

'I hope to. There's nothing I'd like better. It's the villains who . . .'

And there he was! Suddenly he was thinking about the telephone again.

'Good evening, gentlemen.'

'Shall we see you next Saturday?'

'Maybe.'

He did not feel let down. He had had the weekend away which he had made up his mind to have, but he couldn't expect that his worries and responsibilities would not follow him into the country.

'When do you want to leave?'

'As soon as we've had a bite to eat. What have you made for dinner?'

'Old Bambois came and offered me a tench, which I have baked.'

He went and looked greedily at the swollen skin, a beautiful golden colour.

They drove slowly, since Madame Maigret was even more nervous at night than in the daytime. Maigret switched on the radio and smiled as he listened to the warnings to drivers and then to the news.

It was mainly about foreign politics, and the superintendent gave a sigh of relief on discovering that there was no mention of the Rue Popincourt case.

In other words, the killer had behaved himself. No crimes. No suicides. Only a little girl kidnapped in the Bouches-du-Rhône. They were hoping to find her alive.

He slept better than he had the previous night, and it was broad daylight when a lorry whose silencer seemed about to split wide open woke him up. His wife was not lying beside him.

She must just have got up, for her part of the bed was still warm and she was busy in the kitchen making the coffee.

Leaning over the banister, Madame Maigret watched him walk heavily downstairs, a little the way she would have watched a child going off to sit a difficult examination. She knew hardly any more than the papers did, but what the papers did not know was with what energy he tried to understand, how much concentration he had to have over certain cases. It seemed as though he identified himself with the people he was hunting down and that he went through their anguish with them.

By chance he found a bus with an open platform and so could go on smoking his first pipe of the morning. He had hardly arrived in his office when Superintendent Grosjean telephoned him.

'How's it going, Maigret?'

'Very well. What about you? What news of your ruffians?'

'Contrary to what one might think, it's Gouvion, the poor little look-out, who is being most useful to us, and who has enabled us to find witnesses for two of the burglaries, one at the Château de l'Epine, near Arpajon, and the other at a villa in the Forest of Dreux.

'Gouvion often stayed at his post for three or four days, watching the comings and goings. He would go and have a bite to eat or a drink in the neighbourhood.

'I think he'll break before long and he'll talk. His wife, who used to be a dancer at the Châtelet, is begging him to.

'They are all four at the Santé, in separate cells.

'I had to keep you in the picture and to thank you again. What about your case?'

'It's coming on slowly.'

Half an hour later, as he expected, the editor of the morning paper wanted to speak to him.

'Another letter?'

'Yes, except this one didn't come in the post but was pushed through our letter-box.'

'A long letter?'

'Long enough. The envelope says "For the attention of the writer of Saturday's article on the Rue Popincourt crime."'

'Still in block capitals?'

'He seems to write very fluently like that. Shall I read it to you?'

'Please.'

'"Dear Sir,

"I have read your most recent articles, Saturday's in particular, and although I am not able to judge their literary value, I have the impression that you are really looking for the truth. Some of your colleagues are not of the same mind and, ever on the hunt for the sensational, print anything, even if they contradict themselves the next day.

"I have, however, one complaint to make to you. In your last article you speak of 'the madman of the Rue Popincourt'. Why this word, which first of all is hurtful and secondly sets out a judgment? Because there were seven stabs? No doubt, for you say a little farther on that the murderer struck like a madman.

"Do you know that you can do a lot of harm by using words of that kind? Certain situations are painful enough in themselves not to be judged in a superficial manner.

"I do not ask to be treated with kid gloves. I know that in everyone's eyes I am a killer. But I would prefer not to be annoyed in addition by words which are probably stronger than intended by those who use them.

"Apart from that, I must thank you for your objectivity.

"I can tell you that I have telephoned Superintendent

Maigret. He seemed to me to be very understanding and I want to trust him. But how far does his profession oblige him to play a part, let alone set traps?

"I think I shall telephone him again. I feel very tired. Tomorrow, however, I shall go back to work.

"On Friday I went to Antoine Batille's funeral. I saw his father, his mother and his sister. I want them to know that I had nothing against their son. I didn't even know him. I had never seen him before. I am truly sorry for the evil I have done them.

"Yours very sincerely."

'Shall I print it?'

'I don't see why not. On the contrary, it will encourage him to write again and in each letter he tells us a little more about himself. When you have had it photographed, send it to me. There's no point in sending over a messenger.'

The phone call did not come until ten minutes past twelve, when Maigret was wondering whether to go for lunch.

'I suppose you're calling me from a café or a bar near your office?'

'That's right. Were you waiting for me?'

'I was just going out for lunch.'

'Didn't you know I would ring?'

'Yes, I did.'

'Have you read my letter? I expect they read them to you over the telephone. That's why I don't send you a copy.'

'You need people to read you, don't you?'

'I don't want them to get wrong ideas. Just because someone has killed, people make assumptions about him. You too, I expect.'

'Well, you know, I've known many of them.'

'I know.'

'When we used to send convicts abroad to prison islands some men wrote to me from Guiana. Others, when they've served their time, come and see me sometimes.'

'Really?'

'Do you feel any better?'

264

'I don't know. At any rate I was able to work almost normally this morning. It makes me laugh to think that those same people who are so normal with me would be quite different if I only said one little sentence.'

'Do you want to say it?'

'There are moments when I have to hold myself in. With my boss, for example, who looks down on me from a great height.'

'Were you born in Paris?'

'No. In a little town in the provinces. I won't tell you which, for that would help you to identify me.'

'What did your father do?'

'He is chief accountant in a . . . let's say, in a fairly big firm. The man who can be trusted, you know the type. The fool the bosses can keep at work until ten in the evening and make him come in on Saturday afternoons, not to mention Sundays.'

'What about your mother?'

'She's an invalid. As far back as I can remember, I can see her always ill. It seems it was caused by my birth.'

'You haven't any brothers or sisters?'

'No. That's why. She does her own housework, though, and keeps the house very clean. When I was at school I was one of the cleanest pupils, too.

'My parents are proud people. They wanted me to be a lawyer, or a doctor. But I'd had enough of studying. So then they thought I would go into the firm where my father works, which is the biggest employer in the town. I didn't want to stay there. I felt I was suffocating. I came to Paris. . . .'

'Where you suffocate in an office, don't you?'

'But when I leave it at the end of the day nobody knows me, I'm free.'

He was talking more easily, more naturally than the previous time. He was less afraid. His silences were less frequent.

'What do you think of me?'

'Haven't you asked me that already?'

'I mean in general. Forgetting the Rue Popincourt.'

'I think you're one of tens, of hundreds of thousands in the same situation.'

'Most of them are married and have children.'

'Why have you never married? Because of your ... illness?'

'Do you really think the things you're saying?'

'Yes.'

'Every word?'

'Yes.'

'I can't understand you. You aren't at all what I imagined a superintendent in the Police Judiciaire would be like.'

'A superintendent is like anyone else. Even at the Quai des Orfèvres, we're all different from each other.'

'What I don't understand most of all is what you said to me the last time. You said that it would take you twenty-four hours to identify me.'

'That's right.'

'How?'

'I'll tell you that when I see you.'

'What is your reason for not doing it and not arresting me straight away?'

'Supposing I were to ask you what was your reason for killing?'

There was a silence, more notable than the others, and the superintendent wondered if he had not gone too far.

'Hello,' he called.

'Yes.'

'I'm sorry I was so brutal. You have to look at things right in the eye.'

'I know. That's what I'm trying to do, believe me. Maybe you think I write to the papers and ring you because I need to talk about myself. Really it's because everything is so wrong.'

'What is wrong?'

'What people think. The questions they'll ask me in the assize court, if I ever get there. The Public Prosecutor's charge and even, perhaps most of all, my lawyer's defence.'

'You're thinking so far ahead already?'

'I have to.'

266

'Do you expect to be giving yourself up?'

'You think I will, soon, don't you?'

'Yes.'

'Do you think I'll feel better for it?'

'I'm sure you will.'

'I'll be shut in a cell and treated like a . . .'

He did not finish his sentence and Maigret did not interrupt him.

'I don't want to keep you any longer. Your wife will be waiting for you.'

'She certainly won't be worried. She's used to it.'

Another silence. It seemed as though he did not want to cut the thread which linked him to another man.

'Are you happy?' he asked shyly, as if that question obsessed him.

'Relatively happy. That is, as happy as anyone can be.'

'I've never been happy since I was fourteen, not for one day, not for an hour, not even for a minute.'

Suddenly he changed his tone.

'Thank you.'

And he hung up.

The superintendent had to go up to Magistrate Poiret's office in the afternoon.

'Are you making any progress with your investigations?' the magistrate asked with the touch of impatience common to all magistrates.

'It is almost over.'

'Does that mean that you know who the murderer is?'

'He rang me again this morning.'

'Who is he?'

Maigret took the enlargement of a head photographed among the crowd in the sunshine on the Quai d'Anjou from his pocket.

'That young man?'

'He's not as young as all that. He's in his thirties.'

'Have you arrested him?'

'Not yet.'

'Where does he live?'

'I don't know his name, or his address. If I have this photograph printed, people who see him every day, his colleagues, his concierge, anyone, would recognize him and wouldn't hesitate to tell me who he is.'

'Why don't you do it?'

'That is the question which is worrying him too and which he asked me this morning for the second time.'

'Had he phoned you before?'

'Yes, on Saturday.'

'You realize, Superintendent, the responsibility you are taking on yourself? A responsibility, moreover, which I share indirectly, now that I have seen the photograph. I don't like that.'

'No more do I. But if I moved too quickly he probably wouldn't let himself be arrested but would rather settle it once and for all.'

'You are afraid he may commit suicide?'

'He has nothing else to lose. Don't you agree?'

'Hundreds of criminals have been caught and the number of them who have attempted to end their lives . . .'

'And what if he is precisely one of those?'

'Has he written to the papers?'

'A letter was put in the letter-box of one newspaper office, yesterday evening or in the small hours this morning.'

'That is a well-known pattern, I think. If I remember my courses in criminology correctly, that is usually the way with paranoiacs.'

'Yes, according to the psychiatrists.'

'Don't you agree with them?'

'I don't know enough about it to contradict them. The only difference between them and me is that I don't divide people into categories.'

'It is necessary, however.'

'Why is it necessary?'

'In order to pass judgment, for example.'

'It is not my place to pass judgment.'

'They were right to warn me that you were difficult to manage.'

The magistrate said it with a slight smile, but he meant it, nevertheless.

'Would you agree to a bargain? It is Monday now. Shall we say that if on Wednesday at the same time . . .'

'Go on.'

'If your man isn't under lock and key by then, you will send his photograph to the papers.'

'You will really stick to that?'

'I am letting you have a delay which I consider to be sufficient.'

'Thank you.'

Maigret went back down to his own floor and opened the door of the inspectors' office. He didn't particularly need them.

'Are you coming, Janvier?'

Once in his office he went over to open the window, since he was hot, and the noises from outside thundered into the room. He sat down at his desk and picked up a curved pipe which he smoked less frequently than the others.

'Anything new?'

'Nothing new, chief.'

'Sit down.'

The magistrate had not understood a thing. For him, criminals were defined only by this or that article of the penal code.

Maigret too sometimes needed to think aloud.

'He rang me again.'

'He hasn't decided to give himself up?'

'He wants to. He's still hesitating, as one might hesitate to jump into icy water.'

'I suppose he trusts you.'

'I think so. But he knows I'm not on my own. I've just come down from upstairs. When the magistrate begins to question him he will unfortunately have to take notice of some realities.

'I know a little more about him. He comes from a small town in the provinces, he didn't want to tell me which one. That means that it is a very small town, where we would have no difficulty in picking up his traces. His father is a chief accountant, a man who, as he says not without bitterness, can be trusted.'

'I can see that.'

'They wanted to turn him into a lawyer or a doctor. He didn't have the courage to go on with his studies. Nor did he want to go into the same firm as his father. Nothing original there, as I told him.

'He works in an office. He lives alone. He has a reason for not getting married.'

'Did he tell you what it was?'

'No, but I think I can guess.'

Maigret, however, avoided saying anything more on the subject.

'I can't do anything but wait. He will undoubtedly ring me again tomorrow. I have to send his photograph to the papers on Wednesday afternoon.'

'Why?'

'An ultimatum from the magistrate. He doesn't want to bear the responsibility of waiting any longer, he says.'

'Are you hoping that . . .'

The telephone rang.

'It is your anonymous caller, Superintendent.'

'Hello. Is that Monsieur Maigret? I am sorry I hung up on you this morning. There are times when I think that nothing has any meaning any more. I'm like a fly beating against a window-pane trying to escape from the four walls of a room.'

'You aren't in your office?'

'I went there. I was full of good will. They gave me an important file to deal with. When I opened it and read the first lines I asked myself what I was doing there.

'I was seized by a kind of panic and, under the pretext of going to the lavatory, I went down the corridor. I barely took the time to grab my raincoat and hat from the hook as I went by. I was afraid someone would catch me, as if I felt I was being pursued.'

At the beginning of the call Maigret had signalled to Janvier to pick up the second receiver.

'Where are you?'

'On the Grands Boulevards. I've been walking in the crowd for an hour. There are moments when I hate you, when I suspect you of doing it on purpose to send me out of my mind, to put me little by little into a state of mind in which there will be nothing I can do but give myself up.'

'Have you been drinking?'

'How did you know?'

He spoke more forcefully.

'I had two or three brandies.'

'You don't usually drink?'

'Only a glass of wine with meals, rarely a drink by itself.'

'Do you smoke?'

'No.'

'What are you going to do just now?'

'I don't know. Nothing. Walk. I might have a seat in a café and read the afternoon papers.'

'Have you sent any more letters?'

'No. I may write one more, but there isn't much more left for me to say.'

'Do you live in a furnished room?'

'I have my own furniture and I have the use of a kitchenette and a bathroom.'

'Do you do your own cooking?'

'I did cook my evening meals.'

'And you haven't done so for several days?'

'That's right. I go home as late as possible. Why are you asking such pointless questions?'

'Because they help me to understand you.'

'Do you do the same with all your customers?'

'That depends on the case.'

'Are they so different one from the other?'

'Men are all different. Why don't you come and see me?'

There was a nervous little laugh.

'Would you let me leave again?'

'I couldn't promise you that.'

'Well, you see . . . I shall come and see you, as you say, when I have taken a definitive decision.'

Maigret almost told him of the magistrate's ultimatum,

271

then he weighed the pros and cons and decided to remain silent.

'Good-bye, Superintendent.'

'Good-bye. Don't let it get you down.'

Maigret and Janvier looked at each other.

'Poor man,' murmured Janvier.

'He's still fighting himself. He is quite lucid. He isn't cherishing any illusions. I wonder if he'll come before Wednesday.'

'Didn't you get the impression that he had begun to hesitate?'

'He has been hesitating since Saturday. Just now he is outside, in the sunlight, in the crowd where no one takes any notice of him. He can go into a café and order a cognac and they'll serve him without paying any attention to him. He can go and have a dinner in a restaurant, or sit in the darkness in a cinema.'

'I know what you mean.'

'I'm putting myself in his place. From one hour to the next. . . .'

'If he were to commit suicide, as you fear, it would be even more definitive.'

'I know. But he must know that. I only hope he doesn't keep on drinking.'

Light currents of chilly air drifted through the room and Maigret looked at the open window.

'Well, what about a drink?'

And a few minutes later they were both seated at the counter in the Brasserie Dauphine.

'A brandy,' ordered the superintendent, which made Janvier smile.

CHAPTER SEVEN

TUESDAY was a terrible day. Nevertheless Maigret arrived at his office quite gaily. It was such a truly spring day that he had walked from the Boulevard Richard-Lenoir, sniffing the air, the smells from the shops, looking round from time to time at the bright and gay dresses worn by the women.

'Nothing for me?'

It was nine o'clock.

'Nothing.'

In a few minutes, in half an hour, one of the editors or chief reporters would ring him to tell him about another letter written in block capitals.

He expected it to be a decisive day. He was ready for it and he laid his pipes out on his desk, chose one with care and went over to the window to light it, looking out at the Seine which sparkled in the morning sun.

When he had to go to the briefing, he had Janvier sit in his office.

'If he rings, get him to wait and come and get me at once.'

'Right, chief.'

There was no telephone call while he was in the director's office. There wasn't one by ten o'clock. There was still none by eleven o'clock.

Maigret went through his mail, filled up forms, his mind abstracted, and at times, as if to make the time pass more quickly, he went in to the inspectors' office, taking care to leave the door open. Everyone knew he was worried and nervous.

The telephone which did not ring created a sort of vacuum which made him uneasy. He felt something lacking.

'Are you sure there has been no call for me, Mademoiselle?'

In the end it was he who rang the newspaper offices.

'Haven't you had any letter this morning?'

'Not this morning, no.'

The day before, the first call from the man in the Rue Popincourt had come at ten minutes past noon. At noon Maigret did not go downstairs with the others. He waited until twelve-thirty and once more asked Janvier, who was most up in the case, to relieve him.

His wife did not ask him any questions. The answers were only too obvious.

Had he lost the game? Had he been wrong to trust to instinct? Tomorrow at that time he would have to go to see the magistrate and admit his defeat. The photograph would be printed in the papers.

What the hell could that idiot be doing? Maigret felt surges of anger.

'He was only trying to make himself interesting and now he has dropped me. Maybe he's laughing at my naïveté.'

He went back to the Quai earlier than usual.

'Nothing?' he asked Janvier mechanically.

Janvier would have given a lot to have some good news to give him, for it upset him to see his chief in such a state.

'Not yet.'

The afternoon was even longer than the morning. Maigret tried in vain to get some interest in his routine work, using the time to deal with the paperwork which was overdue. His heart wasn't in it.

He imagined all possible hypotheses and rejected them one by one.

He even rang the police emergency first-aid section.

'You haven't been called to any suicides, have you?'

'Just a minute. There was one during the night, an old woman who gassed herself, out by the Porte d'Orléans. A man threw himself into the Seine at eight o'clock this morning. We were able to save him.'

'What age was he?'

'Forty-two. A neurasthenic.'

Why was he doing all these things? He had done what he could. It was time to face reality. He wasn't hurt at having been hoaxed, but at seeing that his intuition had been wrong.

That meant that he was no longer able to make contact, and in that case . . .'

'Damn, damn and damn!'

He had said that at the top of his voice, alone in his office, and he picked up his hat and went, coatless and alone, over to the Brasserie Dauphine where he drank two pints of beer one after the other, standing at the counter.

'No telephone calls?' he asked on his return.

By seven o'clock he had had no call and he resigned himself to going home. He felt heavy and was not at peace with himself. He took a taxi. He found no joy in the sunshine, nor in the colourful street noises. He could not even have said what the weather was like.

He started to climb the stairs heavily and stopped twice because he found himself a little out of breath. A few steps away from his landing, he saw his wife watching him come up.

She had been waiting for him as if she were waiting for a child coming home from school, and he was almost angry with her. When he got up to her, she merely said in a low voice:

'He's here.'

'Are you sure it's him?'

'He told me so himself.'

'Has he been here long?'

'Almost an hour.'

'Weren't you afraid?'

Maigret suddenly had a retrospective fear for his wife's safety.

'I knew I wasn't in any danger.'

They were whispering outside the door which was shut to.

'We talked.'

'What about?'

'Everything . . . Spring . . . Paris . . . the little truck-drivers' restaurants which are disappearing now. . . .'

Maigret went in at last and saw, in the living room which was both dining room and sitting room, a man, still young, who stood up. Madame Maigret had taken his raincoat and he had laid his hat on a chair. He was wearing a navy-blue suit and looked younger than he really was.

He forced himself to smile.

'Forgive me for coming here,' he said. 'I was afraid that over there, at your office, they wouldn't let me see you straight away. One hears so many things. . . .'

He must have been afraid of being beaten up. He was embarrassed. He searched for words with which to break the silence. He did not realize that the superintendent was as embarrassed as he.

'You're just as I imagined you would be.'

'Sit down.'

'Your wife has been very patient with me.'

And, as if he had forgotten about it until that moment, he pulled a Swedish knife out of his pocket and held it out to Maigret.

'You can have the blood analysed. I haven't cleaned it.'

Maigret put it down carelessly on a table and sat down in an armchair, facing his visitor.

'I don't know how to begin. It's very difficult to . . .'

'I'll start by asking you a few questions. What is your name?'

'Robert Bureau. Bureau like a bureau, a desk. You might say it's symbolic, since my father and I . . .'

'Where do you live?'

'I have a little room in the Rue de L'Ecole-de-Médecine, in a very old house at the end of the courtyard. I work in the Rue Laffitte, in an insurance company. Or rather, I used to work there. That's all over with now, isn't it?'

He spoke those words with a melancholy resignation. He had calmed down, and was looking at the restful décor around him as if he wished to fit himself into it.

'Where do you come from?'

'From Saint-Amand-Montrond, on the Cher. There is a big printing firm there. Mamin and Delvoye, who do work for several publishers in Paris. That's where my father works, and in his mouth the names Mamin and Delvoye are sacred. We lived in a small house near the Canal du Berry—my parents live there still.'

Maigret didn't want to hurry him, to get to the important questions too quickly.

'You didn't like your town, then?'

'No.'

'Why?'

'I felt I was being stifled there. Everyone knows everyone else. When you walk down the street you can see the curtains at the windows twitching. I've always heard my parents saying: "What would people say?"'

'Were you good at school?'

'Until I was fourteen and a half I was top of the class. My parents were so used to it that they scolded me if I had one mark less than perfect in my exercise books.'

'When did you start to be afraid?'

Maigret had the impression that the man he was talking to turned paler, that two little hollows appeared near his nostrils and that his lips grew dry.

'I don't know how I've been able to keep the secret until now.'

'What happened when you were fourteen and a half?'

'Do you know the area?'

'I've been through it.'

'The Cher runs parallel to the canal. In places it's ten yards or so away from it. It is broad and shallow, with stones and rocks which allow one to wade over it.

'The banks are covered with rushes, with willows, with bushes of all kinds. Particularly around Drevant, a village about three kilometres from Saint-Amand.

'That's where the local children usually go to play. I didn't play with them.'

'Why not?'

'My mother called them little guttersnipes. Some of them used to bathe in the river quite naked. Almost all of them were the children of workers at the printing works and my parents made a great distinction between wage-earners and white-collar workers.

'There were about fifteen of them, maybe twenty, who played together. There were two girls among them. One of them, Renée, who must have been thirteen, was very well developed for her age and I was in love with her.

'I've thought a lot about all this, Superintendent, and I wonder if it would have happened anyway in different circumstances. I suppose it would. I'm not trying to find excuses.

'One boy, the pork-butcher's son, made love to her in the undergrowth. I caught them unawares. They went to swim with the others. The boy was called Raymond Pomel and he had red hair like his father, whose shop my mother patronized.

'At one moment, he moved away from the others to relieve himself. He came close to me without knowing it and I took my knife out of my pocket. I released the catch and the blade flicked out.

'I swear I didn't know what I was doing. I struck several times and felt as if I was freeing myself from something. For me, at that particular moment, it was absolutely necessary—I wasn't committing a crime, or killing a boy. I was just stabbing. I went on stabbing him after he had fallen to the ground, then I went away quite peacefully.'

He was animated and his eyes shone.

'They only discovered him two hours later. They hadn't noticed he wasn't with the group of twenty children any more. I had gone home after washing the blade in the canal.'

'How was it that you had this knife when you were so young?'

'I had stolen it from one of my uncles some months earlier. I had a passion for knives. As soon as I had any money I bought one which I always carried in my pocket. I saw this Swedish knife at my uncle's house one Sunday and I took it. My uncle looked for it everywhere without even thinking of me.'

'Why did no one, your mother for example, ever find it?'

'The wall of our house, on the garden side, was covered with Virginia creeper. Its thick growth framed my window. When my knife wasn't in my pocket, I hid it where the vine was thickest.'

'Didn't anyone suspect you?'

'That's what surprised me. They arrested a bargee whom they had to release again. They thought of all possible subjects, except a child. . . .'

'What was your state of mind?'

'To tell you the truth, I felt no remorse. I listened to what the women said gossiping in the street, I read the Montluçon paper, which spoke of the crime, without feeling myself in any way concerned.

'I watched the funeral procession go past without any emotion. For me, at that time, it already belonged to the past. To the inevitable. It was nothing to do with me. I don't know if you can understand that? I think it is impossible to do so if one hasn't been through it oneself.

'I kept on going to school, where I had become abstracted and where my marks got lower and lower. I must have grown somewhat paler and my mother took me to our family doctor, who examined me perfunctorily.

'"It's just his age. Madame Bureau. The boy is a bit anaemic."

'I think that I didn't feel as if I belonged to the real world. I wanted to run away. Not to run away from any possible punishment, but to get away from my parents, from the town, to go far away, anywhere. . . .'

'Aren't you thirsty?' asked Maigret, who was very thirsty himself.

He poured two brandies and water and held one out to his visitor, who took it and drank avidly, draining his glass in one gulp.

'When did you realize what had happened to you?'

'You do believe me, don't you?'

'I believe you.'

'I have always thought that no one would believe me. It happened without my noticing it. As time went on, I felt myself more and more different from other people. Stroking the knife in my pocket with my fingers, I would say to myself:

'"I've killed someone. No one knows about it."

'I almost wanted to tell them, to tell my fellow-pupils, my teachers, my parents, like one boasts about something one has done. Then, one day, I found myself following a girl along the canal. It was the daughter of one of the bargees and she was going back to the barge. It was winter and it was already dark.

279

'I told myself that all I had to do was to run a few steps, to take my knife out of my pocket . . .

'Suddenly I began to tremble. I turned around without thinking and ran back to the houses at the edge of the town, as if I would feel safer there. . . .'

'Did that happen to you often after that?'

'When I was a child?'

'At any time at all.'

'About twenty times. Most of the time I didn't have a particular victim in mind. I would be outside and suddenly I would think:

'"I shall kill him."

'I remembered much later that when I was a child, when my father hit me and sent me to my room to punish me, I used to growl the same thing:

'"I'll kill him."

'I wasn't necessarily thinking of my father. The enemy was all mankind, man in general.

'"I shall kill him."

'Would you mind giving me another drink?'

Maigret poured him one and poured one for himself at the same time.

'How old were you when you left Saint-Amand?'

'Seventeen. I knew I'd never pass my exams. My father couldn't understand and worried about me. He wanted me to go into the printing firm. One night I went off without saying anything, taking with me a suitcase and what little I'd saved . . .'

'And your knife!'

'Yes. I've meant to get rid of it a hundred times and could never bring myself to do it. I don't know why. You see . . .'

He was looking for words to express himself. One could tell that he wanted to be as truthful and precise as possible, which was difficult for him.

'In Paris at first I was hungry and, like so many other people, I unloaded vegetables at Les Halles. I read the advertisements in the papers and I went everywhere that had a place to offer. That's how I got into an insurance company.'

'Have you had any girl friends?'

280

'No. I made do, from time to time, with picking up a girl in the street. One of them tried to slip an extra banknote out of my wallet and I almost took out my knife. My forehead was drenched in sweat. I staggered out. . . .

'I realized that I had no right to get married.'

'Were you ever tempted to?'

'Have you ever lived alone in Paris, without relations, without friends, and have you gone back to your room in the evening, alone?'

'Yes.'

'Well then, you'll understand. I didn't want to have friends, either, because I couldn't be frank with them without risking being imprisoned for the rest of my life.

'I went to the Saint-Geneviève library. I devoured psychiatric treatises, always hoping to find an explanation. Of course I didn't have the background training. When I thought my case corresponded to a particular mental illness, I would realize that I didn't have such and such a symptom.

'I became more and more distressed.

'"*I shall kill him* . . ."

'I ended up with these words on my lips and so I would run home and shut myself in and throw myself down on my bed. It seems that I would lie there groaning.

'One evening a neighbour, a middle-aged man, knocked at my door. I took my knife out of my pocket mechanically.

'"What do you want?" I called through the door.

'"Are you all right? You're not ill? I thought I heard you groaning. I'm sorry."

'He went away again.'

CHAPTER EIGHT

MADAME MAIGRET appeared in the doorway and made a sign which Maigret did not understand, so far away was he from those surroundings, then she murmured:

'Would you come in here a minute?'

Back in the kitchen, she whispered:

'Dinner's ready. It's after eight. What shall we do?'

'What do you mean?'

'We have to eat.'

'We're not finished.'

'Maybe he could eat with us, could he?'

He looked at her, amazed. For a second this proposal seemed quite natural to him.

'No. There mustn't be a properly-set table, no family dinner. That would make him feel terribly ill at ease. Have you any cold meat, any cheese?'

'Yes.'

'Well then, make some sandwiches and bring them in to us with a bottle of white wine.'

'What is he like?'

'Calmer and more lucid than I had feared he would be. I'm beginning to understand why he didn't get in touch with me in any way all day. He needed to step back, to see things in perspective.'

'See what things?'

'Himself. Did you hear any of what he said?'

'No.'

'When he was fourteen and a half he killed a boy.'

When Maigret went back into the living room Robert Bureau, embarrassed, muttered:

'I'm keeping you from your dinner, aren't I?'

'If we were at the Quai des Orfèvres I would send out for sandwiches and beer. There's no reason why I shouldn't do the same here. My wife is making sandwiches for us and will bring them through with a bottle of white wine.'

'If only I had known. . . .'

'If you had known what?'

'That someone could understand me. You must be an exception. The judge won't have the same attitude, or the jury. I've spent my whole life being afraid, afraid of stabbing someone else without meaning to.

'I have watched myself, so to speak, at all times, wondering if I wasn't about to have an attack—at the slightest headache, for example.

'I've consulted I don't know how many doctors. I didn't tell them the truth, of course, but I complained of violent headaches which were accompanied by a cold sweat. Most of them didn't take it seriously and prescribed aspirin.

'A neurologist in the Boulevard Saint-Germain did an E.E.G. According to him, I have no brain damage.'

'Was that recently?'

'Two years ago. I almost wanted to tell him that I wasn't normal, that I was a sick person. Since he didn't find out for himself . . .

'When I went past a police station I wanted to go in and say:

'"I killed a boy when I was fourteen and a half. I'm afraid I may kill again. It ought to be cured. Shut me up and have someone take care of me."'

'Why did you never do that?'

'Because I've read so many things. At almost every trial the psychiatrists give evidence and often they're laughed at. When they talk about diminished responsibility or mental deficiency the jury doesn't pay any attention. At best, they bring the sentence down to fifteen or twenty years.

'I forced myself to manage alone, to recognize when an attack was coming on, to run and shut myself up in my room. It worked, for a long time. . . .'

Madame Maigret brought them in a tray of sandwiches, a bottle of Pouilly Fuissé and two glasses.

'I hope that will do.'

She went out quietly to eat alone in the kitchen.

'Help yourself.'

The wine was cold and dry.

'I don't know if I'm hungry. There are some days when I eat hardly anything and others, on the other hand, when I'm ravenous. That may be a sign, too. I look for signs everywhere. I analyse all my reactions, I attach importance to my slightest thought.

'Try to put yourself in my place. At any moment I might . . .'

He bit into his sandwich and was the first to be surprised to see himself eating naturally.

'And I was afraid that I might have been wrong about you. I had read in the papers that you were human and that you sometimes went against the Public Prosecutor's Office. On the other hand, I've heard of your interrogations *à la chansonnette* —you treat the prisoner gently and kindly to make him feel at ease and he doesn't realize that you're dragging it all out of him.'

Maigret couldn't help smiling.

'All cases aren't the same.'

'When I telephoned you I weighed every one of your words, every one of your silences.'

'You came in the end.'

'I had no more choice. I felt my whole world falling apart. Wait! I'll make you a confession—yesterday, at one particular moment on the Grands Boulevards, I had the idea of attacking somebody, anybody, in the middle of a crowd, of striking out all around me, savagely, in the hope that someone would kill me.

'May I pour myself another glass of wine?'

He added, with rather sad resignation:

'I shan't drink any more wine like that for the rest of my life.'

For a moment Maigret tried to imagine what Magistrate Poiret's expression would have been if he had been able to hear this conversation.

Bureau continued:

'There were three days of torrential rain. They often talk about the moon and its effect on people like me. I watched myself. I didn't notice that my impulses were stronger or more frequent at the time of the full moon.

'It is rather a certain intensity of the weather that has an effect. In July, for example, when it's very hot. In the winter when the snow is falling in huge flakes.

'You might say that nature has a period of crisis and . . .

'Can you understand?

'That rain which went on incessantly, the squalls, the sound of the wind rattling the shutters of my room, all that combined to put my nerves on edge.

'In the evening I went out and began to walk in the storm. After a few minutes I was soaked and I raised my head on purpose to get the lashing of the rain full in the face.

'I didn't hear the warning signal, or if I did I didn't obey it. I should have gone home instead of keeping on. I didn't notice where I was going. I walked and walked. At one particular moment my hand gripped the knife in my pocket.

'I saw the lights of a little bar in a dark little street. I heard footsteps in the distance, but that didn't worry me.

'A young man in a light-coloured jacket came out, his long hair plastered to his neck, and I was triggered off.

'I didn't know him. I had never seen him before. I hadn't seen his face. I struck at him several times. Then, as I was going away, I realized that I hadn't yet reached the moment of release, and I went back to strike him again and to lift up his head. . . .

'That's why they talked about a madman. They also said a nutcase.'

He stopped talking and looked around him as if he were surprised to find himself where he was.

'I am really mad, aren't I? It isn't possible that I'm not ill. If only I could be given treatment. . . . That's what I've been hoping for for so long. But you'll see, they'll just send me to prison for life.'

Maigret didn't dare answer.

'Aren't you going to say anything?'

285

'I hope they'll give you treatment.'

'But you wouldn't count too much on it, would you?'

Maigret emptied his glass.

'Drink up. We'd better go straight over to the Quai des Orfèvres.'

'Thank you for listening to me.'

He emptied his glass in one swallow and Maigret poured him another one.

Bureau hadn't been very far wrong. At the trial, two psychiatrists gave evidence that the accused was not insane in the legal sense of the word but that his responsibility was greatly diminished since he found it difficult to resist his impulses.

The defence counsel begged the jury to send his client to a mental hospital where he could be treated.

The jury accepted the attenuating circumstances, but still condemned Bureau to fifteen years imprisonment.

After which the judge, after coughing, pronounced:

'We realize that this verdict does not completely agree with the facts. At present, alas, we have no establishments where a man like Bureau may be given effective treatment while remaining under strict surveillance.'

Standing in the box, Bureau looked for Maigret and gave him a smile of resignation. He seemed to be saying:

'I knew that's what would happen, didn't I?'

When Maigret left the court his shoulders were a little more bowed.

Epalinges, April 21st, 1969